D1428284

Regatta

Libby Purves

FLAME

Hodder & Stoughton

First published in 1999
by Hodder & Stoughton
A division of Hodder Headline
First published in paperback in 2000
by Hodder & Stoughton
A Flame paperback

A CIP catalogue record for this title is available from
the British Library.

ISBN 0 340 71881 1

Typeset by Palimpsest Book Production Limited,
Polmont, Stirlingshire
Printed and bound in Great Britain by
Clays Ltd, St Ives plc

Hodder & Stoughton
A division of Hodder Headline
338 Euston Road
London NW1 3BH

to Tom and Caroline Stevens
and their river

The town of Blythney and all its inhabitants are purely fictitious. To create them meant taking certain liberties with the geography of coastal Suffolk, for which the author apologises.

Chapter One

The man on the quay was old, but his hands were strong and sure. As the child watched, hidden by a clump of reeds, he stooped to pick up something from the heap at his feet. He ran a glinting knife through damp fur, and with one deft movement turned the creature's coat inside out. It was like some gruesome conjuring trick: where a moment before he had held a dead but unmistakable rabbit, now he had a piece of butcher's meat in one hand and a limp tangle of fur in the other.

The old man tossed the fur into the river, and the current bore it swiftly away downstream. The skinned carcass he laid in a green plastic box before reaching unhurriedly for the next.

He had done three rabbits and was reaching down for the last one when the child erupted from cover and confronted him.

'That,' she said indignantly, 'is gross.'

He had thought he was alone. The small stone quay stood aloof from the main river buildings, modest and unfrequented. Two hundred yards downstream the larger quay, on its modern concrete pillars, jutted importantly out over the fast-flowing bend in the stream. Even on a quiet evening of early summer the big river pier had a relentlessly busy look, fringed with muddy dinghies and set among the jumbled buildings of boat yard and sailing club and the long slipways below the car park. An air of hurry and consequence always hung around Grenden Quay: masts tapped and clinked, flags fluttered, and the webbing slings on the boat hoists swung in the impatient breeze.

But the small quay, upstream, was just itself: a stubby stone rectangle punctuating the long curve of green marsh and brown water. It had no buildings or slipways, nor any car park; the most intrepid of the Blythney off-roaders would not have attempted the narrow, muddy and treacherous track along which the child had walked, a small dark figure against the sunset. Coker's Quay was a place to walk to in solitude for contemplation of the river's flow, or to arrive at silently by boat, and trudge across the open marshes to the town.

Local lore said that it was the first of all the landing places, and had been there since before history bothered with this bleak corner of East Anglia. The puzzle of it was that its stones were not local – indeed in this land of mud and reed and shingle there was no such thing as local stone – yet nobody knew for certain where they had been brought from, or when. When the repairs were done in the 1960s by the local history group, granite was brought from Cornwall which oddly matched the damaged fabric of the ancient quay; oddly, because why would Cornish stone have come here to the easternmost edge of England, so long ago? One winter-evening lecturer had told a sleepy half-full Blythney hall that it must have been the ballast of some long-sunk ship, of a Viking ship perhaps, or a particularly adventurous Saxon trader. But then, why had no ancient timbers ever been found here, as they had on the River Deben further down the coast? And why was Coker's Quay so far upstream? Logic would dictate a landing place at Grenden, where the river flowed fast on the inward bend, and the land was hard enough for a waggon to come right to the waterside. Who had wanted a second quay, so awkwardly placed amid mud and wet marshes? Smugglers? Hermits? Outcasts?

Idle as autumn smoke, tales and theories had long swirled around Coker's Quay; the town had traditionally been a little proud of its mystery. But even that benign curiosity and respect for the unknowable past was fading today. It could not compete with the bright, relentless spirit of holidaymaking that pervaded the modern town. There was even talk of a marina development which would surround and subsume the little quay; only the problem of building a roadway prevented it. For the moment, Coker's stayed a lonely place, fit to be visited by lonely people.

'That is gross,' said the child's voice, and the old man turned, his knife in one hand and the rabbit, dangling from its dead ears, in the other.

'Hello,' he said. 'Where did you spring up from?'

The little girl ignored the question.

'What you doin' to them rabbits?' she asked fiercely. Her voice was not a Suffolk voice but harder, sharp and staccato, as if she had come from a place where people breathed less deeply.

'I'm skinning them for a pie,' said the man promptly, and as if in deliberate defiance of the cross little face before him, he ran the knife neatly down the final cadaver and

3

whipped its skin off over its head, like a vest. The inside of it glistened, nastily.

The child paused, captivated by the neatness of the action but struggling to hold on to her original partisan indignation on behalf of the rabbits. The trick was too good though, too masterly for her young honest mind to dismiss as mere brutality.

Finally, as if unwilling to give him the satisfaction, she asked in a grudging tone, 'Where'd you learn to do that?'

The man tossed the skin into the tide, then stooped to lay the rabbit down in the box and fit the lid on top of the meaty load.

'In the army,' he said. 'You never know when you'll have to catch your own food.'

The child considered. 'You can get it in shops now,' she said, still combative. 'You can even get rabbit. In the supermarket. I saw.'

'Still dead, though, isn't it?' said the old man. 'And I bet it had a worse life than this lot. Living in some hutch.'

'Where'd you get them, then?' The girl was edging closer now, drawn by the allure of argument.

'The dog got them,' he said. 'On the heath.' He pointed to the darker line of bracken that divided the pale marsh from the sky. 'Snap! Dead in a minute. Better than anything that happens on a rabbit farm, believe me. My lady wife doesn't like my dog, but she does like making rabbit pie. So the dog and I get back into her good books by paying tribute, like any conquered tribe.'

The child kept silence again. The old man kept his silence too, and began to strap the box of dead rabbits onto some contraption that stood by him on the uneven surface of the old pier. It looked like a battered porter's trolley but with wider, spongier tyres, like the ones she had seen on the dinghy launching trolleys down at Grenden Quay. When he had nearly finished she spoke again.

'Did you kill people, in the army?'

He did not look at her, but pulled the last strap tight. 'Yes,' he said. 'I did.' He glanced away into the distance beyond the marsh, and gave a piercing whistle. Out of the gathering dusk, fast and silent, his dog sped towards him.

He turned back to the child. 'Getting dark,' he said. 'You should be home for supper, shouldn't you?'

'Home!' said the child with biting scorn. 'As if!' But she turned, without a farewell, and walked along the riverbank path towards the town. Looking after her, the old man saw that she was limping badly.

The rabbits were graciously received by Marion Glanville, who promptly withdrew to clean and chop them, with the help of a fortifying glass of sherry on the draining board. Her old hands were steady and precise, and her old bone-handled knife well-sharpened. Soon there was no rabbit, only meat: cubed and tidy and piled beneath a bowl to protect it from the prowling grey cat. When she had finished, she came through to the shabbily comfortable sitting room to replenish her sherry before the cooking began. Her husband was reading, his back on a cushion and his long legs swung over the arm of the sofa like a boy sixty years his junior. At Marion's approach Harry Glanville put the book down, sat up properly and pulled off his reading glasses.

'Do you know,' he said, 'I think I met Sheila's latest project down by the river tonight.'

'The holiday child from London? It's a bit early, isn't it?' She was a bright, interrogative little woman, spry in her seventies, and most of her sentences ended on an upward inflection. 'I know Sheila's boys are back this weekend from Ampleforth, but the council schools don't break up until the middle of July, do they?'

'I did wonder,' said Harry Glanville. 'But I think Sheila mentioned there was some special arrangement. Brat got expelled from school or something, so she offered to have her early.'

Marion poured her second glass of sherry, and sat down opposite her husband. 'Well,' she said, 'you have to admire that niece of yours, doing all this welfare work as well as coping with her own three. And Simon. What's the child like?'

Harry considered. 'Not coal-black, but blackish,' he began.

'You have to say "mixed race" now, dear,' interrupted his wife. She had a portfolio of social work herself, and was regarded as the household expert on what would "do" in these altered days.

'Well, never mind that,' said Harry. 'She's got some sort of bad foot. Limps. Looks like an old injury, because she limps pretty fast and doesn't seem to make a thing of it. I rather liked her. Told me off for skinning the rabbits.'

'Did she, now!' said Marion. 'You set her right, I hope. These city children! Think meat comes naturally in plastic packets!'

'She wasn't all that bothered. Not really.' He yawned, and reached for his book and his glasses again. 'Asked if I killed anyone in the war.'

Marion grimaced. 'Did you tell her you were Sheila's uncle?'

'No. I thought I might, then I had a feeling she was enjoying a bit of independent status. Out on the river bank, chatting up mad old men with rabbits. Didn't want to spoil it by being part of the big warm Sheila family.'

Marion nodded with complete understanding.

The Glanvilles' house, insouciantly and rather elegantly shabby, lay at the top of the town behind the water tower, commanding a wide view of marsh, heath and river. The road to these top houses was dusty and unmade and led nowhere, but in the hierarchy of Blythney this was a point of pride. No holiday visitors used it as a short cut, and nobody risked their springs by driving fast; even in the frenzied days of late July and August there was a brooding quiet about these houses. Most of them were inhabited by retired couples, with the exception of the mellow Queen Anne façade and the landmark wavy brick wall that indicated the boundary of the Markeens' little empire at the Hall. It was, without doubt, the classier end of town. You could, as Alaia Markeen frequently said, turn your back on all the seaside business if you wanted to.

Where Sheila and Simon Harrison lived, right on the front in a tall brick house called Seafret, the summer would arrive with more éclat and a great deal more noise. Sheila had no wish whatever to turn her back on 'the seaside business'. She loved it all: the arrival of London friends to open their holiday cottages, the warm tantalizing smell of fish and chips curling across from the high street, the rattle of rollerskates on the Edwardian promenade and the vista of gaily striped windbreaks on the pebble beach.

She loved the way that her two spare bedrooms filled, from June to September, with successive waves of children's schoolmates, young couples, overspill relatives from friends' small holiday cottages, and waifs and strays sent by the Country Hosts Association. She was in love with the clumping racket on the stairs, the impatient yells of shrill or gruff young voices, the trails of sand and pebbles over the worn seagrass matting in the corridor, the oars leaning up in the porch and the casually dumped lifejackets and bikes in the hall.

Sheila loved the carnival and the regatta and the outdoor concerts and the Summer Theatre and the children's opera group and the picnic circle and the Country Club. She loved the splashing of the beach and the bright skimming life of the summer river. Not least, she loved her own ability to make monumental stews and chillis and lasagnes for twenty people and to preside, beaming pinkly, over a crowded table in the big kitchen which occupied most of the ground floor. Summer was Sheila's time: her reign as queen of holiday Blythney.

In the winter she was busy enough too, of course. There were committees and governorships and bazaars and fundraising for St Bernadette's and her prized seat on the Social Work Review Commission, which took her to London two days a month, expenses paid from Ipswich station. But the summer was Sheila's joy. The festivity and freedom of her summers quite made up for the odd nagging sense she sometimes felt in the duller days of winter, when all the children were away at school: a suspicion that she should have hung on to a proper job in a proper office. In spite of Granny's money. That one day, she and Simon would be left face to face, with no tumbling young to distract them from one another, and that unless she had another all-absorbing world to retreat into, this would not be a happy moment.

But then, as she often said to pale, irritated London friends, 'It's wicked to take paid employment from someone who really needs it, and a family is a job, isn't it? And when your own littles have grown up – bless them! – there are always other needy mites you can give a helping hand to!'

Sheila's use of expressions like 'needy mites' was, oddly enough, the thing which most divided her from her contemporaries. She was, after all, barely forty. Perhaps being raised by a grandmother, not a mother, had caused her verbal sensibilities to skip a generation. However it was, she spread a certain palpable discomfort which fortunately she never noticed herself.

For the past five years, Sheila had ruthlessly enlarged her summer family by way of the Country Hosts Association, which offered holidays (without their parents and separate from their siblings) to underprivileged children. Baffled tots from Hackney and Deptford, Forest Gate and Brixton, had been delivered by brisk London social workers and plunged into Sheila's summer frenzy of pleasure. Startled infants with no prior knowledge of J.M. Barrie had found themselves parading the streets on Blythney carnival day dressed as Peter Pan and the Lost Boys; burger-fed babies had sat at her big table staring suspiciously at portions of cheese-and-lentil bake; and when Sheila swept up the river at the helm of the big motor-dory in the uncertain Suffolk weather, a succession of bewildered faces had peered over the gunwale, and uncertain little feet had stepped out onto the muddy sand of the river beaches.

There had been happy successes and sullen failures. Some visitors had made tolerably friendly relationships with the Harrisons' own children – especially when Douai was young enough not to have fully grasped the notion of class divisions – and at worst there had been armed truces, in which each faction stayed within its own territory and ignored the other. It was all the same to Sheila. In her happy and partly imaginary world all children lived in one big enchanted glade, presided over by her benevolent self.

She was in presiding mood now, telling her thin, dour husband Simon about her plans for the new child.

'They'll have a wonderful time. I think it might be all for the best, having an older child than usual. And for a whole three weeks! She can have a lovely time with Douai and Vincent on the river, and if Joan's really set on this French venture of hers we can see if the Cottens' Manchester cousins want to come down for the regatta and have her room. Their Alison and Dondie are just about the same age as Anansi, aren't they? Give or take a year? And they could all have fun together. If you got the other Whitecap out of Uncle Harry's garage, they could do some races – obviously Douai's in the Laser Two handicap in the mornings but there's the afternoon series . . .' She paused, half aware that her husband was not listening with any enthusiasm, but then ploughed on.

'Oh, but of course, Anansi will be gone before the junior regatta, such a shame – maybe if we contacted her family now we could extend it for a bit. The more fresh air the better, with these children, and apparently the mother just hardly cares!' Sheila smiled, strangely heartened by the thought of lesser mothers hardly caring.

Simon Harrison scowled. The happier his wife got, and the nearer the dreaded summer approached, the deeper his scowl would grow. He slapped cutlery down crossly on the table and said, 'You can't make them play together, you know. They're not five years old any more. Douai's a year or more older than this child, and if he's having this Yorkshire friend down from school, he's not going to have much time for whassername – Anansi – is he? Anyway, Anansi's supposed to be a male name. Some folk hero in West Africa.'

'Oh,' said Sheila airily, 'they'll all muck in together. A big gang's so much more fun! I've block-booked on the tennis course at the Country Club to get them going! Mixed doubles!'

'When do Vincent and Douai get here?' asked Simon, pulling side plates out of a wall cupboard.

'The Cottens are picking them up from King's Cross at six,' said Sheila. 'Then they'll all come down together. About eight thirty, probably. They're so good. I do feel awful about us not being able to collect them. But with you not driving, and them living in Islington anyway—'

Simon slapped down the last plate and left the room. A twelve-month ban was bad enough when you were stuck out in the sticks, without your bloody wife for ever throwing it in your bloody face. Grabbing his waxed coat from the untidy hall – for it was beginning to drizzle – he stepped out onto the damp promenade in time to see the dark, slight, limping figure of the black child moving towards the house.

Tennis! he thought contemptuously. Did Sheila have no eyes? Or imagination?

The child looked hesitantly at him in the greying light, recognizing a familiar of this unfamiliar house. Simon ignored her, lowered his head and walked hard in the opposite direction.

Chapter Two

It was Anansi's third night at Seafret.

On the first evening she had arrived late, off a train that stood for an hour idle at Witham and lost a further hour between Manningtree and Ipswich. Miss Archenlaw, the lady with the red nose from the Country Hosts Association, had spent the whole trip fretting visibly about her own homeward journey. She had also made it clear to Anansi that children not travelling in a group, or on the correct date, were a great burden to the organization and a considerable nuisance.

Miss Archenlaw had not said these things outright. There had just been a few pointed observations about behaviour, linked to some headshaking about people who got themselves excluded from school. She had also informed Anansi in half a dozen different ways that she was very lucky to be going to such a nice place with such a nice family, and for an extra fortnight too. More than most of 'their' children got.

'It'll give your mother a nice breather,' she said. 'It's quite a job being on your own with two kiddies, especially with Kyra being so little.'

Anansi had not replied; but as she looked out of the train window at the darkening countryside, it seemed to her that she saw her mother and Kyra, pale drowning faces, looking back at her. She blinked, fiercely, and as the wobbling view resolved itself she saw that it was only her own face, bleached in reflection, and the long lugubrious features of the escort.

She, her shabby, shiny little backpack and her plastic carrier bag of shoes were briskly handed over to a large blonde lady. Miss Archenlaw had said, 'Be good, now!' dabbed her red nose, and hurried for the last train back. The big blonde had said, 'Hello! *What* a journey! These trains! Come on now, everybody calls me Sheila!' and put Anansi into the front seat of a weirdly long, square-backed car.

As she was driven through the darkness, a deeper darkness than she had ever seen, the child clung to some kind of handle on the car door, her right hand on her breast to hold the seat belt away from her. She had rarely been in any car, and the unfamiliar webbing of the belt cut painfully into her neck.

Panic rose, but Anansi was used to panic. She quelled it with practised ruthlessness, leaving only a hunched bleak place inside herself, a black hole of vague sadness edged with rage. But she had lived with that hollow place inside her for so long that she hardly noticed it. Eventually she fell uncomfortably asleep.

When the car stopped at last it was on a road with only one side. To the right lay a row of big houses, their lit windows urban and familiar. But to the left there was nothing. Less than nothing, and a strange sound, and some surface on which the glints of the streetlamps made moving patterns.

'We're right on the sea!' said the woman who wanted to

be called Sheila. 'In the morning you can just pop on your swimmers and run down the beach for a dip! It's pebbles, though, so you'll want sandals.'

Anansi was too tired and shocked to understand this talk of popping and swimmers. The next morning, looking out of the window, she saw for the first time the illimitable wastes of the grey North Sea and realized that she had indeed travelled right to the edge of the known land. The window was deep, its sill lower than her waist; she felt that she might topple through it, and when Sheila came to call her for breakfast Anansi was kneeling, holding on to the sill, mesmerized by the appalling sea.

'Thrilled!' said Sheila later to Penny Tranmere in the hardware shop. Penny was after a new colander, and Sheila was buying sandpaper for a pine bedside cabinet which she was rubbing down for Douai's room. Douai would have much preferred a space-age plastic one. Sheila beamed at her friend and said, 'I went up to get her this morning for breakfast, and she was just gazing out at the waves. It's a joy to see the way these little mites *blossom* in this environment!'

'She's not so little, this one, is she?' said Penny. 'Simon said she was nearly twelve. Though if that was her sitting on your front wall this morning, she looks more like eight.'

'Bit of a *problem family*,' hissed Sheila, holding up her three sheets of sandpaper. Penny's present occupation was a piece of research on early satirical drawings; for a moment, she thought, behind the sandpaper Sheila's broad face took on the look of a Hogarthian gossip hissing behind an ivory fan. 'Her mother has a two-year-old by a different father, and apparently things haven't gone at all well since the wee one was born. There's been talk of putting this one into

15

voluntary care. She's had several spells in children's homes to give her mother respite. Unmanageable at school.'

'Can you and Simon cope?' said Penny doubtfully. 'I mean, if she's unmanageable . . .'

Sheila beamed again. 'Watch us!' she said. 'You know I'm a great believer in the healing power of a Blythney summer!'

Penny, who had her own reasons for keeping conversations with Sheila as short as possible, smiled some incoherent answer and decided, after all, not to bother queuing with her colander. She hung it back on the peg, glanced meaningfully at her watch and gave a narrow-shouldered shrug. With her white collar and pale glossy bob, she was as neat and pretty in her pink canvas smock as Sheila was stout and straggly in her blue one. The knowledge gave her obscure, guilty satisfaction.

'Well, good luck. 'Byee!'

''Byee!' said Sheila.

Anansi's first day had been – yeah, all right, she thought with surprise as she hunched into her bed that night. There were no other children in the house yet, which was a reprieve. Having met Sheila she was dreading the possible arrival of her daughter, the big, confident girl Joan whose portrait in rather garish oils smiled down from her bedroom wall. But Sheila said that she might miss Joan who was backpacking round France and would not give a date for her return. 'Well, you know how they are in gap year!' Sheila laughed, mystifyingly.

Even more than that she dreaded the boys. Vincent, she divined, being at the lofty age of fifteen, would have little interest in her. But Sheila had shown her a picture of Douai who was 'nearly a teenager!' and she feared the worst.

It was pronounced Dowey – weird name! He was called after an abbey in France, Sheila said, 'very special to us English Catholics'. To Anansi, Douai's chiselled, pinched face boded no good. He did not have the look of a boy who would take kindly to a girl near his own age being dumped in his home. Sheila had explained about boarding school, and Anansi – whose finer feelings few people appreciated – was miserably conscious of the awkwardness of her being here first. These kids were coming to their rightful home, from distant weeks of exile. Why should they find her, a cuckoo in their nest? Was that fair?

She remembered the first time she ran away from the Home to her own home, and found Kyra born. One of the teachers at school, the nice one, had told her about baby cuckoos. Squatting in other birds' nests, taking food off their mothers. At the thought, the bleak hollow place inside her seemed to suck with a sudden violent spasm, threatening to draw her strength and peace into it and make her hit and spit. No, Douai would not like her. Why should he?

But he was not here yet, and her first breakfast had been a silent tête-à-tête with Simon. Sheila never sat down for breakfast, preferring to bustle in and out of the room issuing a stream of suggestions for everybody's daily activities. When she had finished, Anansi asked if she could go for a walk.

'Of course!' Sheila had said gaily. 'Safe as houses, in Blythney! You don't need to worry! We shan't be worrying!'

Anansi, who had been sent out alone in Deptford for fags and groceries since she was five, blinked without comprehending Sheila's meaning.

'Did I oughter have a key?' she said interrogatively.

17

Another gale of laughter from the big lady. 'Gracious, no. We only lock up at night, here.'

During that first morning Anansi quartered the alien little town, looking at people and shop windows with close and curious attention. She was puzzled by the combination of richness – look at the cars, and the prices in that shop with the sweaters! – and a certain unnerving simplicity. There were ladies whose hair and faces and bearing proclaimed them richer than anybody Anansi knew but who wore sloppy jeans rolled up, and scuffed cloth slippers with rope soles, and whose neat small breasts jutted against shapeless tops that looked, she thought, like they were made of old sacks. There were men with loud, confident voices – businessman voices, rich voices – but they wore baggy pink canvas shorts, the very ownership of which would have stripped all vestige of personal confidence, for ever, from any street-smart guy Anansi had ever known back home.

There was no video shop, nor any of the familiar names: no Woolworth, no Smiths, no Boots, no Kwiksave or Asda. Instead there was a chemist's which had all the ordinary things but also had old-looking coloured glass bottles high on shelves, and a funny sign with a bowl and a stick. The little newsagent's had familiar mags and papers but again it was odd; there were dark wooden shelves and real glass bottles with sweets in, and a big shelf of expensive books. The fruit shop, its stands spilling onto the pavement, seemed comfortingly familiar at first. But when you looked more closely, it was not quite right. All the expensive stuff – strawberries, melons – was left out on the pavement unguarded, while the carrots and potatoes were away in sacks inside. There was no curry house, no Chinese, no McDonald's, but a cafe with little tables and two striped

18

umbrellas outside it, and pubs with tubs of flowers that nobody seemed to have messed with.

Were rich people stupid, or what? wondered Anansi. They left stuff out for anyone to nick. Not a set of bars in the place either, except in the little jeweller's; but here again was a surprise. Nothing dressy or glittery, but a lot of plain things that looked like orange plastic, at prices which shocked her very much. She liked the shop with the pale pine furniture outside it, and timidly reached out to touch the soft waxed sheen of the wood. You could see how it was put together: little tongues of wood sloped to fit in between other tongues at the edge of the drawers and where the legs met the table tops. She had always loved 'built things', where you could see how the parts fitted together. She spent some time looking, with close attention, at cabinets and chests and tables with price tags worth, she again saw with amazement, months and months of anybody's Giro.

One strange shop made her stand for a while, intrigued. It had carpet on the floor and white empty spaces, and on the walls were paintings in heavy frames, each with a private spotlight trained on it. The man behind the counter – more like a posh desk, really – sat quietly writing in a book, and through the window Anansi could see two or three people walking around, looking at the pictures with equal quietness. She squinted, trying to make out what the pictures were of. One had a church in it, but she could not be sure of the others. More than the pictures she liked the peaceful look of white, cool space. And a cat statue, nearly cat size, made out of some kind of smooth, shiny, dark-brown stuff with pale golden gleams coming from it where the light fell.

To her horror, the man at the desk looked up and smiled at her. He was small and thin, with dark hair curling down over his collar at the back and a wide mouth which continued disconcertingly as a dark scar up his cheek. He raised his black brows and cocked his head on one side, as if to motion her into the gallery. Anansi fled, with all the speed her lame foot allowed, until she was several doors away and could breathe the comfortingly familiar petrol smell of the little garage.

On that first afternoon Sheila took her in the car again, with the belt sawing into her neck. 'Just a little drive round, to get your bearings!' said her hostess with a gale of her now familiar laughter. First she showed her something called the Country Club, where under a leaden sky a man was driving a roller over some grass tennis courts. Then they drove back along the bumpy, sandy road behind the town until they came to another unmade track alongside a high bank. On one hand there was flat country with coarse grass and puddles; on the other, a long bleak ridge of piled-up shingle.

Sheila pulled the car in and said, 'Come on. Have a look at our river.'

Anansi followed her up some steps set into the shingle bank, and looked out to sea. Its expanse still made her shudder, with a queasiness of fear. She had taken to shutting the curtains as soon as she walked into her room and saw that vertiginous grey view.

'I thought that was the sea,' she said, 'not a river.'

'Behind you,' said Sheila.

Anansi turned, and for a moment felt a wave of panic. Water on both sides. She saw now that the grass and puddles on the other side rapidly gave way to a river, wide and shiningly brown, which ran parallel to the long, straight sea beach, with only fifty metres of shingle bank and foreshore dividing water from water.

She blinked, and slowly turned right round. In a moment, looking along the straight line of the river, back along the track and out again to the sea, she understood how the landscape fitted together. They were standing on a wrinkle of stones and sand and rough grass which separated the two expanses of water, sea to her left and river to her right. When she turned round and looked past the car and the rough road, it became apparent that the squeezed strip of land rapidly widened out into marshes and dark, scrubby heathland. She saw that this was the place where the river suddenly gave up shadowing the coastline and bent inland. Marsh, heath, river and pebble beach were all equally strange to her; she had no words for any of them. At the point where the river bent, there was a long white hut and a concrete pier jutting out over the water.

'That's Grenden Quay,' Sheila was saying. 'The sailing club. We mainly sail on the river, though of course the boats can be dragged down to the sea – we put out a sort of wooden slipway, it's *tremendous* fun – but the main racing's all on the river. Oppies, Mirrors, and of course Toppers and Lasers these days – goodness, it's changed since Simon and I were children! And the Whitecaps, obviously, because they're a local class ever since nineteen forty-seven – and the keelboats. Swallows, Squibs – even Dragons!'

Anansi did not listen to this gibberish. She was learning to blank out Sheila as she blanked out teachers at school. Instead, she frowned with the effort of taking in this odd, wet, empty landscape. There was a crane by the pier – a little crane, but a familiar outline. A memory stirred painfully inside her: a walk by the docks, years ago when she was little, with a tall man holding her hand. She could remember the upward stretch of her arm; the physical

21

memory made her wriggle her right shoulder. A word came back that she had rarely used.

'Is it the *Thames*?' she asked.

'No!' said Sheila merrily. 'Gracious, no. The Thames is three or four rivers south of here, down the coast. This is the Blyne and Grend.'

'Blynen . . . ?' tried Anansi.

'No. It's called the Blyne from here to where it hits the sea, all that straight line – seven miles of it. Then the Grend,' she gestured inland, upstream of the great bend. 'Same river, but as soon as it bends, it's called the Grend. See, you can remember it that way. Blyne in a line, bend makes it Grend.'

Anansi withdrew her attention from Sheila halfway through this explanation, and continued to stare at the river. It did not alarm her as much as the grey-brown wastes of the North Sea had done, but it held her gaze in the same way. Sheila would have just said 'Thrilled!' but if Anansi could have explained, she would have said that she was gazing at it in the same spirit as you might gaze at a freak or a road accident.

Rivers in pictures were blue; this one was brown, ruffled by the afternoon breeze and stirred up into odd rough whirlpools and eddies near the quay. The whole sheet of water was moving; she could see that from the way the ripples went. There were boats on it, none of them moving but all facing the same way, presumably tied to underwater things that she could not see. If she looked hard she could see water flowing past their sterns, sucking them into position with their sharp bows upstream, tugging at chains and ropes. On the far bank a few cows grazed.

'When the others get here,' Sheila continued – for she had not stopped talking while Anansi stared at the river –

'we'll get our motorboat launched, and you can learn to sail the Whitecap with Douai.'

The child turned her big eyes on Sheila, unbelieving. 'I've never been in a boat,' she said. 'That's scary.'

'No, it's not!' cried Sheila, with a rollicking laugh. 'It's tremendous fun. And perfectly safe. You wait!'

Anansi turned and limped back down the steps to the car.

She thought about these things that night, in the room over the sea. Once she got up and closed the curtains, to shut out the emptiness; but a few moments later she thumped out of bed again and went over to re-open them. When at last she slept, the dream about the fuckilla man came back.

It was a while since it had come, but in her sleep she winced from it. He was coming closer, blocking out the light, and his foot swung back and kicked her ankle, hard. The ankle was sticking out because she was sitting on the floor. In the dream Anansi knew it was her fault for leaving her foot sticking out where he might fall over it. The remembered pain shot through her bones, and in the wide Blythney bed she curled her dark small body into a ball.

There was always a high complaining voice in the dream, saying, 'Leave 'er! Leav 'er, I told yer,' and then the man's voice, far louder, would say, 'Fuck off, you fucker. I'll fucking kill her.' The fuckilla man, she had called him in her head when she was small.

The dream would change then, into a different time with her foot still hurting, and her on the floor crying and nobody hearing. Usually she woke herself up, in a private way she had learnt, before the floor-crying bit had gone on for too long. A few years ago, before Kyra was born, a particular morning had come after this dream and brought with it a

23

new awareness of her lame, twisted foot. Anansi had asked her mother how it got bent.

'You got run into by a car,' her mother Tracey said at first. 'When you was first walking.'

Anansi had argued, and told about the dream. So the story had changed.

'You got attacked,' said Tracey. 'We dunno who did it. I found you and took you to the hospital.'

But there was no hospital in the dream, and it was her mother's voice saying, 'Leave 'er.'

Anansi, doggedly rational and perfectly familiar with the upsets of various schoolmates' lives, had long since worked out that the man, who she was convinced had truly kicked her, was at some time part of the domestic circle. So after Nanna Beverley was dead and Kyra was treacherously born and Kyra's dad was in and out of the house, out of his bloody head half the time, a man to be kept clear of at all costs, she confronted her mother. Things about fathers, bad things, were beginning to stir in her understanding. They did not, from what Kyra's dad said, always like being 'landed' with bloody kids. Sometimes they lashed out.

'Was it my dad that did my foot in?' she asked baldly.

And her mother had been angry and said, 'He was a bastard, your dad. Said he was a prince, back in Africa. Thass why you got that wog name. Bloody Jamaican, it turned out. Cook in the army or something. Never bleeding cooked for *me*. Good riddance.'

So Anansi knew that her father had named her, and lamed her, as well as leaving her. Which was, as her waking self knew, all *well* out of order. Tracey said good riddance, but a small strange part of Anansi was sorry, in the dream, every time he vanished. It was a lovely voice, deep and ringing. And it was definitely out of order, not having a dad.

* * *

The dreaded boys were due to arrive on her second full day at Seafret, in time for supper; she hoped very much to be out of the house, so that she could appear after them, humbly, and thus demonstrate that she knew she was an outsider and not a cuckoo. Hence the riverbank walk to the quay where she had held her first Blythney conversation with the old man who had the dog and the rabbits. Old men, Anansi knew, were often flashers or worse, but she had no particular fear of them. You nutted them in the stomach and they crumpled up; she had seen it done enough times. She could have pushed this one into the river if he tried anything on. But he didn't and he was OK, in spite of the rabbits. No, if any man disturbed her in this new place, it was Simon. He hardly ever smiled, whereas his wife smiled and laughed all the time. There was, Anansi thought consideringly, something really, really weird about that.

Simon Harrison, walking away from the house in the grey evening light, was working himself into a worse temper every minute. Summer! God, summer! Kids and mess and quarrels, and no sanctuary to run to. Sheila thought nothing of using his back bedroom study for passing guests. Blythney men with town jobs – Don Harper with his first-class season ticket to London or Alan Tranmere who drove up to Colchester three times a week – would grumble humorously at this time of year about being chained to the treadmill and freed only for weekends and the brief Saturnalia of Blythney Regatta.

'Tremendously clever of you,' Alan Tranmere would say with his prematurely senatorial rumble, slapping his great gut with laughter. 'Tremendously clever to be a damn writer – stay at home all you like, go sailing when you feel like it, eh?' The Londoners with holiday homes were even worse – Bethie and Hugo Cotten and the Rattrays and the Ward-Williamses were for ever cooing about how absolutely *marvellous* it must be for Simon and Sheila to live full-time in 'this glorious place', close to the reeds and the river and the sea. After winter weekends of walks and pubs they would come for a last drink before driving home on Sunday night. Sitting in Sheila's kitchen, with the wind howling balefully along the empty promenade outside, Eric Rattray and Bethie and the others would mourn complacently about their return to comfortable homes in Hampstead and Islington. Simon, speechless with envy and irritation, would gulp his Scotch and think with horror of another bleak week of Blythney life.

Now he walked on, rapidly, heading southward out of the small town's grip. There was a time once, he said to himself, jumping down onto the shingle below the end of the prom, there *was* a time when he had planned to have a flat in London, and at least a half-life there, near the Groucho Club and the launch parties and the bookshops and British Library and the buzz of literary London. Ten years ago, when Joan was eight, they still lived in the cottage outside town and it was becoming clear that the little boys would absorb all Sheila's devotion for the foreseeable future. At that time he had contemplated a most agreeable form of semi-separation for himself. His first book, *Against*, was a critical success: *The Sunday Times* said it was 'witty, savage, premonitory of a grim fin de siècle – the most promising first novel of the new decade'. In the *Telegraph* it was 'a breezy, brilliant *point du départ* for a major new talent'. Several colour magazines had come down to interview this fresh talent and photograph Simon

26

in his lean-to writing den, and the literati had raved for a fortnight about this voice from a Suffolk shed which had challenged the city with its 'rare blend of sophistication and brutality'.

His advance on that book, of course, had only paid off the overdraft built up while he wrote it. But the advance on the next book would surely yield the flat in Soho and the freedom not to spend any more time than he could bear with Sheila and the children. The cottage was small and the shed leaky; he could plead pressure of space.

But then Sheila's grandmother died and left her Seafret, that seven-bedroomed brick tower cut from half an Edwardian hotel. And since Sheila's parents were long dead, and her uncle Harry steadfastly refused his share, she also got all the money. That should have made things easier because it effectively took the last shreds of family responsibility off Simon. It was not a major fortune, but it meant that Sheila could give up her part-time jobs, keep house and send the children to those sinister Catholic schools she was so fond of. And he could have his pied-à-terre in London, fuelled by a fat advance on the next book, and take only as much family life as he fancied.

Simon had been so sure of this future that he had begun composing lines in his head for the next round of publicity interviews. 'I need the stimulus of the city, Sheila and the children need Suffolk. We find our marriage is reinvigorated by the mix of experiences we bring to it.' But despite the critics' gushing honeymoon, *Against* had sold indifferently in hardback and, more humiliatingly, hardly any more in paperback. Meanwhile Simon, excited out of any sense of caution by the first reviews, had spent too long playing off rival publishers for the next advance. He gambled for a month too many, and found to his chagrin that instead of going up, the offers began to go down.

His agent, Nadia, was sanguine, and told him that this often happened with a critical success – readers were so *slow* to latch on to the next big thing – and that matters would adjust themselves because a talent like his would always come through. Nadia, he now saw, was not all that bothered. Nadia, after all, had plenty of other clients. Nadia persuaded him to accept the far lower advance now on offer, and gradually withdrew into a studied vagueness, returning fewer and fewer of his calls.

With the prospect of the London flat gone, Simon wrote his second and third books in a heavy-hearted and irritable state in the top floor back bedroom of Seafret, against a background of Sheila's new, grandmaternally-financed, domestic idyll.

How can a man write witty and savage chronicles of a decadent fin-de-siècle Britain if, when he looks out of the window, he sees not tower blocks and roof gardens and the vans of heroin dealers but quiet, primitive grazing marshes and a ruined Martello tower?

It was impossible, and it was clearly Sheila's fault. When Simon got to the end of a satirical double-edged soliloquy paralleling cracked concrete and crack cocaine and broke for a cup of coffee, he would descend to the kitchen and find his head brushing against bundles of dried bay leaves and onions as the warm comforting smell of dumplings assailed his nostrils. While his mind turned over various brutally witty ways of describing decadent nights in an Armageddon city, his body was for ever falling over tricycles and buckets and spades in the hall, and being fed on wholesome roast chicken and rice pudding. While his gaunt, nymphomaniacal heroines were shooting up or turning tricks in concrete underpasses, the author would raise his head from composition to find the ever-broader shadow of his wife falling across the page and her relentlessly jolly voice saying, 'Wash hands! I'm just doing the gravy!' or 'Don't forget, we're going to the Cottens for kitchen sups' or 'Could you pick up Douai from Cubs? I'm all over flour!'

Simon thought – he had to think, for self-respect's sake – that this was the reason that his work never again lit the brush fire of critical acclaim. Whatever the reason, the sales of *Glow Job* and *Dead Pretty* were barely enough to keep him in whisky, let alone buy a London flat. He did, once, drive into Ipswich to an anonymous-looking building society to try for a mortgage, but was turned down as having 'no regular income'. The rage this slur engendered prevented him from trying again. By now he was contributing nothing at all to the family finances, which seemed to disturb Sheila not one whit. As to the wider wellbeing of the family, it was all he could do to prevent the poison of his failure seeping out into every word and gesture. In his rare moments of shame about this, he thought that it was as well the boys were at boarding school. He did not think of Sheila with any shame. It was, after all, her fault.

And now, without so much as a driving licence, he was again facing a Blythney summer of children and picnics, boating and jollity and the counterfeit envy of prosperous Londoners. The prospect seemed to Simon, as he walked fast along the shingle path on the sea wall, more intolerable than ever before.

Still, when he reached the bombed shell of the old Martello tower and stepped into the darkness of its ruined walls, Penny Tranmere was waiting for him in the short skirt he liked her to wear; without knickers, as he liked her to be. They did not speak. They rarely spoke beforehand.

The woman leaned, provocatively silent, against the dank wall; the man stepped forward into her darkness. With a groan, Sheila Harrison's husband folded Alan Tranmere's wife in his arms, and eased his rage and failure on her warm upturned lips and keen bony body.

Chapter Three

Sheila finished Simon's job of laying the table just as Anansi sidled into the kitchen. She smiled away her own dark thoughts, and greeted the newcomer with practised boisterousness.

'Hullo – ullo! You're just in time for the big welcome!'

Anansi winced. She had not stayed out long enough. She would, after all, be a cuckoo in the nest. Perhaps she could go up to her room. Above her head across the doorway hung a faded banner with the words 'WELCOME HOME!' embroidered on it in ancient chain stitch in five clashing colours.

Sheila followed the child's eyes. 'Yes, we always put that up. Ever since Joanie first went away to St Mary's. Bit of a tradition!'

Anansi nodded, scuffed her feet irritably for a moment and then said, 'All right if I go upstairs a bit?' She turned, and began to climb the stairs by the kitchen door.

'Don't be long!' yodelled Sheila after her. 'The boys will be *dying* to meet you!'

A car pulled up outside. Anansi, on an impulse, locked herself safely into the lavatory on the landing.

Vincent Harrison had always reclaimed his territory in the same way at the end of term, and now that he, too, was a boarder, Douai reproduced his brother's every movement. They burst in, dropped their biggest bags on the floor just inside the front door, and growled 'Hi, Mum!' at the beaming figure in the kitchen doorway. Then they thumped up the stairs to fling open every door and throw coats and sweaters and backpacks around, blurring the hateful tidiness of their rooms like tomcats spraying their boundaries. Then they burst out of their own rooms again and roamed around the landings and the other rooms of the tall house. From her locked cell, Anansi could hear them, thundering up the stairs beyond her landing and towards the top of the house.

'Oh, wicked! Dad got his new computer!'

'What speed's the modem? Dad! Can we try it on the Net?'

'He's not here. We'll ask later.'

A thump, as of somebody jumping down a flight, and a commanding rattle.

'Who's in the bog? Da-ad!'

Anansi froze, but the bolt held. Thump, and another rattle. It was her own bedroom door being opened.

'Who's in here?'

'The CHA kid, I s'pose.'

'Boy or girl?'

'Girl, I think Mum said.'

'Uh.'

Anansi thought that the higher of the two voices must be Douai. Dowey. She listened as they crashed up to the top landing again for another look at the computer, and then jumped and slid down towards the kitchen.

'Whass for supper, Mum? We had an awful pie at the service area.'

'Dow was nearly sick in the car.'

'I *so* was not.'

'You were green.'

'Only -ish.'

'Grass green, arse green.'

'Shithead!'

'Boys! Really!' Sheila sounded warmly, purringly thrilled, not reproving at all. 'Now, you must meet Anansi.' She raised her voice in a happy shout up the stairwell. 'Anansi dear! The boys are here!'

Slowly Anansi came down the stairs, holding the banister on the side of her lame foot so that she did not seem to limp. Two faces looked up at her, familiar from the photographs, deadpan and unsmiling.

'Hi.'

'Hi.'

'Hi,' said Anansi.

As she went into the kitchen she paused just behind the door so she could hear Douai's voice from the hall behind her, saying to his brother, 'I thought it was gonna be another little one, that Mum could look after, like the usual ones.'

'Nah, she said nearly *your* age. A little fwendy-wendy for you.'

'Eleven! Shit, I'm not looking after her.'

The other voice whispered, and there was an explosion of giggles.

Simon and Penny reached their respective homes at around

the same time. Simon, returning on foot to the tall brick house on the promenade, greeted his sons without much visible enthusiasm but, Sheila noticed with relief, also without the wound-up rancour he had shown before he stormed out. Penny Tranmere used her little car, discreetly parked near the Yacht Club, to drive the quarter-mile back to the smart cream-coloured house where Alan was in the process of dismissing the local childminder for the evening.

'You go off, Janet,' he was saying as she walked in. 'It's gone seven. Penny'll be back any minute.'

As Penny reached the kitchen, her two daughters turned identical faces to her, the same straight fair hair hanging neatly around Katie's six-year-old solemnity and Suzie's four-year-old grin.

'Mum's back. Mum, we went to Jamie's house and saw his puppy.'

'Can we have a puppy?'

'They've had their teas,' said bun-faced Janet, shrugging on her coat. 'And pudding. Night night, my little darlings. Be seeing ya. Tomorrow afternoon, Mrs T?'

'Yes. Thank you.' Penny leaned over her children, her face self-consciously turned away from Alan. It was never easy, this coming home from assignations with her body still singing and burning. She dared not touch him for hours, for fear he would feel the difference in her. She also felt a prick of shame for having picked a quarrel as an excuse for her outing.

Alan, however, appeared to have forgotten it, which was subtly annoying of him.

'Good drive? Did you get the sherry?'

'I didn't go for sherry.'

'You said you were—'

'No, I said you drink too much whisky. Which you do.

I only said that sherry would be better for you, if you must drink before supper.'

'Oh, I thought you were going out to get some sherry.'

'No.'

The two girls began clamouring again about the puppy. Alan, mumbling something which sounded like 'Dogshit', poured himself another whisky and made his portly way towards the sitting room.

In another sitting room, behind the elegant serpentine wall at the top of the town, Alaia and Jonny Markeen drank companionably together. They sat on white sofas which shone, spotless, against the deep rose of the carpet; their child Marta sat curled in a broad wing chair nearby, reading with voracious attention.

'I saw a wonderful little face today,' said Jonny, swirling pale sherry in his glass and looking down into it as if it was a crystal ball. He screwed up his intelligent, monkey face with the effort of clear remembering, and the scar on his cheek whitened. Alaia, on the other sofa, looked across at her husband with affection.

'On canvas or in real life?'

'Oh, very real. A little girl, middling dark, lovely East African head, with her hair cropped short. Beautiful brow, big eyes, but thinner lips than you'd expect with that head. Mixed race, I should say. Something blighted about her – pain around the mouth. I'd like to see a smile, or a rage. But when I looked at her she ran for it.'

Alaia laughed. She was used to her husband's pre-occupation. He had been a painter of portraits when she first knew him as a fellow art student in Paris: starveling, intense, driven, and unable to walk down any street without alarming at least one total stranger with a disconcertingly hungry

35

stare. He never wanted to paint conventional beauties, and only once in their courtship drew her, in fierce black pencil and without conviction, during an uncharacteristic bout of anxiety to please.

Alaia did not mind; enough others had wanted that. Nor had she minded that his painting made so little money, although it was a secret relief to her when abruptly and flamboyantly at the age of thirty-five, after ten years of married life and the conception of Marta, he had declared his creative phase over. Jonathan Markeen, in 1989, turned his back on painting and penury, took to dealing, and made a great deal of money very quickly. The gallery – all his galleries – had been spectacularly successful, and had brought them to this peak of cultured comfort in Blythney Hall.

The Hall could not be farther from Les Halles. It had stood here, in wider parkland, at the time of Queen Anne when only the straggle of fishermen's cottages and the church made up Blythney; it had queened it over the little town long before the development of Victorian and Edwardian seaside brick villas, and still reigned with effortless supremacy. The Markeens found it piquant that, courtesy of their dwelling alone, they had within five years come to be regarded as an inevitable part of modern Suffolk squirearchy. The people at the Big House.

Alaia played the part with brio, threw garden parties for the hospice fund and sat as a governor of the primary school. She drew the line only at the Yacht Club ball. Jonny was a generous sponsor of town and county charities, had a lifeboat tin in the gallery and gave a marine painting every year for the Retired Fishermen's Benefit Draw.

But together, sometimes, in the evening they would rock with laughter at it all. Jonny's grandfather, bastard and nameless son of a Creole seaman, had made up his own surname, *Marraquine*, only in order to marry his Albanian gipsy wife and open a wine shop in Marseille with money from a dead man's pocket. His father Raoul had changed it to Markham in shame and embarrassment when Grandfather was shot dead by an absconding Grandmother Marraquine in 1954, cutting their only son off, penniless, at art school in London. After Raoul's own death Jonny and his two sisters had got together and adjusted the family name again in memory of Grandfather Marraquine – of whom, being ironically-spirited moderns, they were now quite proud.

As for Alaia herself, her mother was an exiled Polish Jew and her father a Smithfield meat porter who christened her Alison. None of these picaresque antecedents were widely known in Blythney; indeed one or two Blythneians with particularly short and flexible memories used to say they had 'known all the Markeens for yonks, our families have always been friends'. It was generally assumed that Jonny's scar was achieved while hunting, rather than in a bar in Montmartre when he was nineteen. A vague sense hung around that the couple had come from somewhere else, but most people assumed this to mean Norfolk.

Now, Alaia watched Jonny frowning into his glass, trying to remember the new dark child's face, and asked, 'Where's she from, do you think?'

'Well, I asked Alan Tranmere. He came in for the bronze cat for his wife. He reckons she must be one of Sheila Harrison's East End waifs. Like all those little brats last year who were in her boat when Hugo Cotten had to tow it off the mud. But this one was a lot older. And Alan reckons she's the only one, and doing double time down here because she got chucked out of school.'

'So she's in for the full Sheila Harrison Summer Experience, poor little toad,' said Alaia reflectively. 'With those louty boys. What the hell can she make of this place, a kid like that?'

'All I know,' said Jonny, 'is that she was looking into the gallery. And ran away when I nodded at her to come in.'

Marta, who had been gradually unwinding herself from her book, looked across to him.

'Is she a little poor girl, Daddy?'

'I would imagine so,' said her father. 'Sheila supports a charity for taking disadvantaged inner city children on holiday. I'm not so sure I wouldn't rather give them the money. Let the whole family go on holiday together. Can't see the advantage in being bossed around by Sheila's horrible brats, myself.' He always talked to his nine-year-old daughter as if she were his own age.

Marta flicked back her dark hair and frowned. 'The family might be horrid. Like a wicked stepmother family.'

'True.'

'Anyway,' persisted the child, 'I'd like to have a little poor girl for a friend. I could give her some of my things. Can we get her to come and play?'

Alaia was opening her mouth to say 'What a good idea', but Jonny spoke first, swiftly.

'You *never*,' he said with sudden sternness, 'you *never* make a friend of someone just because they're poorer than you. Poor people aren't like pets you can buy.'

Marta considered, not apparently feeling herself reproved at all. 'Well,' she said, 'I could look at her face, like you did, and decide. Then it wouldn't be for her poorness, only her face.'

'Fine,' said Jonny. 'Fine, if it's her face.'

When Marta had wandered off to wash her hands for

supper, Alaia said: 'Do you think Simon Harrison's off the rails again?'

'Well,' said her husband – who took, to her pleasure, a most feline and un-English delight in gossip. 'He came into the gallery this week, and yes, I should say so. Ranted on a bit about the Booker Prize judges – you know how he thinks I'm an intellectual and more worth his notice than the pink-faced philistines of the town. Then I said he must be pleased to have the boys home this weekend, and he went off at the deep end. Seems terribly annoyed with Sheila.'

'Ah,' said Alaia. 'He always gets extra annoyed with Sheila when he's having a fling, doesn't he?'

'Most unfair,' said her husband. 'I thought the whole point of affairs was that they made you nicer to your wife, out of guilt.'

'What a very French attitude,' murmured Alaia. 'So who do you think it is?'

'Don't know. Poor old Sheila. She does mean well, you know.'

'Why did they get married?'

'That isn't the question' said Jonny. 'The question is why did he stop liking being married to her?'

'Because she got preoccupied with the children?'

'Nah. No man minds that. Not if they're his children. I'll tell you the reason, because he's done a good bit of ranting about it. He went off Sheila because she doesn't like his books. Thinks they're just gratuitously pessimistic and violent and dirty.'

'Well,' said Alaia consideringly, 'they are, actually.'

'Indeed,' said Jonny. 'But one is an Artist. One has a right to expect one's wife to admire one's work. Or at least pretend to.'

'Oh, does one?' said Alaia. 'God, I wish I got on with Sheila Harrison. I feel so sorry for her. Perhaps I should have her round for coffee and a cheerful chat.'

'You,' said Jonny, 'are exactly like Marta. You want a "little poor girl" to patronize.'

His wife threw a pale pink silk cushion at him.

At Seafret's supper table Sheila prattled gaily, Vincent and Douai shovelled food into their mouths and responded monosyllabically to their mother's questions, and Simon played sullenly with his broccoli, his mind elsewhere. Only once did Douai speak to Anansi, who ate quietly at the end of the table, her big eyes taking in the family scene.

'Why are you called Anansi?' he asked abruptly, between mouthfuls.

'My dad was a chief, from Africa,' she said, as she had said a hundred times before, in school. 'It's a African name'.

'It's a man's name,' said Douai. 'Not a girl's. It was in a book at school.'

Anansi wanted to say 'It's my name', but was silent.

'Does your dad tell you about Africa?' asked Vincent, with some interest.

But Sheila jogged his elbow, and frowned theatrically, shaking her head and mouthing what looked like *'Gone!'*

'Yes,' said Anansi. 'He tells me 'bout lions.'

Douai sniggered. He had seen his mother's gesture. Anansi heard him snigger, and returned silently to her food.

Chapter Four

The Londoners began to drift down for the summer. Bethie Cotten and her children, freed from London day schools, arrived to open up the summer house; Maurice and Jane had twin cousins coming down, Alison and Dondie, who when the Cotten house filled up would stay as agreed in the Harrisons' spare bedroom but eat and spend the days with their relatives. Hugo Cotten came down every weekend, slipping into his alternative summer life with practised ease, changing from city suit into seaside canvas at seven o'clock each Friday. The Hamptons, Poppy and Andy, did the same, so the Harrisons had neighbours on the seafront. Eric Rattray brought pale pregnant Susannah down and installed her firmly in his mother's house 'for the fresh air and rest' while he drove the Porsche back up towards the lights of London with a song on his lips.

The houses on the promenade were filling up, casting off their empty winter gloom; in the council estate on the edge of the town and the villages beyond, cleaners and waitresses and barmaids and teenage washers-up began to find seasonal work advertised again, and took it gladly.

Sheila Harrison's kitchen and cluttered front room were always full of people, mostly children and young teenagers. Grania Hampton, a sultry blonde of eleven, had a crush on Vincent and hung about endlessly on pretexts like bringing her brother Mark to see Douai's new rollerblades. The red-headed Cotten twins rushed in and out to see their cousins, dragging behind them waves of friends and smaller hangers-on from the other holiday houses. Like a plague of locusts they would denude the kitchen of biscuits and drinks, and then settle, carpeting the front room with their sprawling limbs, to watch cartoons while the rain swept down in sheets outside the window. For the weather had not yet, as Blythneians put it, 'settled'. It was an article of faith that it would eventually 'settle', even if it took until mid-August to do so. Meanwhile a series of depressions whirled over southern Britain, spending their force at last in brief sharp gales and downpours over the East Coast before passing out over the sea.

Vincent and Douai, despite their size and energy, preferred not to go out much in the rain during the first days of the holiday. Their school set great store by a healthy outdoor life, and once released from it they thankfully set up computer games in Vincent's bedroom, shut the curtains and remained holed up in a fug of smelly socks and half-eaten pasties. Douai smuggled in cans of lager; he was better at getting drinks and cigarettes illegally than his elder brother, and thus was tolerated in the lofty circle of fifteen-year-olds.

For most of the day Sheila energetically cooked quiches and pasties and cakes for the freezer. 'We'll need plenty of picnic food,' she said happily, 'once the weather settles. You'll see, Anansi, we just *live* on the river when the summer comes.' She listened constantly to Radio Four, and often rang the BBC duty office on her kitchen telephone with complaints about it. Once, hanging about unnoticed in the chimney corner, Anansi heard her pick up the telephone, dial, and register a strident complaint about an interview on the *Midweek* programme.

'I'm a social worker,' Sheila was saying, 'and for the last hour I have been *inundated* with calls from people who were distressed by the comments made by the woman who spoke about her eczema cure.' Anansi, who had been in the house all morning and knew perfectly well that the phone had not rung even once, marvelled quietly but said nothing. Privately, she thought that Sheila might be a bit weird in the head, but as Sheila was the nearest thing she had to a protector in this odd place, she kept her counsel.

In fact, she was beginning to feel oddly weak. At school and on the familiar streets, if people gave her grief or showed no respect Anansi lashed out, not always wisely but sometimes too well. She had made herself quite a name for it. If you were a crip, you had to. But in Blythney she could not lash out. Something about the brisk, smiling, holiday gentility of the place inhibited her. She was fazed, mistrustful of the very politeness of people: the way that ladies who bumped her in the street said, 'Oh, I *am* sorry,' and the way men stood aside for her at the counter when she ran errands to the newsagent. 'After *you*, young lady.' The old world, the real world, seemed to recede and become less real. Twice Sheila had asked her if she would like to write to her mum ('Such a pity you can't phone – but she's cut off, you say?') and offered her paper and pens. Anansi, the bleak dark place inside her tugging uncomfortably, refused with some abruptness. She could write, and Tracey could read, but in each case only just. And what could there be to say?

Simon, unable to work with the tides of children in the house, slept late, ate lunch at the pub and took long walks in the rain, particularly towards evening in the direction of the ruined Martello tower. One section of its roof gave reasonable shelter from the downpour, and although Penny often mentioned plaintively that she did have the key to the Tranmere parents' unused caravan at the other end of town, and that it would be nice to lie down, Simon stubbornly insisted that they kept to their old place and position.

'The next book,' he said, pushing her roughly against the old stone wall in the gloom, 'is called *Martello*. It's going to be the one, the big one. I can't break the mood.' So Penny had just said, 'Aaaoh!' and, 'Yes, yes, it's going to be a marvellous book, I can *feel* it is,' and acquiesced to everything. They never talked much, exchanging only incoherent expressions of mutual admiration and practical arrangements for the next meeting.

Anansi took walks too. Sheila had given her a plastic coat which she mysteriously called an Oily, with a hood. It was not cold and Anansi found that if she wore her cycle shorts and bare legs, it did not matter that the rain could wet her legs, as they dried so fast in the wind. Usually she walked down past Grenden Quay towards the small stone pier she now knew enough to call Coker's. Often the old man was there.

'Hi,' she said, on the second occasion. This time he had no rabbits, but appeared to be lowering something over the end of the quay, his attention on the water swirling past it. Eventually he straightened up, raindrops glistening on his springing grey hair.

'Hi,' he said. 'Just doing my mooring.'

Anansi looked blankly at the rope. Harry Glanville chuckled, and said, 'Look.' He stooped again, hauled up a wet tangle of rope, and began to pull smoothly on one strand of it. A wooden boat with a mast, which had been bobbing quietly on the water, began to move towards him as if summoned by remote control. Then he selected another strand of the rope, pulled again, and the boat withdrew to its first position.

Anansi laughed, pulled out of herself by brief delight. 'How'd you do that?'

'The rope runs through a pulley, out and back. I fix the pulley to a ring on the bow of the boat, almost on the waterline. When I go out sailing, I fix it to a little floating marker, so I can pick it up again. It saves hauling the boat onto the beach and getting muddy at low tide.'

'D'you go in that boat?'

'Yes. It sails. It's called a Whitecap. White top to the mast, see.'

'The lady – Mrs – Sheila – she's always talking about Whitecaps.'

'Yes. She's got two. One complete wreck, and one just about viable. It's in my garage. She hardly ever sails now, prefers her motor-dory, and the boys only like the fast plastic sort of boat.'

'You know her? The lady – Sheila?' Anansi was incredulous, and not best pleased. This damp quay world was her own place, her discovery. She was not sure whether she wanted it to be connected back to the nervy, noisy world of Seafret.

'Yes, I know her. Actually, I'm her uncle.'

Anansi tried to digest the absurd notion that the large and commanding Sheila could have such a thing as an uncle. It occurred to her, almost with a shock, that Sheila must even have had parents.

'Was you her mother's – um – brother, then?'

'No. Her father was my brother, Maurice. He died just before she was born. Twenty years after the war ended. But he was hurt in the war, and he never got over it.'

Anansi paused. It had seemed momentarily as if the old man was no longer talking to her, a child acquaintance, but to someone far older and on nodding terms with war and grief and hurt. Instinctively, she stayed quiet, and looked out over the water to where his eyes also rested at a spot just beyond the moored boat. As she hoped, he went on:

'Maurice was my younger brother. Five years younger. He shouldn't have died first.'

'Did he get wounded in the war, then?'

'In his head.' Harry glanced sharply at her, suddenly noticing her age again. 'Shouldn't you be cutting along home?'

Anansi, suddenly and firmly, sat down on an old upturned dinghy with a hole in it. 'I like hearing about people's dads,' she said with stubborn finality. 'Where they go, an' that.'

'Well,' said Harry, yielding. 'He got badly hurt, and he had to hurt a lot of other people. With bombs. That turned his mind a bit. You know?'

'Like the druggies? We got druggies down where I live.' The old man winced slightly, and said, 'Not quite like that. But bad enough. He lost his mind in the end, and jumped in the river.'

'Could he swim?'

'Nobody can swim,' said Harry enigmatically, 'if they fix themselves up so they can't.' He had said more than he meant to, and began gathering up his damp sail bags and putting them on his fish-box cart.

Anansi did not move. Her big serious eyes were on him. 'He got drowned, then?'

'He did.'

She looked out at the brown water and the dripping banks. The rain had stopped but moisture hung in the air as if it, too, had the power to drench and drown.

'Here?'

'More or less. You don't want to think about it.'

'People's dads,' said Anansi. 'You have to think about it.'

'Have you lost yours?'

'Yeh. Never saw him. He was in the army. My mum says he was a bastard.'

'Don't believe everything people tell you.'

A shadow crossed her face, then, 'Nah,' said Anansi. 'I don't. 'Cept I believe about your brother.'

He inclined his head in solemn acknowledgement of this compliment, and eased his trolley down onto the path. 'So you see,' he said, 'your hostess Sheila never saw her father, either.'

'Had 'n uncle, though.'

'Not the same.'

'No.'

Anansi looked at Sheila that night – beaming, dispensing curry to her big sons, matriarchal power radiating from her every pore – and held her new knowledge safe. She was so wrapped in her thoughts that she did not hear the plans they were making for the next day: the first of the sunny days, the official and long-awaited beginning of the Blythney Summer.

Chapter Five

The weather forecast which had excited the flurry of planning the night before was not wrong. Bright morning sunlight streamed into Anansi's room at Seafret, and danced through the houses, waking with golden warmth the Cottens and the cousins, the Tranmeres and the Hamptons and the Rattrays (for it was Saturday, and all the London arrivals were safely gathered in between the watery arms of the sea and the Grend). The wind, however, blew fresh out of the south-east and bent the distant trees that screened Blythney Hall.

Jonny Markeen looked out of the bedroom window and said to Alaia, 'I might take a boat out. Bit windy for Marta, do you think?'

'Yes, I do think,' said Marta's mother. 'You go. Take in a couple of reefs.'

'Not that bad,' said Jonny. 'Tell you what, I'll ask Alan Tranmere if he fancies a shakedown in the Flying Fifteen.'

'Ugh,' said Alaia. 'Is there racing?'

'I thought probably not, but the flag's up.'

She moved to his side, taking his arm. The two of

them looked out towards the river, and saw the Yacht Club flag slowly climbing the mast, hauled up no doubt by the Hon. Sec.'s long-suffering wife. On the rutted track towards Grenden Quay, a procession of four cars passed, each towing a tall, rocking trailer with a slender boat hull cradled in it.

'Oh God,' said Alaia. 'Summer's here.'

Sheila was hauling Anansi's arm into a sleeveless padded jacket, and fiddling with the zip.

'This'll do you,' she said, stripping it off again and handing the jerkin to the child. 'And you can wear Douai's old shortie wetsuit.'

'Mu-um!' said Douai.

'Rubbish, it's unisex, and it doesn't fit you now.'

'I won the Mirror Cup in that wetsuit. It's a sacred relic, OK?'

So, still mystified, Anansi found herself instead wearing a spongy jacket rather too big for her, and some neoprene shorts with a hole in them and V. HARRISON lettered across the buttocks. She was holding the blue-and-white waistcoat which Sheila called a BA. 'Buoyancy aid, to stop you sinking!' she said. 'Off we go!'

Vincent and Douai followed their mother and Anansi down the track, muttering to one another. The wind was easing slightly, and Vincent said to his brother, 'I wish you could crew the Laser Two with me. I don't want Dondie. He's a dork, and he won't go on the wire.'

'I can for the race. This afternoon. Only this morning Mum says I have to take *her*.'

'Yeah. Nancy-pantsie. "Give her a sail,"' he mimicked his mother's voice. '"She'll pick it up in no time."'

'Sad.'

'Very sad.'

'Very, very, very sad!'

Sheila was bombarding Anansi with her usual confusing surplus of information: 'Dow's going to take you out in the Mirror, the Cottens' Mirror, the green-and-red one. Not racing, of course – just up the river to Coker's and back, to give you the idea. I'll probably be out on the water in the rescue boat – it's a training morning here, so there's plenty of cover.'

'I never been in a boat,' protested Anansi. 'I might just watch.'

'No-ho-ho!' cried her hostess. 'It's not the same!'

'She could go in the rescue boat with you,' proffered Vincent. 'Then Dow could crew me, and Dondie could take the Mirror with Alison.'

But Sheila knew that she was right, and protests were swept aside in repeated assertions that they would all, repeat all, have an absolutely lovely time doing it her way.

The Tranmere children were too young, in Penny's view, to join in the Saturday morning club training session. Some of the more seasoned Blythney set put their infants into pram dinghies as soon as they were out of prams, and read them *Swallows and Amazons* before they could walk straight, but Penny was not 'old Blythney'. It was Alan who had been here on boyhood holidays with grandparents and roamed the river with Andy Hampton and Susannah Rattray's brothers and tomboyish Bethie Cotten and giggly Sheila Harrison (Glanville, as she then was). These children of the halcyon 1960s had sailed and camped and quarrelled together, a self-assured and self-sufficient tribe; then danced and flirted on through the 1970s at the Yacht and Country

Clubs, coming back from university or college in extravagantly flared jeans with triangular Paisley-pattern inserts above the boot. They all had collections of profoundly embarrassing photographs of one another to prove it.

Some, of course, had drifted away; but a hard core of Blythney holiday children never had. These survivors had not, it seemed, wanted to take the hippie trail or find new kinds of holiday or even take their boats further afield to tougher regattas. All they wanted as adults was to earn enough to come back to the town every summer, have their own holiday house, sail on the river and drink with the same people they had drunk with since their first illicit tot of Merrydown apple wine at ten years old. Ideally, like the Hamptons, they married one another. The imported spouses like Penny Tranmere and Simon Harrison were outside all this, and prone to spend the Blythney summers resenting it a little.

One of Penny's subtler revenges on the system was to rule, very firmly, that neither Kate nor Suzie should be taught to sail before they were at least eight. Their early childhood at least should be hers, not Alan's, and certainly should not be colonized by his dreadful hearty friends like Sheila Harrison and Andy Hampton. So this morning she stayed away from the river to lean on the blue Aga in her clean, beautiful kitchen. Against a background of thumps and shrieks from the children and their friends upstairs, she was unburdening herself to Susannah Rattray, who sat despondently pregnant in the big rocking chair waiting her turn for a grumble.

'Alan's gone off sailing with Jonny Markeen. Really, he did promise we'd go to Ipswich and look at futons.'

'Eric's down at the Yacht Club too. Talking to some chap about Dragons. Honestly!' Susannah had a faint, querulous voice, and held her bump with both hands as if it might float away.

'The thing is,' continued Penny Tranmere remorselessly, 'I don't know what it is with me and Alan these days.' She paused, waiting for a prompt. Susannah, however, was off on her own tack.

'I know – they don't *think*. I keep saying to Eric that this nine months is the last time we'll have just to be together, just us, before we become a family and have to compromise. And he's in London all week, so you'd think on a Saturday we could do something together.'

'Oh, Alan's *here*, all right,' said Penny, deftly snatching the ball back. 'Breathing down my neck – literally – all the time. And I do feel I'm someone who needs space.' She shot a sidelong glance at Susannah, to see whether she had picked up the subtext about her not liking Alan breathing on her bare neck. To emphasize the point, she reached inside the collar of her crisp blue shirt, pulling apart the V at her neck and massaging the soft skin as if it itched.

Susannah, recognizing the signs, sighed and obediently said, 'Things not going any better in that area, then?'

'No!' said Penny. And, with a pleasing sense of throwing herself headlong off a cliff, she ploughed on, 'To be quite honest, Suze, I don't mind any more. Prefer it that way. There's someone else. I mean, I'm having – well, a thing, really.'

This was far better than the usual unspecific current of complaint. Susannah forgot her own troubles in the heady excitement of vicarious adultery.

'You aren't! You mean—'

'Yup. The full monty.'

'How long?'

'A couple of months now.'

'God! I mean – who? And how? I mean, where?'

Penny smiled, and wriggled her thin shoulders. She was not prepared, yet, to give away chapter and verse. That was not the purpose of this conversation. The purpose was to talk, long and intricately, about her own feelings and needs and the fact that this was something to which she had been driven by Alan's crassness and bedtime sleepiness and his bluff, proprietorial, husbandly way of smacking her bottom without proper respect when he came into the kitchen to refill his glass. Which was, in Penny's view, rather too often. No wonder he had lately been more or less – oh, it was a horrid word, wasn't it? – impotent.

So talk she did, leaning the disrespected bottom on the Aga and letting the stove's insidious warmth creep around her thighs as she spoke – without names or places – about her Martello tower liaison with Simon Harrison.

Sheila Harrison was at this moment climbing into the rescue boat with a nimbleness surprising in a woman of her size, and untying the rope from the pontoon while Andy Hampton fired up the engine.

'See you out there!' she called to Anansi who now stood, stiffly trussed up in her rubbery clothes and life jacket, looking at the river. Beside her, Douai yanked bad-temperedly at the rigging on the Mirror dinghy, and a red sail climbed its little mast and pulled itself into shape. In a moment he had raised a smaller sail, which flapped noisily in the wind, shaking the small boat on its trolley.

'I don't really want to come, not really,' said Anansi, in the first spontaneous sentence she had ever spoken to this angry, narrow-faced, contemptuous boy. 'You could go with one of your friends. I could watch.' She spoke placatingly, her pride buried beneath growing fear.

Vincent, who was rigging a sleeker and more complicated boat nearby, looked up.

'Dondie,' he nodded towards a vacant-looking, red-haired boy who was twanging the wire stays irritatingly at his side, 'could take the Mirror out solo rig and you could come with me, Dow, and let Anansi watch. It's quite windy. Just for this time, it might be better. She could go out with me later on, I've got more weight to keep the boat steady.'

Douai bit his lip. First his mother dictated his day, and now his brother was implying – for he was not fooled by the line about weight – that he was not a good enough sailor to give this sulky black girl a first lesson. He could see no end to the coming frustration. For another three and a half bloody weeks, until the bloody girl went, Mum would be nagging him to take Anansi out and tag her along with him every day on the river, because she was 'his age'. As if! When Andy came down to stay, what would he think? Andy had a spiteful tongue: he would tell the boys at school the sort of crap company that Douai kept. Better if she did come out with him, and capsize a few times, and get put off sailing for good. That would keep her out of his hair.

So, 'No,' he said to Vincent. 'If we don't do what Mum says, she'll go on and on.' To Anansi he said, 'Come on, you.' He jerked his head towards the water, and began hauling the little green-and-red boat along on its trolley. The wind took the sails as he turned it, and the wooden boom banged from side to side. Anansi followed him down the long concrete slope to the swirling water, helpless to refuse, limping carefully on the weedy, slippery surface.

Douai walked into the water, holding the boat with one hand, and said to her, 'Take the trolley back up above the tide line.'

She pulled it up, and left it next to another trolley. The small task, easily completed, made her feel marginally better. Glancing back towards the slipway, she wondered whether she should just walk away, back towards the clubhouse, and refuse to have anything to do with this.

But then, looking up towards the white building, she saw someone on its topmost wooden balcony. In the upright soldierly form and shock of vigorous silver hair she recognized the old man from Coker's Quay. The soldier, the rabbit skinner. Something shifted in her head, and pressing her lips together the little girl walked back down the slipway and said, 'So? Whatchya want me to do?'

'Get in. Over the side, there. Sit there. Hold on to the top of that board and when I say "centreboard down", push it down.'

Anansi obeyed, glancing up again at the man on the balcony. When she sat as directed the boat seemed about to tip over; she clutched the board, but it wobbled in its slot. The rippled water moved the boat sideways, up and down, and finally in a toppling heave to the other side as Douai climbed in. Nothing was stable or predictable, nowhere was safe. Douai was hauling in a rope, bracing his legs, sitting on the side. The boat was flying forwards, the smaller sail still flapping with a sound like gunshots. They narrowly missed a sharp post sticking up out of the water. Anansi whimpered.

'Pull in that rope next to you. Hard!' commanded Douai. 'And sit on the edge.'

Anansi could no more sit on the edge than climb the mast. She slipped and slid, her thin bottom on the damp varnish of the seat, her twisted foot unable to find a purchase. When she pulled on the jib sheet, the small sail filled with another deafening crack and the whole boat heeled sharply over. She let it go.

'Get it *in*! Sit on the *side*!' shouted Douai. The wind had momentarily gusted up again, and his hands thrilled to their control of the vibrating helm and sheet. The dark, flailing, helpless figure was an impediment to this mastery and an affront to his maleness. He was not a *nanny*! She let go the jib sheet and the sail flapped again. As she turned, vague but still trying obediently to capture the hysterically flapping rope, Douai saw with a shock of displeasure that the white panel on her small buoyancy aid bore, in felt pen and in his own former hand, the words DOUAI HARRISON.

He lunged forward and caught the sheet himself, capturing it neatly between a pair of sprung plastic jammers. The boat heeled again and picked up speed, and he saw that he would have to turn before he hit a moored Flying Fifteen.

'We're going to do a thing called tacking,' he said. 'The boat will lean over to the other side, so you move when we come through the wind. When I say "Lee oh", let that sheet go and grab the other one.'

Anansi took none of this in. The bucketing, lurching, flying progress of the boat across the water was too new and too shocking for her to spare any thought for details. She clung on, turning her cropped head to and fro, breathing too fast.

Douai was immoderately annoyed. Right, he thought, *right*. He was not spending four weeks of his precious summer looking after this stupid dorky girl. No way. He saw a gust coming towards him across the water, a dark patch on the sunny surface. He had been spilling wind to keep the boat upright, but now he pulled in the mainsheet hard, and felt the Mirror begin to heel more steeply. Anansi stumbled forward, catching her knees on the centreboard case, and water began to come in over the gunwale below her. She screamed. A grab at the centreboard made it rise unsteadily in its casing, and the boat began to heel further.

Until that moment Douai had not been sure whether he would do it; certainly he could even now have brought the boat upright and into smooth progress back upriver merely by letting the mainsheet run through his hand. But the scream did it. He hauled in hard on both sheets, let the boat wallow for a moment with its gunwale under and Anansi clinging to the centreboard, then, when he was sure of capsize, he threw himself neatly over the far side and slid into the cold water.

For a moment, pulling himself round the stern to look at his useless crew, he thought that she had gone straight down and vanished. There was no bobbing figure in a blue-and-white life jacket, no spluttering companion such as he was used to joke with at such moments. Nothing.

Then an arm came from beneath the sail as it floated quietly on the water, and he pulled it. When she came out, her eyes were closed and from her mouth came an inhuman sound. 'Ah-ah-ah.' He had never heard panic or met shock. All his own lessons had been wisely and carefully conducted by professionals, and his first capsizes staged with decorum, in little wind. Nor had Douai Harrison ever been hit or threatened except casually by his peers; never locked out of his house in the dark, never hidden from drunks in the alley between the flats. He did not recognize shock, or the fear of death. He saw only a girl behaving like a wimp. But as the sound continued, and as he helplessly held on to Anansi's bony arm, conscience at last twisted in him, an unfamiliar alien gnawing.

'Come on! Hold on to the boat and I'll get it upright!'

She would not open her eyes at first. When the boat had glugged over, heavy with water, and the boom smashed on her head as she fell, she had heard Harry Glanville's words: 'Nobody can swim if they fix themselves up so they can't.' In this river Sheila's father had drowned. Perhaps these rubber clothes, this strange fat waistcoat, were a way of fixing her up so she could not float or swim. For a moment pure panic shot through her: she was being murdered, just as her grandmother had always warned her she would be if she stayed out on the streets late. Murdered.

But then the buoyancy of the jacket pulled her up, and she realized that her head was held above the lapping water. Salty water. But it wasn't the sea, it was the naffing river, wasn't it? She could see nothing but redness, and something was pressing her down again: the sail. She was stuck under it. It was at this moment she threw out her arm to meet Douai's, and began making the shocked awful noise that frightened him. When he pulled her out, she closed her eyes against the sunlight.

Then Sheila was there, somehow, leaning over the front of a rubber blown-up boat. She was saying something. It was 'Whoops!' Then, as a man loomed up beside Sheila and expertly drew Anansi out of the water, Sheila's voice went on, 'Well, your first capsize! What a morning! Everyone's all over the place!'

The man laughed, and patted Anansi on her life-jacketed back. 'All right, sunshine?' said Andy Hampton. 'Stay in the RIB for a bit, what?' He was an open-faced, youthful-looking man with a tuft of blond hair falling over his eyes. Unselfconsciously, he threw an arm round her to steady her as she tried, wildly, to stand up.

'No, sit down. Take a breather for ten minutes. Hold tight, we've got another casualty up by Coker's. Maurrie Cotten's turtled his Topper.' He twisted a grip by his hand

and the boat accelerated, throwing back sheets of spray and forcing Anansi back against Sheila's bulk.

'Don't worry about the boat, Douai's got it up already – look, he's off!' said Sheila.

Anansi, still shocked, stared around her. Douai's red sail was streaking downwind now, and around him more red sails, and a fluttering, skimming insect swarm of others: white, striped, brown, purple, gay primary colours and bright neons. Three or four other boats, she saw, had capsized; their sailors, apparently unworried by this, were balancing on the centreboards and hauling them upright again to clamber aboard and streak off. By the time they reached Maurrie Cotten he, too, had almost righted his boat, so the rubber boat stood by, its engine idling, while the boy pulled his flat craft upright.

'Go for it, Maurrie!' shouted the blond man. 'Go and show Mark how it's done!'

'I've lost my *hat*,' said the boy crossly, floundering aboard on his stomach.

'Oops – it's over there. Hold tight, troops!' Andy spun the rubber boat round and streaked downriver. He fetched the floating baseball cap, spun again so that Anansi closed her eyes in bewildered nausea, and threw it to the boy, who by now was keeping pace with sail flapping, leaning forward to fiddle with a baler. His wet red hair flopped forwards over his eyes.

'Thanks.' He sat up, put on the hat back to front, hauled in his sail and sped off. Sailing boats were around them in all directions, moving fast, zigzagging from tack to tack with great graceful sweeps of their masts, bedecking the whole of the river's homely brown face with bright random colour and movement.

Anansi began to shiver, and only by great effort did

not cry until she was back ashore, alone, limping up to the changing rooms.

Simon Harrison was in the Yacht Club bar with the Cotten parents and Eric Rattray.

'Was that your youngest just went over?' asked Eric.

'Dunno. Was it?'

'Oooh, *men*!' said Bethie Cotten. 'You are awful. You hardly care at all, do you?'

'There's rescue cover,' said Simon. 'Silly little arse, he's always dry-capsizing just for fun. He'll break his mast again, sticking it in the mud, and cost me.'

'It is, it's Douai Harrison in our Mirror,' said Hugo Cotten, peering through the miniature field glasses he sported round his neck all through the sailing season. 'So it'll cost me, not you, you toad.'

'They've taken the crew off. Oh, it's your little black lady.'

'Sheila's doing,' said Simon. 'That kid is hating it here already, and now she's let Douai half drown her. Perhaps she'll send her back now.'

'You usually have little wee ones, don't you, Sime? And weeks later than this?' Bethie was curious, looking out at the small shivering figure as the rescue boat approached the pontoon. 'What are you doing with this one?'

'Christ knows. Drowning her, by the look of it. Oops, there goes your Maurice again. That child is such a chancer!' Simon sucked at his drink.

In the corner, unremarked, Harry Glanville put down his half-finished coffee and gathered up his jacket to leave the room.

'I suppose I've always been emotionally adventurous,' said

Penny Tranmere, massaging her bare brown neck with complacent pleasure. 'Alan might find out, but if he does, it's sort of fate, isn't it? It'll be meant. It would mean that I'm meant to be with – Him. But I don't know. Some things are too intense to last. Particularly with artists.'

'Who is it?' asked Susannah, irritated now, and resolving to leave as soon as possible and go down to the club for a drink. 'Go on, I'll keep it to myself, honestly. Is it one of Jonny Markeen's pet painters?'

Penny turned towards her. 'All right then,' she said. 'Promise you won't be shocked. It's—'

'Mummeee!' Suzie Tranmere sashayed into the room, wound from head to foot in expensive shawls, a dripping carton of Ribena in her fist. 'I'm a princess, but Katie and Sally say I'm not!'

'Oh my God!' shrieked Penny. 'That Pashmina cost *five hundred pounds*!'

Susannah sighed, and decided it was time to go. She knew from long experience that these moments of rash confidence, once broken, took at least twenty minutes to recover. At the Yacht Club there would at least be a drink and Bethie Cotten, who was always willing to discuss the minutiae of pregnancy for hours on end. Another day would do for Penny's demon lover.

Chapter Six

Emerging from the changing room, Anansi looked nervously into the club bar. Nobody took any notice of her. Beyond the plate glass and the terrace she could see the black rescue boat moving between the fluttering yachts on the water, and Sheila still aboard, her blonde hair flying loose on one side from its bun. After a moment's hesitation Anansi went back into the changing room and threw her wet towel and gear down on the bench next to Sheila's things. The second time she emerged she was unencumbered. She stood for a moment, thin in her cycle shorts and T-shirt, and swung her arms in a windmilling, chimpanzee motion. She was alive. She began to feel normal. With normality came the sly, hot return of anger. Experimentally, she kicked the white-painted wall with the toe of her bad foot, and relished the contact. She kicked it harder.

This time Simon Harrison, momentarily alone at the bar, turned and saw her. For almost the first time since she had arrived, he spoke directly to his house guest.

'Took a dive, did you?'

She nodded, speechless. These extraordinary people seemed to take near-drownings and desperate rescues very lightly indeed.

'I see you're not going out again.' Simon, had she known it, was looking at her bony knees and elbows, her twisted foot and cropped round head, and feeling an unaccustomed twinge of guilt. With her hard little face and starveling body this child was an incongruity here, a thing from the world he wrote about rather than the world he lived in. She belonged, he was thinking, in one of his own fictional settings: against leprous concrete and obscene graffiti, in a street scene where crack dealers slipped consignments to hopeless wan young mothers who tucked white packets behind the baby in its pushchair. It worried him to see this child's face here in Blythney among the tans and pink cheeks of an affluent, anachronistic Enid Blyton summer set. When Sheila did her holidays for smaller children he had been able to ignore them; they were unformed babies, big living dolls. But this child was already hardening in the mould: city, cynical, underclass.

Indeed Simon, although he would have been indignant at the charge, had as firm and immobile a set of notions about society as any Edwardian dowager. What Anansi was, as far as he was concerned, she always would be. His children's pleasures would not, and could not, ever be hers. She was inappropriate here. He could have rationalized these feelings into a dislike of middle-class patronage, but the plain fact was that the child's solid presence in his family's world unsettled him. These abrupt inquiries were the nearest he could come to being placatory. So was his unfatherly disparagement of her erstwhile skipper.

'Douai's not nearly as good a helm as he thinks he is.'

'He did it on purpose,' said Anansi. 'He's a fucking

murderer.' She turned, and walked out onto the terrace, head down, picking her way furiously through the tables where couples chattered in the sunlight and watched their skimming, speeding children tame the wind to their gay sails. Simon stared after her, leaning his elbow on the bar and finishing his drink in one mouthful.

'Stroppy,' he said to himself, aloud. There was an unwilling note of admiration in his voice.

Anansi reached the river path, putting distance between herself and the clubhouse. Her halting steps took her, without thought, upriver towards the little stone quay. When she reached it the old man was there, sitting on his fish-box barrow, as if he had never left the place.

'I saw you at that club,' she said. 'On the high bit.'

'Yes,' he said. 'I was looking at some charts, in the chart room. Maps of the river.'

'I fell in,' she said.

'Capsized,' said the old man. He was doing something to a piece of rope with a penknife and a sharp steel spike. 'Not your fault. You weren't on the helm.'

'What *is* a helm?' she asked irritably. 'The man said Douai was a bad helm. Whassit mean?'

'The helm is the steering gear of a boat. So the same word is used of the person who steers it. Just as the rudder directs the boat, the helmsman directs the rudder. The rudder dictates which way the boat goes; the helmsman controls the rudder. So he is responsible for whatever happens to the boat. Including unnecessary capsizes.'

'The water,' said Anansi after a brief silence, 'was salty.'

'Yes.'

'That's weird. It's a river.'

'A tidal river. It goes down to the sea, and comes up

from the sea. More of this stuff here is salt sea water than fresh water off the land. So it tastes salty.'

'I think it's creepy,' said Anansi flatly. 'I'm not going in no more boats.'

The old man pushed the sharp steel spike between the strands of his rope and pulled one strand round, to tuck it in beside the steel prong.

'You're right,' he said. 'Tidal rivers *are* creepy. Not a lot of people understand that. Rivers are assaults on the land. Fingers of sea, reaching in to quiet, comfortable land places. Cargoes can come up the river, and sailors needing shelter. But enemies can come up rivers in the darkness too, and strike at the heart of things. It's easier than landing on the beach, and more deadly.' He glanced sideways at Anansi, his sharp blue eyes inquiring. 'Do you understand any of that?'

She was silent. He, too, stayed silent, quietly splicing his rope. She watched his hands for a moment, feeling no pressure to answer. The tide was low, and the sailing boats were keeping clear of Coker's Quay; it was as if the two of them were talking in another world, far from the circling, swaying, speeding gaiety of the coloured boats.

At last the child said: 'Yeah. I get it. You could come right up the river, in the dark, without making a noise like you would on the road. You'd be in the middle of somewhere, like, suddenly.'

'Right,' said Harry Glanville. 'In war, that happens.'

'Here?'

'A thousand years ago, they say, invaders came up the Blyne and Grend. They sometimes find things from ships, buried under the fields. Some people say the invaders built this quay.'

'You were in a war,' said Anansi suddenly. 'You killed people, you said. Did you come up a river and do it?'

'Yes,' said the old man. 'I did.'

'In a motorboat?'

'No. In a canoe.'

'With a gun?'

'We had small arms, but the main thing was bombs, d'you see? We put them on the sides of warships in a big naval harbour. In France. There were German warships there.'

'Did you get away?'

'Well, obviously I did,' said Harry acerbically. 'I'm here, aren't I?'

Anansi crowed with sudden laughter, as he had meant her to.

When Susannah Rattray reached the Yacht Club, the children were already coming in from their practice, hauling dinghies up the slipway and shouting shrilly to one another. She looked at them with the apprehensive affection of pregnancy – would her dear, secret, inner baby ever be so large, so competent, so full of shouts? – and stepped heavily up the terrace and through the open doors to the bar.

Bethie Cotten was there, telling Maurrie to hurry up and get his wet things off. When he had gone, Susannah sat down confidentially beside her friend and said, 'I've just been talking to Penny.'

'Oh?' Bethie Cotten was not enamoured of Mrs Tranmere. In point of fact, few of the Blythney wives were. There was a reckless, dangerous quality about Penny despite her outward demureness, and a good number of them were very well aware of their husbands' interested glances.

Susannah settled, arching her back and pushing her

discarded sweater down to support the curve of it against the cruel weight of her bump.

'She's having an affair.' She had not meant to pass on the news so crudely or so rapidly, but was goaded to it by her irritation at the memory of Penny's coyness.

'Oho,' said Bethie. 'London, or here?' Hugo's last few solitary outings unrolled in her methodical mind.

'She didn't say,' said Susannah.

'Does Alan know?'

'Would he?' Susannah laughed, without much mirth. 'I didn't get the impression it was going to last. She said something about an artist.'

'Uh,' said Bethie Cotten, relieved. Hugo Cotten could not, by any stretch of fantasy, be described as an artist.

The morning's doings on the river were discussed that night around the Harrison table in the usual baffling code. Anansi listened more carefully than normal, given her own involvement. Douai was badgering his mother.

'I ought to have my own Laser Two. It's spastic, at my age, crewing for Vince all the time, and they need more boats in the fleet.'

'Don't use spastic in that sense, darling. Cerebral palsy is a real and tragic condition.'

'Bo-ring!'

'Douai! You'll go to your room before pudding if you don't behave.' But Sheila, Anansi noticed, still beamed with overflowing maternal fondness on her youngest child.

He, too, saw this and persisted, 'So can I get a Laser Two? There's three in *Yachts and Yachting*.'

'Not for this summer.'

'Well, I'm not sailing the Whitecap.'

'Why, darling? All your friends—'

'It's spas— it's too slow.'

'There's a lot of skill in sailing slower boats too,' said Vincent piously.

'Dickhead.'

'Douai!'

Anansi removed her attention from them. Sometimes, suddenly, she felt a cold shivering at the thought of the morning's capsize. She lived again the sudden darkness, the water forcing itself into nose and ears and mouth, the terror at the whining roar heard through the water as the engine of the rescue boat approached. She had not remembered this at first, had thought that the first sign of rescue was Sheila's looming bulk over the black rubber tube. Now details of the time in the water were beginning to return. Douai had grabbed her arm. She had not known whether he meant to drown her or to save her. The approaching engine had sounded like a great wasp. Fumes had blown over her, into her face, as it came from upwind.

She looked at Douai now, thin-faced, indefinably sour around the mouth. When a pause came in the bickering she spoke to him directly.

'Did you go on sailing, after we went in the water?'

'Yup,' said Douai. 'Obviously. Got to get going again after a capsize. It's spastic going off in the rescue boat.'

'How'd you get back in the boat?' She sensed his contempt, but suppressed her rage in the need to know these new things.

'Stand on the plate, haul upright, and roll in. Peasy. Get yourself off the wind, flip the self-balers *if* you've got them, which that rubbish Mirror does not have. Sad.'

'Suppose it sinks?' said Anansi, persisting despite the layers of mystification which were building up.

'Can't. Buoyancy tanks, see? Full positive.'

'Unless the bungs come out,' said Vincent.

'Which they sometimes do!' Sheila added, laughing uproariously and drawing a glare of positive dislike from the silent, preoccupied Simon at the other end of the table. 'The Cottens are always using plastic caps off Nicolas rosé bottles instead of proper rubber bungs, so they pop out under pressure, and glug glug glug!'

It seemed to Anansi that the family at Seafret spoke many words without ever making her any the wiser. Whereas the old man on the quay spoke few and made her wiser every day. When she had walked out to Coker's Quay that morning, sore-hearted and humiliated, she had been intending to go back later and demand – as she knew was her right – to be returned home straightaway. She had rehearsed the telephone call to the Country Hosts Association. 'I'm not staying here. They're loonies. I haven't settled, see? I got a right to go home. Else I'll ring Childline.'

After her conversation with Harry Glanville she had changed her mind. The call could wait. Her fear of the river, still strong, was mingled with fascination. When she fell asleep, listening to the soft washing of the sea on the pebbles, she dreamed of silent, living, rippling tendrils of water prying into the soft helpless land, bringing dark shapes of invaders. After a while she was herself the invader, skimming over the water as she had done that morning in the short mesmerizing moments of speed before the catastrophe. Upriver she sped, into the heart of the enemy camp, and in her hand was a warm, wild, glorious bomb. To show them.

Harry Glanville, leaning back on the pillows next to his wife's white hair and tranquil sleeping face, stayed awake and also thought of rivers. His were fringed with reeds, seeping away through shallow creeks into marshland. Long and low, camouflaged and laden, he paddled through the shallows to join the main river. His flotilla moved unseen around him, dipping their paddles quietly in the cold water. There were miles to go before morning, upstream with the tide towards the basin where the great ships lay, waiting to be sent violently to the riverbed for ever.

He did not know why he had told the thin black child about it, on the quay. Probably just because she had asked. And something about her, absurdly but insistently, always reminded him of warfare. It was not only that he pitied her lonely and precarious state; there were plenty of others like her to pity. It was stronger than that, a tug of fellow feeling; her face had in it battlefields and strategies and reckless courage in the face of insuperable odds. He felt an instinct he had never felt towards his great-nephews or niece, or any of his godchildren. When Harry saw Anansi he wanted, in an obscure way, to arm her.

Chapter Seven

It was two more days before Anansi found out Simon's secret. On those days the boys sailed and cycled with their friends and Anansi kept clear of them. She helped Sheila without enthusiasm around the house ('Isn't it nice to be girls together! Now, how good are you at pastry?'). The housework made her remember her grandmother, Tracey's mother: Nanna Bev, who was killed by the lorry in Romney Road when Anansi was six. Nanna used to make pastry. Tracey bought it, frozen, if she had any money, but reckoned the chip shop pies were better anyway.

Twice a day Anansi took patient, limping walks while Sheila flitted brightly around the town, greeting newcomers with 'More swallows! This *does* make a summer!' She also spent a lot of time harassing the boat yard on Grenden Quay about getting the engine fixed on her big dory 'so we can start having some real picnic days!'

Simon and Penny generally met each evening at the Martello tower. Penny continued, with increasing plaintiveness, to mention the relative comfort of the caravan;

Simon continued to insist that their dank and comfortless trysting place was essential to his creative flow. The brutality and briskness of their couplings fulfilled a need in him. Now that the summer visitors were arriving and Alan Tranmere had friends to meet in the bar of the Anchor and Hope before supper, the most convenient time for Penny was the hour afterwards, just before the summer dusk. She would leave him to baby-sit while she took her evening walk.

Simon was, as usual, free to leave his house at any time with no explanation and without demur from the ever-bright Sheila. 'Off out, darling?' she would say to the slamming door. 'That's right – some fresh air!'

Anansi marvelled silently at this. In her experience the comings and goings of men did not take place without shrill angry shouts of 'Where you going? Well, don't bloody come back, then!' or, conversely, 'Get out, or I'll have the police.' She herself was equally anxious to get out of Seafret after supper, since the boys' circle and the noisy Cotten cousins (who had now moved in by night) used it for assembling before their own evening excursions. The visitors had no sense of territory, and often she would find five or six of them sprawled across the big bed in her room, or using her window to throw water bombs on friends in the front yard below. They would look round at her with healthy, polite, inscrutable faces that showed no aggression, but Anansi would wither and shrink back, abashed.

Generally, her evening walk took her along the edge of the marsh to Grenden and then upstream to see whether Harry was at his station on the smaller quay. Twice she was disappointed. Once he was nowhere in sight, and nor was his fish-box cart; on the second occasion she saw him, but not on the quay. He was afloat in his little brown-sailed boat, sailing upriver and vanishing behind the reeds and round the river's bend. That was on an evening of extraordinary splendour, when the whole expanse of water was gilded and reddened in streaks by the sunset, and the trees stood black and stark on the hill which Harry had told her might be a Viking burial place. Men lay there, he said, who had come up this river in boats long ago and taken the inhabitants by surprise.

On the third evening he was not there, and again his boat was missing from its mooring by the little quay. His handcart was by the steps, though, and Anansi reasoned that he must be coming back before the darkness fell. Rather than return to Seafret she walked back along the path, and onto the sea wall. From the clubhouse came sounds of laughter and clinking glasses. A few children were tidying up their boats by the slipway or swinging on the railings. She hurried past. As she did, a shrill voice called to her.

'Anansi! Hi-i!'

This was such an unusual occurrence that she stopped in her tracks and turned, uncertain and almost fearful. The Blythney children had not, apart from Douai's capsize, mistreated her at all. They had simply passed over her, edited her out, not bothered with her. She was aware of this with a mixture of relief and pique: never in her short turbulent life had she felt so invisible. Not in the council children's homes, not at school, not on the street or the landings of the flats had she ever been so neutrally treated. She had been chased, threatened, punched, all but raped; had made short-lived friendships and violent enmities. She had been cursed and – when she was far smaller – cuddled. When Tracey needed her to fetch some puff or a white packet from the corner boys, she had been wheedled and flattered. But she had never before been politely ignored, and it galled her.

The girl calling her was familiar from the club and the gatherings of children at Seafret. She was dark, her hair and brows as black as Anansi's own, but her skin was a white girl's and the hair was straight and lustrous. A little kid, shorter even than herself. Martha. That was it. No, Marta.

'Hi-yee!' said Marta Markeen. 'I wondered where you got to in the evenings. Do you want to come in and have a Coke?'

'In there?' said Anansi incredulously.

'Yah. We can go in the bar in the evenings now. Junior members. You can be one when you're eight. I'm nine. But we have to drink it at a table and not the bar. You coming? I've got treats money off my mum.'

'Nah,' said Anansi stiffly. 'I got stuff to do.' She walked on along the sea wall, but the little girl trotted after her.

'Please. Be friends. Go on.'

This open appeal halted Anansi in her stride, and she looked down at the smaller child in surprise.

'Why?'

'Well – 'cos I like knowing new people. You could tell me about London. I've only been there two times since I've been remembering. And only to the pantomime anyway. But I was in London when I was a baby, in my dad's old house.'

'I'm only here for a bit,' said Anansi. 'What's the point?'

'I could write to you when you go home,' wheedled Marta. 'Oh, go on. You could come on a picnic in my dad's boat. It's got sails.'

'I done that,' said Anansi. 'Sailing's crap, OK? I nearly frigging drowned.'

'I know. Everyone told me. But that was Douai's fault,' said the child severely. 'My dad is a much better sailor than Douai Harrison. And our boat is bigger. It has a lead keel that's so heavy it couldn't turn over. Mirrors' keels are only wood.'

'I'll think about it,' said Anansi, to get rid of her. And then, sarcastically, 'That all right for you?' She gave the little girl one of her special hard, don't-fuck-with-me stares, but it seemed to have no effect.

'OK,' said Marta happily. She glanced back to the clubhouse and saw the tall figure of Alaia on the steps, swinging a set of car keys and looking around her.

'That's my mum. I think I have to go home. She might have let me stay if you'd come in for a Coke.'

'Right,' said Anansi, ignoring the reproach. She limped on, obscurely exhausted by this conversation and anxious to leave the spot where it had taken place. To ensure her complete escape she went on further and faster than she intended. As the ruined Martello tower grew closer, her curiosity began to rise. Weird thing! The curve of its massive walls seemed to hypnotize her, and she went on walking and finally dodged through the shallow remains of its moat until she could touch it. The sun's warmth was still in the old stones, and she put her flat palm on the surface, marvelling at the contrast with the chilly evening air.

There must, she reasoned, be a way in. Cautiously, without noise, she moved round the circumference on the coarse sea grass, and at last found what she was looking for. A doorway, ragged with dereliction, facing inwards towards the river. From the town side of the sea wall the tower had looked complete and unvanquished, but now she could see what the bomb had achieved half a century before. Part of the far side of the circular wall had fallen inward, leaving a pile of rubble old and stable enough to be interwoven with grass and moss like a rockery.

Carefully she picked her way over the stones until she stood in the doorway.

It was darker inside than out, although there was hardly any roof left, and a cool, musty smell came from the interior. She wrinkled her nose in surprise: no smell of urine. She was used to railway bridges and subways, and the dark damp walls made her expect the acid smell of piss as a matter of course. But this ruin smelt only of salt decay. It was the same kind of smell as you got up at Coker's Quay when the tide was low and the old man was working on his mooring ropes. Anansi stood for a moment breathing the concentrated smell of salt riverbank, and found an obscure comfort in it. The black space inside her lightened momentarily.

Then she saw the couple: at it, over against the far wall. It was not a new sight to Anansi. Since babyhood she had witnessed the sexual act plenty of times, through half-closed eyes in her mum's bedroom, and outdoors too, in concrete alleys and night-time underpasses. And it was on telly often enough, although it never looked so jerky or uncomfortable there as it did in life. With detached coolness she surveyed the pair for a moment. The man's back looked vaguely familiar. After a moment, it was entirely familiar. It had, after all, been turned on her often enough during the past week.

The woman, whose eyes were closed and whose head was tilted back, was the one they called Penny. It was strange to see her there, against the damp stone wall like a tart, when she had always seemed so neat and clean and rich. Soundlessly and still unseen, the child stepped back through the doorway. She could look at the tower another day. The old man might be back at the little quay by now, anyway.

He was. Anansi arrived just as Harry Glanville's dinghy glided up neatly to its mooring. Looking down, she watched him pull up a green washing-up liquid bottle which was floating, tied to a piece of thin rope. The rope was fixed to a thicker one, which he hauled up green and slimy and pushed through a ring she had never noticed, down near the waterline at the front of the boat. Then, while she sat with legs dangling on the end of the stone quay, Harry pulled down his sail and tied it up in a neat sausage which he laid in the bottom of the boat. After a few more minutes' tidying and lashing, he looked up at her and said, 'Hi. Save me getting wet, would you? Pull the top line.'

She stooped to pull the boat in; magically, it glided towards her until Harry could reach the quay ladder. It stopped, lightly aground, a stride away from the ladder, and the old man had to stand on the dinghy's wide foredeck, pressing it into the mud, and make a flying step to the lower rung.

'Thanks,' he said. 'Nearly got a pair of brown socks there.'

Without being asked, Anansi pulled the lower line and made the dinghy pull itself off the mud and glide back to its place. Harry climbed up, groaning slightly as his stiff knee landed on the damp stone.

'Had a good day?' he asked.

'Ord'nary.'

'I've been all the way up to Catley,' he said. 'Three miles upriver. You can get right past the marshes into

79

ordinary farmland when the tide's high. I had to swing the mast down to get under the bridge.'

'Yeah?' Something stirred within Anansi, tightened round her heart at the notion of gliding through changing country on the wide ribbon of water, infiltrating the unknown land. 'Like when you went up the other river, with bombs?'

'Well, in France we never landed. Just put the limpets on the ships and paddled like hell before the big bang.'

'If you got enemies, and they don't have any respect,' said Anansi, 'it does good to chuck them a bomb, right?'

'If you've got a bomb,' said Harry consideringly. 'And if they really deserve it. But I wouldn't recommend it in peacetime. Bombs are a bit final. You can't just apologize and undo them.'

'There's no difference really between wars and ordinariness,' said Anansi. 'It's never exactly a peacetime, is it? People still fighting and quarrelling and puttin' people down. Everywhere.'

'When you look at it calmly, and comparatively, and from the perspective of having seen a real war,' said Harry, 'believe me, peacetime it is.'

But Anansi had stopped listening. Something had occurred to her.

Once any child's first week in a holiday placement was over, it was Miss Archenlaw's responsibility to contact the hosts, speak by phone to the child if possible, and file a very brief report to the committee of the Country Hosts Association, confirming that all was well. The committee secretary would then pass on the news of the child's successful holiday, in a rather formulaic style, to the parents (or, more likely, parent).

Generally, this was bland routine; when a placement was really going wrong the hosts would have been on the phone far earlier. Or, occasionally, the child itself would be remonstrating strongly against the circumstances of its supposed holiday. This week had been more troublesome than usual, with a querulous call from a twelve-year-old boy who hated his youth camp at Broadstairs and wanted to return as fast as possible to the stimulating urban pursuits from which, notionally, the CHA was protecting him. There had also been a call from a distraught couple in Norfolk whose charges, aged five and seven, enjoyed themselves mightily round the farm and the ponies all day but devoted the nights to soaking several full sets of bedding apiece. Also, their language was shocking the family's grandmother.

These troubles Janice Archenlaw had handled with a calm, professional competence which she was herself the first to appreciate. The boy had been reminded that his therapeutic holiday was part of the condition of his discharge following the theft of three car radios, and that while Broadstairs Youth Camp might be dull, it had to be considerably better than youth custody. The couple in Norfolk had been persuaded to wring out bedding and block Granny's ears for a few days more because they were, after all, doing a wonderful and worthwhile good deed for these very deprived children, and possibly changing their lives. After many years with the charity, Janice now said these things automatically. But they were none the less convincing – and calculatedly shaming – so the Norfolk couple knuckled under.

Ringing Sheila Harrison would, after all that, be a pleasure and a relief. Mrs Harrison had been taking in CHA children for five years, with never a complaint from the hostess. The children themselves had varied in their reaction from dazed and acquiescent to moderately enthusiastic ('They've got a real *boat*, an' a beach with waves. Only they never have no burgers'). Certainly Sheila would not whine or repine over a bit of simple bed-wetting or a few unchildlike verbal obscenities.

Before Miss Archenlaw could make the call, however, the director herself came in.

'Janice, have you checked up on Anansi Cowper?'

'Just about to.'

'Leave it till tomorrow, would you? Social services have been on. There's a police problem with her mother.'

'Oh dear. Drugs?'

'In the baby's buggy. Not a casual thing, a specially-made concealed pocket in the padding.'

'Cannabis?'

'No such luck. Class A, and quite a lot of it. Sounds like crack cocaine to me, though they were a bit cagey.'

'Are they going to prosecute?'

'Yes. But they've remanded her in custody anyway, because it was such a stash. They think she's a regular dealer. It was a tip-off in some operation they're running.'

'Custody!' Miss Archenlaw was shocked. Never, in her fifteen years' service, had a sole custodial parent been actually imprisoned while their child was bucket-and-spading on a CHA holiday. She was a vain and not very imaginative woman, but her instincts were immediately humane. 'Something must be done to get her out. Could we stand bail?'

'They say it will be refused. It's not a first offence.'

'Oh dear, oh dear. What about the baby?'

'Aston Lodge had an infant place. She's there.'

'Oh dear, oh dear oh dear.' Miss Archenlaw swept off her half-moon reading glasses and began polishing them furiously. 'Do you not want me to ring Mrs Harrison? And tell her?'

'Not yet. I need to make them sort out which home can take Anansi when she comes back. It's a shame she isn't profiled as suitable for fostering. I think they were a bit hasty there. The violence at school has been quite rare, and I would have thought a response to stress and to her disability. But there it is. They've lost too many foster parents in these boroughs through sending out violent children. And finding an institutional place is always so difficult in July and August.'

The two women nodded together. Actually, as they both knew, it was next to impossible. Unwanted children seemed to become even more unwanted than usual during the heat of the long summer holidays.

After a pause, Janice Archenlaw said, 'Well, if Mrs Harrison says Anansi's doing well down in Blythney, I still think we should suggest they do look for a foster home. I really don't think she's uncontrollable in a domestic setting. It's just school. She was perfectly fine on the train to Suffolk with me. Actually . . .' she paused, and the director looked at her with narrowed eyes.

'I know what you're thinking. You're thinking, leave her with Mrs Harrison.'

'Well, why not? If it's going well. Our background checks are accepted as equivalent to the ones they do for emergency fostering. The Harrisons passed them all. Mrs Harrison did once say she'd thought of longer-term fostering – though I didn't discuss it with the husband.'

The director frowned, trying to envisage the couple she had briefly met at a Hosts' seminar, one so large and blonde and smiling, the other so thin and dark and sour, volcanic in his resentment at being there at all.

'Mmm, but there was something, something . . . I know, in our profile checks, there was a query about him writing dirty books, wasn't there?'

'Yes,' said Miss Archenlaw. 'Only the one dirty book, way back when we began. But she was so keen and suitable otherwise that you and Duncan decided it was all right.'

'I remember,' said the director. 'Duncan said it wasn't really pornography but probably counted as literature because he didn't seem to be selling many.'

It had been a long day. Together, furnished though their working lives were with the facts of poverty and vice and sorrow, the two women erupted into fits of giggling which took long minutes to subside.

Chapter Eight

The engine was mended. Inside its weathered wooden housing it sang a steady, discreet, throaty song, and when young Nick down at the boatyard pushed the throttle forward, it deepened to a great vibrating roar and shook the white hull and blue gunwales.

'Lovely lot of power there,' he said. 'Push her over the tide, no trouble.'

'It's always been a lovely engine,' said Sheila robustly. 'Good. What do I owe you?'

'Mr Nettles'll do the bill when he got time,' said the boy. 'Awright, then? He says you can leave it by the quay tonight if tha'ss handier.'

So at last Sheila could achieve the first climax of her summer by leading a picnic to Miserley beach. On the morning after Anansi's visit to the Martello tower, in blazing Mediterranean sunshine, she rose at six thirty to defrost and assemble quiches, sausages, fruit pies, a portable barbecue, charcoal, matches, home-made lemonade in old Coke bottles and a special camping kettle that boiled water on no more fuel than two sheets of the *Guardian*. She drove this equipment down to Grenden Quay and loaded it into her waiting boat in a series of baskets and insulated boxes. Then, while Simon and Anansi ate their cereal and the others ambled about noisily upstairs, Sheila leaned on the dresser, with her bottom stuck out in the pose that her husband most hated, and began telephoning.

'Bethie? Picnic? The tide's perfect for Miserley – I can take five littles in the dory, and the big ones can sail up – high water is two o'clock, yes, couldn't be better. Eric and Hugo – well, obviously! If they anchor off in the keelboat, Dondie or Jane or one of them can come and get them ashore in the rubber dinghy if we tow that up behind the dory – and honestly, if Maurrie can't sail back in the Topper we can tow . . .'

Then, 'Penny? We're all off up the river. Yes, all the Cottens, and I think Poppy and Andy are going up with the kids – Grania's getting quite confident on the helm, but Mark will be with her . . .'

Then, 'Susannah? How are you, how's the poor back? Look, we're all off upriver to Miserley. You'd rather drive round? Well, why not? Simon might drive you – he's very excited, his ban ended yesterday, he can hardly keep his hands off the car – Sime! Did you hear that? Sorry, Suzy . . .'

Friends were used having their more communal summer pleasures orchestrated by Sheila. She block-booked for the summer theatre – always the comedy – and for the family proms along the coast at Snape Maltings. She knew exactly how many tents and windbreaks, dinghies and bicycles were owned or could be borrowed by every middle-class family in Blythney. She masterminded the construction of ever more elaborate carnival floats, dragooning idler mothers into intensive sewing bees, at the end of which thirty or forty small children would emerge as very creditable Vikings, or ghosts, or Lost Boys.

In the midst of all this, once every week or so in the high season she would decree a mass picnic. A fleet of dinghies and mother ships with engines would converge amid much shouting and signalling to startle the cows which grazed above the quiet river beach of Miserley, three miles upstream from Grenden Quay. To this end she kept a tide table by her telephone and punched up weather forecasts on Simon's fax machine daily. Now, crooking the telephone in her shoulder and pleating the corner of the latest Metfax, she was shouting instructions to Poppy Hampton.

'No, force four at the most – Grania should be fine to sail up – could they fit with Marta Markeen, if Alaia would let her come? Those two might make a lovely little crew for the junior regatta – if you come with me and Andy takes the RIB, Mark could even go threesome in the Laser with my two, leave the girls to have their little adventure – or maybe your Whitecap? Oh, what a bore – they do spring planks so easily now they're all getting older! Do you want me to have a word with Nettles at the yard? Oh, all right, I see – anyway, the barbie; I've got that, if you just bring sausages or burgers to cover your lot . . .'

At the far end of these conversations, sleepy families would look up from their cereal and supermarket croissants, demur briefly, but then accept that Sheila was, of course, right. The middle-class work ethic was as nothing compared to the strenuousness of their pleasure ethic. Summers must not be allowed to drift away unused. To loll indoors, or even on the porch, was downright sinful. Particularly in Blythney, where it was quite possible that this would be the only day for weeks to combine a convenient tide with bright sunshine and a usable, yet bearable, force of wind.

They knew, all the river-bred families, that if by mischance or idleness they reached the end of the summer without ever having congregated on Miserley beach in the sun, they would feel deprived and depressed all winter. It was a rite. Sheila was its high priestess. They were, in a grumbling way, grateful to her.

Anansi watched and listened, making herself unobtrusive in her corner as the boys and the Cotten cousins stormed downstairs and threw items of breakfast food into their faces and onto the floor. There was, she could see, no possibility at all of her avoiding this boat trip. When Sheila was talking about Simon driving the pregnant Mrs Rattray round to Miserley by road, she wondered briefly whether she should offer to go with them but shrank from putting her suggestion forward. She was wary of Simon and besides, she recognized in herself a nagging, fascinated desire to be back on the slippery living water again, to go round the corner and upstream, penetrating the new landscape as the old man had done in his Whitecap dinghy.

She had also begun to understand enough about this world to know that Sheila would not be going in a sailing boat but a motorboat, and that capsizing was not one of the things such boats were prone to do. Something called 'grounding' had been mentioned in the context of the motor-dory, with the usual gales of Sheila mirth, but this had a solid and reassuring sound to it. If there was ground, you could get out and frigging walk on it, couldn't you?

She was further reassured by being given only the DOUAI HARRISON buoyancy aid, and no rubber jacket or shorts, which might have implied a coming immersion.

Sheila did say, 'Now, remember your swimmers!' but Anansi understood, from careful attention to the subtext of the noisy breakfast conversation, that swimsuits were only needed because some of the children liked to run into the river from the sandy strand where the picnic took place. Some of them, said Sheila, even ran in when the sticky black ooze of half-tide was exposed. 'Rolling in the mud! Nothing but their eyes showing!' chuckled Sheila, on this topic. 'They looked like—' She had been going to say Negroes, but stopped herself just in time.

The gay gallant sails moved over the river's brown surface in the sunlight, leaning and skimming, catching and losing the sun in their zigzag progress. Among them, steady and straight, the three motorboats of the flotilla each cut a neat unhurried wake through the water, lacing it with white foam. Anansi sat at the bow of Sheila's dory, looking down at the parting water and then up at the flowing scenery. Above the bend the river grew even wider, although the boats kept to the centre to avoid the shining banks of mud which still could be seen sloping gradually into the water at the edges. There were reeds in clumps and patches, but mainly the sides consisted of miniature cliffs of mud, falling from grass to slimy flats.

There was another bend a hundred yards beyond the first one, taking the river inland past the dark imposing circle of trees where the skeletons of ancient invaders might be buried; more trees, well back from the bank, stood above some small yellow strands on the right-hand side.

Sheila, at the helm of her laden motorboat, was entirely happy. This was a rarer state than any of her companions would have supposed; if asked, most summer Blythneians and winter neighbours would idly have said that she was 'always cheerful'. In fact, her cheerfulness at home had real, unrecognized effort in it these days. Marriage to Simon was taking its toll, though she would never have spoken of it even to him. The increasing intensity of her management of Blythney summers was, had any of her acquaintance been able to see it, not unrelated to the growing bleakness of the rest of Sheila's year.

But at the helm of her motorboat, with Anansi apparently contented at the bow and Bethie Cotten and Penny Tranmere and her two dear little girls perched chatting amid the picnic things in the centre, Sheila was happy. Her own boys, strong and competent, were skimming past with their bright striped spinnaker out. The other children, all known to her from babyhood, coloured and enlivened the river's bleak face with their sails and their bright T-shirts, and shouted merry insults at one another across the gunwales of their little boats. Andy Hampton chugged past in the rubber RIB with Poppy, who was triumphantly waving a giant box of matches at Bethie Cotten in memory of a previous picnic when nobody had remembered the matches and the barbecue had to be lit with a distress flare. It gave all the sausages a most unpleasant and quite possibly poisonous tang.

All these things, these frivolous summer enjoyments and shared memories, comforted Sheila at a level deeper than anybody could guess; a level where she very much needed simple comfort. Here, on the river which she had sailed in her hopeful girlhood, she was doing good and feeling good, breathing good air and spreading good feelings. She was feeding off laughter, clothing herself in a mantle of jollity she had herself spun. She was a theatrical entrepreneuse, staging a summer, producing well-lit happy memories, doing the show right here. There were worse ways to console oneself.

Simon did not like it, but then Simon did not, on the face of it, really like her very much either. There had been a time – so long ago now that it was difficult even for Sheila to bring it back to life in her mind – when they had seemed happy. Simon liked the Suffolk coastal strip, her beloved calf country. He liked it a little for its own sake (he was a neat and competent racing sailor) but far more for the entrée it seemed to give him into what he had perceived in the early days of his marriage as a raffish artistic community. Musicians, artists, the odd literary figure or doyen of Sunday journalism fetched up here at least part-time; one or two famous faces who in London would have passed him by were familiars down here, locals that he could nod to, or exchange sardonic remarks with in the shops at Blythney or Aldeburgh or Southwold or Snape.

Unlike Sheila, he had never had any interest in truly local affairs or gossip, and abhorred the home-time chatter of the village school gates; nor did he think much of the happy philistine Yacht Club set who surrounded them after the move to Blythney. Still, the Markeens' presence in the town consoled him a little; they were closer to being 'his kind' of people than any of the others. Not, as Sheila thought ruefully, that they showed overmuch sign of recognizing this or liking poor Simon. But he liked to be near them; Jonny chatted to him in the gallery. And Penny Tranmere was somebody he spoke of as having 'a fine perception of artistic values, even if she is married to that fat dolt'.

The rest either bored him, or irritated him into envy with their apparently effortless dim City prosperity. Still, at first Simon had liked Suffolk and liked Sheila for moving him there. He had also very much liked his first baby.

As Jo grew, though, and grew away from him, and showed a marked lack of interest in his books, the younger two seemed merely to irritate him. Simon was not the kind of man who wants sons. Sheila had watched, helpless but determinedly cheerful, as he slowly alienated himself from all four of them: her, Jo, Vincent, Douai. Simon had not so much quarrelled with her as concealed himself behind a veil of irritability and silence. It had been gradual. In Vincent's childhood he had still been at least partly theirs; in Douai's, hardly at all. This probably explained the difference betwen Vincent's more amiable temperament and Douai's unrelenting sourness, thought his mother privately; her youngest son was effectively fatherless.

But here on the river he had fathers and mothers, friends and sails, a skill and a place. She loved to see her sons manning the rescue boat with Andy Hampton, learning to rig their first dinghies with patient Alan Tranmere, or joshing with the Cotten children round a family barbecue where Hugo, in terrible khaki shorts, burnt the sausages and leaped around comically as hot fat spat on his hairy bare knees. Simon would turn up at these occasions sometimes, usually by car and dressed in an unsettlingly urban style of well-pressed leisurewear; it both pained and reassured Sheila to see him there, watching his young sons being vicariously fathered by these amiable surrogate uncles.

He was coming by car today, with Susannah Rattray. That would be nice. Get her some fresh air, and Simon could help her down the steep slope from the road. Sheila had told him to bring a folding chair, for the sake of poor Susannah's back, but he might forget. Still, they had everything else with them. Even if Penny Tranmere forgot something, as she generally did, they could stretch the food easily. Standing at the helm of her boat, mentally counting sausages as so often before, Sheila efficiently pushed away from her all thoughts of her uneasy marriage, and revelled in the river.

Miserley beach was empty, except for an elderly couple with binoculars trying to see a bittern on the reedy island that divided the channel there. When they saw the first boats approaching, they put the binoculars away and walked irritably back towards the car park on the hill. It was not much of a beach: a hundred yards of coarse sand, overshadowed by decrepit spreading oak trees. At anything below quarter-flood the beach shaded rapidly into mud flats which were firm for a few feet before turning to a treacly ooze which could suck off rubber boots and swallow them whole.

Sheila had, as usual, timed the expeditionary force immaculately; the dinghies glided up to the beach to rest their noses on clean sand and be dragged up easily above the tide line, and the motor-dory's bows grounded only a couple of feet from the firm ground. Katie Tranmere, who to her mother's slight annoyance was showing a marked talent for boatmanship, elbowed Anansi aside and leapt from the bow with a rope and grapnel anchor. Little Suzie hung over the side, tipping the boat crazily, and was hauled out by Maurrie Cotten and his cousin Dondie with twelve-year-old efficiency.

'Gaar, you'll have it over, baby!'

'I'se not a baby.'

'Yes you are, baby. There. Here's your bucket and spade.'

Sheila by now had hopped over the side into the mud, helped Bethie ashore, and turned back to Anansi who still remained in the boat.

'Good oh. You start passing things out, Anansi – super!'

Between them they unloaded the picnic equipment, and Sheila spread it out while Anansi continued to teeter, uncertainly, at the bow of the grounded boat.

Douai Harrison looked up from tying the painter of the Laser dinghy to a tree, and saw with irritation that the black kid was looking stupid again. And, by association, making him look stupid because she was staying in their house. He moved towards her and said, 'Come on. Get on the shore. We need to pull the boat up.'

Anansi stood, uncertainly and wobblingly, on the front seat of the boat. She could balance well enough on her distorted foot on land, but could not decide how to tackle – from this moving perch – the wide step-and-jump the others had done. Douai stretched out a hand. He was tall enough for her to reach down to it, and she put a foot on the gunwale and prepared to leap. Douai, however, did not wait for her to find her own balance but jerked her forward, so that instead of landing on the hard sand she slipped down the side of the boat, hitting her bony bottom painfully on the gunwale, and landed feet first in the soft mud.

It was slippery, and as Douai let go of her hand she felt her weak foot give way. She hung for a moment at a hopeless angle, then fell flat in the ooze. A shout of laughter met her misfortune – did these people always enjoy accidents? thought Anansi bitterly – and Sheila pulled her to her feet on the harder sand.

'Oops-ee! Well, might as well get muddy now as later – everyone ends up filthy at Miserley! We can rinse off at high water.'

Anansi, miserably, scrubbed at the mud on her legs and cycle shorts. It was sticky, and smelt of rottenness. She saw the cows looking down from the meadow beyond the oaks, and noticed a cowpat further along the beach. She had fallen in *shit*, and they thought it was funny!

Little Suzie Tranmere trotted up to her, prodded her with a plastic spade and said, 'De brown girl's gone more brown, now!'

'It shows a lot less on you,' said Alison Cotten, without malice. 'Must be handy. You can be as filthy as you like and nobody would know. Except for the clothes.'

'Ali-son!' said her aunt Bethie, warningly. But Anansi, her colour deepening, had moved aside, to rub hopelessly at her muddy T-shirt with a handful of grass. She could hear them laughing. Especially Douai.

Simon and Susannah arrived, and Alan Tranmere caused more shouts of laughter when he paddled up to the beach astride a sailboard with its mast and sail trailing, having failed to negotiate the tricky bend under the church. Sausages spat and sizzled, and Sheila skilfully buttered rolls and balanced them on a cloth spread on the flat bottom of an upturned Optimist dinghy. The other women worked more desultorily, and chatted while the children swarmed the oak trees, paddled in the mud, or rowed Sheila's rubber dinghy out to the little cruiser where Hugo Cotten and Eric Rattray were vainly trying to have a quiet beer. Another Blythney dinghy arrived, unconnected with the Sheila picnic, but managed to capsize ten feet off the beach and become involved in an unnecessarily operatic rescue by three other boats, after which they pooled sausages and drinks with the main party and dripped muddy water unconcernedly onto Sheila's rhubarb tarts.

Anansi stayed apart until the eating began, and then moved unwillingly to join the rest. The mud was now dry on her and beginning to flake off. Marta Markeen, who had arrived under the care of the Hamptons, came and sat down next to her.

'Hello. Will you come to our house soon? We could go in the swimming pool with the blow-up dragon.'

Anansi grunted, but was glad of an artless ally. Marta began plying her with questions through a full mouth, occasionally blowing out crumbs of pastry in her enthusiasm.

'Why are you called Anansi?'

'It's a African name. My dad was a African chief.'

'Oh . . . is he dead, then?'

'No. He has to go and do business things, away a lot. In Africa.' Anansi was not in the habit of romancing publicly about her father, but in this circle of complacently intact families it seemed impossible not to. She added a few more details, satisfied with the unquestioning acceptance the little girl gave them.

Unfortunately, Douai too was listening. 'Is that a pork pie you're eating?' he said. 'Be good if it was. You're telling porkies all right.'

'I am not,' said Anansi. 'And I wasn't talking to you anyway.'

Douai laughed. 'Pork pies, pork pies. Mum,' he tugged at his mother's sleeve, 'is it always wrong to tell lies?'

Sheila had not been listening. 'Of course it is,' she said. 'Father Danvers must have told you that. Lying is always wrong.'

'Is it extra wrong if you lie to children who are too little and stupid to suss it?'

'Well, yes. I suppose so. It would be a form of exploiting

other people's weakness, wouldn't it? Good people don't tell lies. You've learnt that.'

'See?' said Douai to Anansi. 'Only scummy people tell lies.'

'Muddy people,' giggled Grania Hampton, anxious to impress Douai, brother of her adored Vincent. 'Mud is a kind of scum.'

'No it's not,' said Douai scornfully. 'Mud is at the bottom of rivers and scum is at the top.'

He had, to do him justice, already given up his brief tormenting of Anansi. She was not that high on his agenda. She did not matter. But it was too late. Once lit, a fuse must burn to its terrible conclusion.

It took a moment, but then Anansi stood up, the hollow place within her filling with bright, warm rage. Like the time when she did that Tyrone over and got permanently excluded from Washbrook High, thus changing the whole of her world with her anger.

It wouldn't be fists, this time, though. A more sophisticated weapon was to hand.

'If scummy people tell lies,' she said, 'there's a lot of scummy people in your family.'

'Oh?' said Douai coldly. The adults caught the tone of this exchange and fell silent. Above them the oaks sighed; on the shore, slack dinghy sails fluttered in a brief ghostly wind. The river, plaything and killer and highway for invaders, rustled past their feet, the rising tide lapping round the boats and Suzie Tranmere's abandoned bucket.

Douai went on, 'What do you mean? My family aren't scummy liars.'

'Your mum is,' said Anansi. 'She rings the radio and says thing that aren't true. About being a social worker. I heard.'

97

Sheila started, but this had only been a ranging shot. Anansi's big eyes were on Douai, holding him still, threatening him with worse.

'But your dad is an even bigger scumbag,' she said. 'Don't suppose he tells your mum that he's shagging *her*,' she pointed at Penny Tranmere who sat, open-mouthed with alarm, still holding a sausage. 'Shagging her senseless in the Mar-tello tower every night, up against the wall. I seen them. They look pretty stupid, an' all.'

Penny dropped the sausage. It rolled in the sand, coating itself like an unappetizing rissole. Sheila did not look at her, but glanced down and began pleating a paper napkin furiously between her fingers. Simon, who had been leaning on the trunk of the biggest oak tree talking to Andy Cotten, froze. His heart hammered.

It was Marta Markeen who broke the silence, turning her face with blithe trust towards Anansi.

'What does *shagging* mean?' she asked.

The trouble with having a crisis on a river picnic is that you still have to get home the way you came: afloat, in a collection of boats, some of which will have to be towed because the wind has dropped away to nothing. Because of the towing, it is best to wait until the fast flood tide has at least slackened, ready to turn in your favour. So, much as it would have been expedient to abort the picnic party, all the assembled Blythneians realized that it would have to go on until the appointed end after two o'clock, when the tide would be almost ready to turn back downriver towards the town.

Another awkwardness was that towards a high spring tide, Miserley beach begins to shrink dramatically. Usually this is a cause of companionable merriment, as rugs and baskets are dragged together and those not wishing to paddle – the adults – sit in an ever more compact knot on the remaining sand.

This was such a tide. Like the innermost circle of Hell, the party could only contract and intensify. The one small mercy was that Susannah Rattray had the wit to feign dizziness and mop her brow theatrically as she sat above them all on her folding chair in the shade.

'I'm sorry, I – I feel a bit weird,' she said as soon as possible after Anansi's outburst. The child herself had turned and walked away from the group to stand by the tree, with (Marta admiringly thought) rather a grand theatrical air. Susannah said faintly, 'Simon . . . is there any chance of a lift back?'

So they went away. Penny Tranmere, for one crazy moment, wondered if she should follow them. Almost instantly she realized that going off in a car with Simon would solve very little. Nor was she qualified to take the other escape option and simply push off from the beach in one of the children's boats. She would only have ended up aground, or floating around hopelessly and having to be rescued. She was marooned. Alan was looking at her in dawning amazement over a can of Tango; his hand had gone so limp that it was widdling orange liquid all over the quiche on his paper plate.

Finally Penny said, 'I think we should talk about all this a lot later, don't you?'

Sheila's first thought was for the children. It seemed cruel that their innocence about adults should end like this, on a sunny day at Miserley beach with sausages and paddling. Before her own humiliation registered properly she had glanced around and made a mental inventory of the damage. The little Tranmeres did not seem to have taken it in. The Cottens and the cousins looked nonplussed, although that knowing little minx Alison was giggling pink-faced; so was Grania Hampton, while her elder brother Mark did not look as if he had understood. Marta had received no answer to her semantic question, and looked as if she would ask it again any minute. Of her own boys, Vincent had blushed a dull red, turned away from his father and Penny Tranmere and moved the short distance to the end of the beach to throw stones in the water. Douai looked the worst: pale, and pinched, staring into space.

All this she registered in the silent half-minute, the long half-minute, after the departure of Simon and Susannah. As for the adults, she thought it better not to catch any of their eyes. When Penny said it should be talked about later, she nodded agreement.

At last Alan Tranmere saved the situation. 'Quite right,' he said. 'Wind's about my level, I think. I'm going to give the windsurfer another blast.'

And, heroically, he wobbled from the shore, bottom sticking out, hands clutching the curved spar, to execute a series of waterborne pratfalls that they could all watch and laugh at with what must have sounded – to the passing bird-watchers and outside picnickers – like an utterly unforced gaiety.

Anansi herself was not happy. She had thought that when she let off her bomb the damage would be instant and satisfying; all the smug posh people who gave her no respect would somehow be sent to the bottom, like a ship with its hull blown open.

No sooner had she done her deed, though, than she realized how long, how slow, how messy and unsatisfying a carnage she had wrought. The Penny woman's embarrassment she could take without difficulty; smart silly bitch, looking so holy in her little white collar and shagging away like a tart. It was Sheila's face she could not bear to see now. Its dimpled plumpness had gone pale, almost yellow, and although her smile was still there, and her flow of bright talk, it was as if a dead body had started chattering. She did not look at Douai or Vincent.

Also, it was bitterly unfair in her eyes that Simon Harrison had got clean away in his car while Sheila was left to tidy up the picnic things and sit ever closer – as the tide rose round them – to Penny Tranmere. She watched Alan's comic gyrations on the sailboard, and all the tastes of the unfamiliar picnic food rose up, sickening, into her mouth.

Chapter Nine

Simon drove Susannah to her mother-in-law's pink house in mutual silence.

When they arrived, she turned to him and said, 'Thanks. Are you, er, OK?'

'Yes. It was a good idea to go, I think.'

'Yes. I think so.'

He drove home, went to his room, and wondered whether to pack a bag. It seemed rather a theatrical thing to do, though, like someone in a television play about adultery. In the end he lay on the bed in his socks and lit a cigarette and waited, like someone in a television play about prison.

There was no way for Penny to get back to Blythney other than the way she had come, in Sheila's boat. It was slower than the trip upriver; there was less tide, and they were towing a clutter of dishevelled children's boats – the children having opted to crowd into the fast inflatable – and Alan's sailboard. Alan had invited himself aboard the Rattray-Cotten cruiser, where Eric and Hugo discussed sail trim and folding propellers and studiously avoided any mention of Anansi's bombshell.

Aboard the dory Sheila was quiet, Anansi leaned over the bow staring into the water, and Poppy Hampton did not speak either. Penny held her children close to her, rather against their inclination, and turned her pointed, delicate little features into the wind. It sharpened her colour and blew her neat hair back and generally gave her a quite pleasing air of courageous martyrdom.

Later, while Sheila put the boat back on its mooring, Penny smoothed her hair and turned to Poppy Hampton on a quiet corner of the club terrace. With an attempt at a smile she said, 'Oh, that child! It's awful how they're so cynical and knowing when they've been brought up in that underclass way!'

It was not a good opening, and Penny knew it almost straightaway. But a cold sense of dismay was gripping her at the thought of the reckoning with Alan, and she wanted very much to be reassured that her daily girlfriends – except, naturally, Sheila – were on-side and on-message.

Poppy was not. Nor did she particularly like the word 'underclass', which committed the twin sins of being both American and unkind.

'It depends,' she said coolly, 'whether there's anything for them to be cynical *about*.'

'Oh, really! So you believe . . .'

Poppy was old Blythney, born in the cottage hospital, her father the vicar until 1972. Andy's father had been the Bishop's chaplain, a roaring, red-faced hunting parson from Norfolk. The younger Hamptons might now live in north London, but only physically. At the core of Poppy's being were the robust rural Anglican values of a bygone age, and a belief in painfully plain speaking.

'Well,' she said, 'I thought for a moment it was the child having rather a rude fantasy, needed her mouth washing out. But when Simon rushed off without a word of denial and you turned the colour of cheap and nasty paraffin wax . . .'

Penny bridled angrily. 'So I'm condemned without trial, am I?'

'Well, are you having an affair with Simon Harrison?'

'It's more complicated than that,' said Penny with hauteur.

'Ah,' said Poppy Hampton, gathering up her bags to leave the terrace. 'So it's true.'

Penny stared after her, speechless.

'Mummy,' whined Katie beside her. 'C'n I have some scampi fries?'

Before she went home, Sheila knew that she must speak to Vincent and Douai. And, maybe, Anansi. But not together. After telling Anansi with uncharacteristic brusqueness to load the picnic things into the car, she walked heavily down to the dinghy park and found her sons pulling a cover over their boat.

'Sweethearts,' she said. 'About what Anansi said—'

'She's a dirty little *bitch*,' said Douai vehemently. 'I'm going to kill her soon if you don't sent her back to Scumsville.'

Vincent looked at his mother more thoughtfully. 'Will she have to go back now?' he said. 'I mean, Dad won't be very pleased . . .'

'I don't know,' said Sheila. 'But I'd like you two to keep a bit quiet about it all, until Dad and I have had a talk.'

Speechless, red around the neck, they nodded. Like Poppy, they now realized that it was all true.

Sheila looked at them with anxious love. 'What are you going to do now?'

'Go to Maurrie's, watch a vid.'

'Fine.'

Back at the car, Anansi had stacked all the boxes in the boot and closed it. Sheila approached her hesitantly, for once not knowing what she would say. As she opened the driver's door, she felt a hot wave of anger. This *bloody* child! At a picnic, in front of her sons and all her friends! In front of her *boat*, so newly mended. On the *river*! It was a kind of sacrilege. She got in, and Anansi climbed in beside her. Sheila still could not speak.

Finally, when the car was halfway down the track to the town, she said, 'Do you hate us?'

It was such a brief, uncharacteristic question that Anansi shot her a startled glance. But she answered quickly enough. 'Only that Douai. He tipped me in the river on purpose. It was out of order.'

'A lot of boats capsized that morning. It was very windy.' Sheila was absurdly relieved to have something concrete to argue about.

'He hated me being in his boat. He hates me being in his house. I only said it because he was calling me a scum and a liar. He was out of order.'

'Yes,' said Sheila. 'But you didn't make it up, what you said, did you?'

'No.' It was an uncharacteristically small voice. 'No.'

'Well,' said Sheila, and she seemed to grow again in stature and power. There was even enough power to turn and smile slightly at the child hunched in the seat beside her. 'I think from now on it's up to me and my husband and Mr and Mrs Tranmere to sort it all out, don't you? You needn't worry about it any more. Or talk about it.'

She changed up a gear. She was an adult, and a mother, and a carer for the less fortunate. She had power and the responsibilities of power. It was up to her to make everything tidy and cheerful again. Wasn't it?

Penny reached home, her daughters squabbling in the back, in time to take a long, hot shower before Alan arrived. She threw her salt-splashed clothes into the twin dirty linen baskets – for she was a woman who would have separated whites and coloureds in the face of the Last Trump – and stood beneath the roaring torrent of her power shower ignoring the squeals and recriminations between Katie and Suzie in their playroom. She allowed anger to rise in her, clenching her fists under the hot onslaught of the water. Bloody, bloody child! Bloody, black, *underclass*, destructive, mocking bloody child! And bloody Simon, for shooting off with Susannah and leaving her stranded on that hellish muddy little beach for everyone to stare at!

Tears started in her eyes and flowed down her face with the water. There were aspects of the humiliation which she was only now allowing herself to grasp: the child had revealed that it had been done in the dank Martello tower, against the *wall* (underclass!) and now not only the adults but the teenagers had heard about it – those giggling girls and Douai Harrison with his foxy pale sour little face and – obscurely even worse – Vince Harrison, who was becoming a bit of a hunk, a bit Leo di Caprio actually. Oh God, oh God, they all knew! Against the *wall*!

And Simon. In the caravan, she thought savagely, there would have been curtains. No bloody child could have spied on them. But no, his artistic demand was for dankness and cold stone and the threat of discovery. And he had stood there on that foul little grimy beach, not protecting her,

107

looking as pasty and sour as his horrid little son and not at all attractive. And the other women's eyes had looked appraisingly at her, and at him, and visibly wondered how the hell she could do it – and Sheila had not looked at her at all.

And Alan. She switched off the shower, stepped out, and began drying herself on a large white towel. It was wholly characteristic of their marriage that she thought of Alan last. She had never seen him angry; he had not known about either of her previous short affairs and she had no idea what to expect when he came home. She was, however, confident that of all the hideous aspects of this business, Alan was the one she could handle with relative ease.

There was a commotion outside the bathroom. She flung the door open, furious, ready to blow off steam by upbraiding the two round-eyed children who stood looking up at her. But before she could begin, Katie said, 'Mummy. What does shagging mean?'

When she got to the house, Sheila asked Anansi to unload the car, to which, with unwonted meekness, the child agreed. Sheila herself climbed up the three flights of stairs to Simon's study. She suspected that he would be pretending to work. Whenever they argued, his tactic was to retire into ostentatious creativity and pretend to be above such trifles as marital disagreement.

The study was empty, though, and she stood for a moment looking around at his computer, his African statues, and the jagged, unpleasant painting of a corpse which he had bought from Jonny Markeen. She tried to imagine how life would be without Simon, his dark moods and his sulks, his claim to artistic temperament and his simmering resentment at being kept and housed with her grandmother's money. Imagination failed her. These things – West African artefacts, sulks, corpse painting, resentment – would, surely, always be here.

She went down to the middle landing and hesitated, but then bravely stepped into the marital bedroom. There, on his single bed, her husband lay smoking, his muddy socks on top of the bedspread.

'Hi,' he said noncommittally. 'You home, then?'

Sheila stood over him, large and sorrowful. 'Why did you have to choose one of my friends? Here, in the town?' she said. 'I know how it is with you. I know you haven't fancied me for years. But if it was sex, why so close to home? Why did you do it inside *my* life? And in my summer?'

'Well,' said Simon, 'I didn't have a driving licence for a whole bloody year, did I? So I suppose it had to be close to home.'

'I would always,' said his wife with freezing dignity, 'have driven you to the station.'

There was a silence.

'Why Penny?' she asked again. 'Poor Alan!'

'Oh . . .' Simon had sat up on the bed, and stubbed out his cigarette on the saucer of a cold, old, coffee cup. When he did not answer, Sheila spoke again.

'Is it a real thing? That would be the only justification. I could almost respect that, if it was a love match. Are you going to live with her and the girls?'

Simon was genuinely startled this time. Since Anansi's attack, his feelings seemed to have frozen, and his mind worked in slow motion. But the suggestion his wife was now making filled him with hot alarm. Live with Penny Tranmere? And the little girls? Where? On what? How?

Sheila was continuing. 'I wouldn't stop you.'

Simon stood up. 'So,' he said, with a weak attempt at dignity, 'are you saying you want me to leave? You're throwing me out, is that it? The "guilty husband"?' On the words guilty husband, he made ironic quote marks in the air.

Irony was lost on Sheila. 'Well, you are,' she said. 'And if you want to go, you go. I won't stop you seeing the boys. They're old enough to choose.' She turned and walked down the stairs, tears in her eyes.

Anansi raised a small, scared face towards the big woman as she blundered into the kitchen and leaned on the worktop, head down, mouth tight, trying not to cry.

Alaia Markeen usually walked down to the gallery at closing time on Saturday, to stroll through the town with Jonny and perhaps drink a cappuccino before wandering home. Today she first picked up Marta from the Hamptons and listened, with increasing dismay and interest, to her child's spirited account of the day's doings. The knowing Grania Hampton had by now given Marta a translation of the mystifying word, which she had personally retranslated into the primary-school expression she knew best.

'So Anansi said she wasn't the liar, because Mr Harrison is off sexing Mrs Tranmere every day in the Martello tower,' explained Marta, trotting breathlessly beside her long-legged mother. 'But Mummy, I think Anansi does tell *slightly* lies, because when I asked about what her dad said about the lions she didn't even know that lionesses don't have manes like daddy lions, so perhaps she doesn't have a daddy or perhaps he isn't a chief in Africa. But I like Anansi. Not for poor girl stuff, but for her face, like Daddy said.'

Slowing down, Alaia asked, 'What did all the grown-ups do when Anansi had said this stuff?'

'About the lions? They weren't listening, really, they were yakking—'

'No, when she said the stuff about Mr Harrison and Mrs Tranmere.'

'Well, after that Mr Harrison went away pretty quickly with Mrs Rattray—'

'Not with Mrs Tranmere?' said her mother faintly.

'No, Mrs Rattray was poorly so he was being kind. I don't think he's sexing her as well, because she's having a baby in her tummy.'

'And Mr and Mrs Tranmere?'

'Well, they all just chatted about other stuff, but when we were getting in the rubber boat to come back – because, Mummy, it was just *zero* wind, Grania says we could *not* have sailed, so tell Daddy I didn't wimp out – anyway, when we were untying the boat I heard Andy – he says I can call him Andy – telling Mr Rattray that she had guilty written all over her face, and that they'd better drop in on poor old Al later and tell him he was well rid.'

'Umm . . . well,' Alaia stifled a desire to laugh. 'I'll tell you something about all that kind of thing, sweetheart. It's fine to tell me, but it's best if you don't tell anyone else or chat about it. Sometimes grown-up lives are a bit complicated, and you might hurt somebody by mistake by saying things.'

Marta considered, gravely, for a moment. 'Anansi did a bad thing, then?' she asked. 'Because she started it, but it was because Douai called her a liar and a scummy person, and he did make her fall over in the mud. I saw.'

'Anansi probably shouldn't have said it, no,' said Alaia. 'But look, here's Daddy. He must have closed the gallery

ten minutes early, that's nice. We could go home and blow
up the dragon for the pool.'

'Shall I tell him the picnic news?'

'No. I'll explain it later when we know a bit more.'

But Jonny knew already. Penny Tranmere – a woman
he slightly disliked but found useful for researching pictures
about which there was some doubt – had turned up at ten
to five with her hair wet and dishevelled, wearing a sweater
inside out and, even more incredibly, only a towel round
her waist.

'He's going to kill me! Lock the door!' she cried, bursting
into the gallery and seriously alarming an elderly couple
who were poking around near some bronzes in the corner.
'You have to help me! He's gone mad!'

The old couple threw malevolent glances at her and at
the dumbstruck Jonny Markeen, and shuffled out of the
gallery. Their day had already been ruined once, when
they had just spotted a bittern at Miserley and then seen
it frightened off by a crowd of noisy families in boats.
Blythney was not what it used to be.

Penny sat down, trembling, on the chair by the desk
opposite Jonny.

'I'm sorry,' she said. 'There's nowhere else I could go,
not quickly. Look, he's coming!' She glanced through the
wide window. Alan, less fleet of foot than his wife, was
indeed getting closer every minute.

Jonny nipped to the door, but instead of closing it
stepped out into the street and shut it behind him, letting
the lock slide to. His keys were always in his pocket. He
pressed a remote control on the key ring and the burglar
alarm snapped on. Alan, puffing up to him, saw the red
light over the door illuminate and stopped.

'Is she in there?' he said, when his breath returned.

'If you mean Penny, yes,' said the art dealer kindly. 'But I think a bit of cooling-off time might be useful all round.'

Alan deflated, suddenly, and ran the back of his hand over his brow. 'Oh God,' he said. 'And I've left the little girls at home alone. We never have before, not even for five minutes.' He began, noisily and undisguisedly, to cry.

'So,' concluded Jonny to his wife and spellbound daughter, 'we are now going up to the Tranmeres' house to collect Katie and Suzie for tea. Penny is still in the gallery, with a towel on, and Alan is waiting outside. He says he won't do anything extreme, and has definitely finished hammering on my precious window, but he reckons he has to finish talking to her.'

'How on earth did they start chasing around the town?' asked Alaia. 'In a *towel*?'

'She ran away, apparently, though he swears he didn't actually threaten her, just shouted a bit. I believe him. I don't *think* there's going to be a bloodbath in my gallery. Hope not, anyway. He's coming up later, when he's had a word, to have supper and collect Katie and Suzie. I'll go down and reset the alarm later on. I don't see what else I could have done.'

'You are a lovely man, you know,' said his wife. 'You haven't even checked your insurance policy yet, though I bet you're about to.' Jonny grinned. Alaia continued, 'Do you think it would be a kindness if we picked up some of the poor woman's clothes and gave them to Alan so he can get Penny dressed before she goes through the town again?'

'I'm not that lovely a man,' said Jonny. 'I think we should let raw nature take its course, don't you?'

*   *   *

At Seafret, the phone had been ringing for longer than usual. Anansi kept glancing towards it, timidly, wondering whether she should pick it up. At last Sheila regained control of herself and moved heavily towards the dresser where it stood.

'Hello? Oh – yes. Oh. Oh dear. How terrible. Yes, of course. No, don't carry on right now, I get the picture. Should I tell her yet? Yes, probably. Well, you can count on us. I suppose. Though there may be a bit of an upheaval here. Family matters. No, well. Perhaps we should speak tomorrow.'

When she had put the phone down, Sheila turned to Anansi and said, as steadily as she could, 'The Country Hosts Association. Wanting to know whether you were doing all right.'

'What did you mean,' asked the child, 'when you said "terrible", and asked if you should tell me?'

Sheila had endured enough for one day. 'All right,' she said. 'Since you're so keen on the bald truth at all costs. It's your mum. She's been arrested. They aren't going to grant bail, apparently.'

Chapter Ten

At last the small town slept. On the shingle beach, abandoned children's buckets rolled in the uneasy surf, making little chinking sounds on the pebbles. Distant waves glimmered as they rose and fell, picking up the cold light of the lamps along the prom. A chip paper blew capriciously the length of the town, wrapping itself round streetlamps and doorknobs and the canopy of the greengrocer's. The Blyne and Grend, having half emptied itself into the sea by nightfall, stealthily filled up again and covered the naked mud with sluicing, bubbling tide.

Behind the safety of the wavy wall, in an elegant Queen Anne bedroom, Katie and Suzie Tranmere slept peacefully, blonde hair spread into fine clouds on their pillows. They dreamed of the magical blow-up dragon in Marta's pool. Hamptons and Rattrays and Cottens dozed in the blameless flesh-smelling warmth of double beds; Simon and Sheila Harrison lay on their sides, facing away from one another in cold twin beds. Douai and Vincent and the Cotten cousins had opted en masse for sleeping bags on the Hamptons' front room floor, so that they could all scare themselves together, comfortably, with a late horror movie.

Penny Tranmere slept awkwardly on three chairs in the back room of Markeens' Gallery, while her husband sat on the pavement, his back to the door, keeping a lonely vigil. He had rung Jonny on his mobile earlier, refusing supper and asking him to keep the children for the night. 'I can't leave. If I do, she'll run for it. I might not catch up with her for days.' When Jonny kindly said that such a cooling-off period might be a good thing, Alan said, 'No. If she won't talk to me now, it's never. Sorry to be a bother to you, but that's how it is.' Alaia had driven down at ten o'clock with a Thermos of soup, a coat, a packet of sandwiches and a patent American folding cushion with backrest, more usually deployed at outdoor performances of *La Traviata* in the ruins of Framlingham Castle.

'You might as well get comfortable,' she said, 'if you really want to do this all night. The girls went to bed very happy, anyway. They think that you're at work and Penny's got a bit of a headache. Marta completely exhausted them in the swimming pool, so they're too tired to worry. And here, take this.' She handed him a Harrods' carrier bag containing a pair of leggings and some slip-on shoes. 'Jonny said not to, but I say, frankly, poor Penny. Whatever she's done, she deserves trousers. She might come out, if you tell her you've got these.'

Alaia's crisp dark beauty and casual goodwill made Alan, for a moment, want to cry. She had even brought him a suggested cover story to ward off kindly inquiries from Saturday night passers-by. He could, Alaia said, explain that he was just looking after the gallery while Jonny got a man down to sort out an electronic problem with the burglar alarm.

'Thanks, but no,' said Alan. 'Not in the mood for lying.'

There was a rare dignity that night, Alaia thought, about the stout rubicund man. She leaned across and kissed him lightly on the cheek; it was the sort of gesture that she, with her assurance, could get away with.

In the event Alan did not need to lie. There were few curious eyes; even in July Blythney was not a late-night town. By eleven the street was empty, and Alan found that with the backrest rigged on his cushion, he could sleep quite reasonably for half an hour at a time, his back against the gallery door lest Penny escape.

Anansi did not sleep at all; or not until the first light of dawn was filtering in through the sea window.

For most of her life she had known that, one day, Mum would get nicked and not set free. Nanna Bev had said so often enough, clucking disapproval as she dried Anansi at bathtime or fed her supper while Tracey was out with a boyfriend. A secret that the small Anansi knew was that one day, she and Nanna Bev would live together, 'have a little shop, maybe'. Some mysterious thing would happen – 'Good times comin' back,' said Nanna, tapping her nose – and life would be easier and less frightening.

'Your mam was never a good girl,' she used to say. 'I did my best, but she turned out bad. Now, you're a good girl. You can't account for these things.'

She said that for the last time on the night before she was killed by the lorry. She left Anansi with only the bleak certainty that this day, this news, would surely come. She was six by then, and had overheard enough to know.

'You mix yourself up with drugs,' Nanna used to say, slapping down food on the kitchen worktop after one of

Tracey's absences, 'and you stay mixed, and end up inside for good.'

'Oh, leave it,' Tracey would snap. 'What do you know? I'm careful.'

But Anansi knew that things Nanna said were always true. She knew it would happen, one day. Perhaps, she thought, that was why she had never let herself love Mum too much, even after Nanna was dead. 'You're not a natural kid,' Tracey complained. 'You haven't got a proper cuddle in you. That's your bastard dad coming out.'

Perhaps that was why Mum had had Kyra, thought Anansi bitterly, huddling in the bed beneath the dark window to the sea. Perhaps she had Kyra so she could have a proper kid who thought she was great and put her arms up. And now where was Kyra? In care, probably. She was too big to get Mum off, like she had the last time. No, Mum was inside now. No new baby to get her the 'compassion'. No community service order. No probation.

Tracey must have been so bloody stupid. Careless. If she had only been there, thought Anansi, she might have prevented it. She had done, before: had lied brilliantly and inventively, even though it filled her with terror at the thought of prison for herself. She had done it so Kyra could go on having a bathtime mum, like she had had Nanna. If she had been home she might have stopped it.

Instead she was here, and had started a whole load of new trouble. She screwed up everything. Anansi knew that she would dream of the fuckilla man, real bad, if she slept.

But she did not. In the exhausted sleep of dawn, she dreamed of Coker's Quay, and a boat, and a shining river on which she raced and skimmed towards a wide sea and freedom. When she woke up her cheeks were wet with tears.

*　　*　　*

The affair of the Tranmeres and the gallery siege was all around the town by mid-morning. For one thing, the unshaven bulk of Alan was still to be seen camped outside on the pavement, dozing fitfully, at nine o'clock in the morning. The minority who went to church – including Harry and Marion Glanville – met Poppy Hampton and had the whole situation explained with forceful simplicity. There was, as a result, quite tangible irritation among the congregation when the sermon went on for twenty-five minutes; there was a very real risk that by the time they were free to investigate further, the siege would be over. Others got the news door to door, or at the paper shop; by ten thirty several little knots of onlookers had gathered, in an artfully casual manner, at points on the High Street where the gallery frontage was visible.

Jonny Markeen came down to investigate, saw Alan's head lolling against his new glass and Alan's paunch rising and falling on his threshold, and decided that enough was enough. Fashionable though it was in London galleries for 'living exhibits' to lead their lives in public behind labels like 'Sleeping yet living woman 1999' or 'Zoo who?' he did not particularly want, he told his wife, to give free exhibition space to 'Cuckolded lardbucket waiting for wife'. Particularly as his Sunday afternoon sales were usually rather good in high summer.

Accordingly he cut through the alley by the chip shop and along the prom until he reached Seafret. The door stood open, as usual; Sheila had been to early Mass, to avoid being looked at, and was in the kitchen making a sausage plait.

'Hello. Is Simon in?' he asked.

'Upstairs. But he's awake. Simon!' Sheila bawled up the

stairs. She seemed, Jonny thought, very calm. The dark child with the fine face was lurking in the background.

'I'll go up,' he said.

Simon was sitting on the bed, looking, thought Jonny critically, pretty lousy. His thin face was pale, his close-set eyes sunk even deeper than usual. It was not a good face, thought Jonny consideringly; once or twice in the past he had almost managed to think of Simon Harrison as a historical study, a Richard III or minor Borgia; and his youngest son Douai did show promise of startling, if not wholly reassuring, character in a very similar face. But Simon's jowls had a disappointing twentieth-century slackness, and his mouth a modern petulance and lack of set.

Shaking himself out of this portraitist's reverie, Jonny said abruptly, 'You know what's going on, down at the gallery?'

'Is she still in there, then?' Sheila had told him about Alan, rather brutally, when she came back from church.

'Yes,' said Jonny. 'And in my view, it is your job to get her out and take her somewhere.'

'How?' Simon sneered. 'Bloody how?'

'Back door. Up Feaveryear Alley. It's locked from outside, and I have the key. We could get into the back room, signal to her to come out, and then when the coast was clear I would open up and tell Alan there's no point staying there any more.'

'And then what do I do? Fly to bloody Gretna?'

Jonny looked down at him with flickering disgust. 'If you fancy. Just clear up your own muddle, that's all. I will meet you in the alley in ten minutes flat. Bring a pair of jeans or something she can wear.'

The ugly little art dealer had authority; Simon, who had both feared and debunked authority all his life, tried for a moment to stare him down in chippy defiance, but failed and dropped his eyes in acquiescence.

Jonny did not wait for Simon to say anything. He left him and in the hall met Sheila, hanging up some children's waterproofs. Her eyes, he saw, were red.

'This is none of my business,' he said, 'but you might, just might, be better off without Simon for a bit.'

'I know,' said Sheila. 'Oh, I know.'

So Jonny released Penny into her lover's care, and broke the news to a highly disgruntled Alan, softening it with the offer of a hot breakfast up at the Hall with his daughters. Then he opened all the windows in the back office, which smelt rather unpleasantly of shower gel and female panic, and prepared for his Sunday opening.

Penny had no car keys, and Simon could not take the family car on top of his other crimes. Fleeing by taxi with no proper clothes was too complicated and expensive an option to consider. Silently, by common accord, they walked up the High Street looking to neither left nor right of them, and picked up the caravan key from the Tranmere outhouse. Penny tried the house door, but Alan had locked it and there was no sign of life. She longed above all things to take cover, painfully aware of the unflattering hang of Simon's old cords on her skinny frame. They walked across Abbey Farm Marsh to the site where a huddle of mobile holiday homes and vans stood around a grey toilet blockhouse. The caravan smelt faintly of rotting wood and old foam cushions, and when they were safe inside it, they did not fall into one another's arms as fugitive lovers should. Instead Simon sat on the wider of the two bunks and said, 'Now what?'

'Has Sheila thrown you out?' asked Penny. She had not

slept well, and thought with longing of her white clean bed and white damask bedroom curtains.

'Well. She said she'd understand if I went.'

'Alan said, when he was shouting at me through the bathroom door, that if I wouldn't behave like a decent wife I could see how I liked being on my own.'

'But he ran after you.'

'I don't think it was to bring me back. I think he just had more stuff to say. And I think he wanted to hit me.'

'Not Alan,' said Simon with unflattering incredulity. 'Easy-going chap. Probably wants you back, wants to say sorry.'

'I told him he revolted me. In bed.'

'That won't have helped, will it?'

The disappointment in his voice made Penny's lips tighten. 'Well,' she said, 'I am going to get some sleep. You can get my clothes from home. Just some summer things, and everything out of my cabinet in the bathroom. It's the left-hand one. And my bag, and some espadrilles and whatever's in my underwear drawer, in the chest by the window.'

She lay down and closed her eyes. Simon stood for a moment looking at her sparrow body and petulant wide mouth, and felt a shaft of panic go through him like a knife. The old caravan rocked slightly as he stepped out onto the grass.

Sheila had told Anansi that Miss Archenlaw was coming down on Monday to 'sort things out' regarding the rest of her holiday and whether the CHA could be of any assistance in organizing her future care. Anansi nodded, dumbly, and after a moment asked whether she could go out for a walk.

The river drew her. She limped up the dirt road and climbed the sea wall behind the Yacht Club, to stand for a moment looking left at the ruined Martello tower. Turning her back on it, she climbed down again, crossed to the river side and began walking along the muddy track towards Coker's Quay. The tide was rising, dragging the boats' sterns upriver on their moorings, and a few racing boats were skimming around the buoys. At the stone quay she found Harry Glanville, sitting on his fish-box cart and doing something to a brown sail draped across his lap.

'Hello,' he said. 'Doing a bit of mending. Can you sew?'

'Nah,' said Anansi. 'I can't do nuthing, really.' Her tone was unusually despondent.

Harry affected not to notice, but continued, conversationally, 'I gather you let off your bomb. Caused rather a lot of civilian casualties, from all I hear.'

Anansi bridled, stung out of her self-pitying depression by the tone of reproach in his voice.

'That Douai was out of order,' she said.

'You're always using that expression,' said the old man. 'But I am not sure you really have much concept of order. You just lashed out, didn't you? Poor Sheila. With all her friends there.'

Anansi was dumbstruck. She did not come to Coker's Quay to be told off. She turned, but her lame foot betrayed her and she stumbled slightly before she could walk away. Quick as a flash, the old man was on his feet, steadying her. His touch – matter-of-fact, a dry firm hand on her arm and another on her shoulder – loosened something inside her. She turned towards him, looking him straight in the eye.

'I know,' she said. 'I know I shouldn't of.' For the first

time in years she felt herself at risk of shedding public tears. 'It's all a frigging mess, now.'

'Yes,' said Harry. 'Never mind. Sit down, and I'll tell you a story.'

This was relief beyond imagining. 'About the war?' said the child hopefully.

'Yes,' said Harry. 'About the war'.

Anansi took his place on the fish-box, and Harry paced up and down the quay, looking out at the river, talking half to himself. As he spoke, she could see the scene he pictured: canoes on the dark river, moving from open reedy country up to towering dark stone docks, the complicated, dangerous load strapped to each foredeck, the men losing one another in the darkness, afraid to call out. She felt with him the lonely struggle to fix each limpet, silently, to the warships' sides; the silent paddling backwards, the spin round, the heart-stopping moment when the compass needle stuck and the paddler could not see or divine his way out of the imprisoning dock. And then, as the first mine exploded prematurely, the searchlights and the patrol boats.

'The other four,' he said quietly, 'were seen. Two were shot in the water, the other two picked up by the patrol boat. I knew they would be shot. I knew that some pretty nasty things would happen to them first, so they would be glad by the time the shot came. All of them were men I had trained. I knew that my raid was not going to be the one that made the history books as a success. I was angry, and professionally piqued. Did you know soldiering was a profession, Nancy? Not just a heroic sacrifice of the few for the many. It's a career, too, is war. Anyway—'

Anansi sat very still. His voice had changed. She divined that he had not yet told her the worst of it.

'Anyway, the point is that when I got back to the river mouth, there was a German lookout in uniform on the other side of the reeds. He was facing the other way. They had never thought to watch the marsh entry to the river, because it was too shallow. That was the genius of these canoe raids – using water that couldn't carry proper boats. The lookout had his back to me, as far away as that bank there.' He pointed at the placid cows beyond the shimmering Grend. 'I was safe as houses, heading away from him. But I thought about my four friends, and I took my pistol and shot him dead. From behind.'

'Dead?' said Anansi. She looked across the river, measuring the distance to the dreaming cows. 'You musta been a good shot.'

'I was. And it wasn't a war crime, technically, because he was in uniform and on duty. But it's more than fifty years ago, and I still dream of him at least once a week. Because I didn't shoot him for the sake of the war, that boy. I shot him for revenge. My own revenge. He was nothing to do with the people who were going to torture my friends and kill them in the morning. He was just in the same army, and pretty low down it probably, to be made night lookout at a river mouth where nothing ever happened. I shot him because I couldn't get at the real bastards.'

'Ye-eeah!' Anansi's assent was a long, heavy breath. 'You get so frigging sick of getting no respect, being done bad to. So you hit anyone you can get at. In my school they called me a thicko because of the reading. But the one I done over, alright, he wasn't one of the ones who called me that. An' he was littler than me.'

'Lucky you didn't have a gun, then.' Harry had picked

up his sail, and was critically examining its tack, where a half-sewn eyelet dangled the threaded needle.

Anansi was silent for a moment, then with simplicity she said, 'I shouldn't have said that, about Douai's dad and that Penny, should I?'

'No. You should not. Not right out in public. Luckily, everyone concerned is still alive. What are you going to do to make it better?'

'*Me?*' Anansi was astonished. 'I can't do nothing.'

'No reason not to try.'

'My mum's in prison,' said Anansi, veering off the subject. 'They'll put me into care again soon. Then I'll have to run away.'

Her tone conveyed accurately to Harry her meaning: that it would be ludicrous to expect any reparation from a being so helpless and beleaguered by bad luck.

'I don't buy that,' he said abruptly. 'If you've power to harm people, then by definition you have enough power to try and redeem the situation.'

'What did you do, then? For your dead soldier?' asked the child scornfully.

'When they're dead, it's never enough. Obviously. I always used to wish that I could wipe it out by saving someone else's life, really saving it, beyond argument, beyond the call of duty. That never happened.' Harry paused. Anansi was quiet.

He went on, 'But I worked in a German boys' orphanage in Kiel for two years after the war. I was on sick leave because I had a bit of shell in my leg. Leg was good enough to swab floors and teach the boys football. Went back into the army. Served in peacekeeping forces. Never shot anyone again.'

'So you reckon you're all right now?' She was belligerent again, wrong-footed and angry.

'No. None of it was anywhere near enough, but it made me feel a whole lot better. Married my wife, lost my brother, kept an eye on young Sheila, got on with life.'

'I'm a kid,' said Anansi, with diminishing conviction. 'They'll put me in care.'

'Not straightaway,' said Harry. 'I'll tell you one thing you could do, to make Sheila happy.'

'I do stuff in the house. More'n those boys do.'

'No, you can do better,' said the old man. 'You could try to be the thing she dreamed you would be. You, and all the other kids she gives holidays to. You could learn to sail, and muck in with the other kids, and get along, and put on some weight, and laugh a bit, and talk and show your feelings, and prove that she was right to bring you here. You could be a credit to Sheila. You could be the living proof that she's right about her Blythney summers being magic.'

Anansi was silent. These things were almost beyond her imagining. At last, heaving herself up from the fish-box, she said, 'All right. While I'm here. But I expect she'll send me back tomorrow with the lady from the charity.'

'Maybe,' said Harry. 'Meanwhile, I am going to show you how to sew in a cringle.'

Chapter Eleven

Alan Tranmere felt better for the sausage breakfast served to him, in companionable silence, by the divinely sympathetic yet unembarrassing Mrs Markeen. His daughters begged to stay on, and were left ensconced at the Hall under the exaggeratedly maternal care of Marta. Alaia drove Alan discreetly home to his back door, and left him to the luxury of a hot shower and a shave.

Emerging purified, he threw his clothes in the nearest linen basket (cavalierly ignoring Penny's rules about whites and coloureds) and sat down at the kitchen table with a cup of coffee. The events of the day and night before were taking on the unreal air of a feverish dream. He pulled the telephone notepad towards him, and began to write a list.

Ring Janet re care, it began. *?? some nights resident?*

Also Mrs B., re packing up P. things.

Solicitor: Ipswich better? re desertion, custody. cf. article in Telegraph *re paternal cust., try Internet?*

Alan did not think of himself as a romantic man, despite his agonized pursuit and vigil. If pressed, he would have said that he ran after Penny in order to get everything straight, as quickly as possible. He had hoped, perhaps, for a convincing denial; he might have settled for penitent tearfulness and a promise of amendment. Faced with defiance, however, he had little difficulty in hardening his own position – his *wronged* position – into a manful programme of action. To be cuckolded (Alan liked the robust old words best) was bad enough. But for the man concerned to be that rat-faced, sour-tongued little failure Simon Harrison was unbearable to any man of spirit. So was the memory of his wife, towel clutched round her narrow body, berating him for being inadequate in her bed.

Cold, spiteful little madam! Not a bit of warmth in her from Day One, he now saw; just disdainful submission to a lifelong meal ticket. Unnatural mother, too. One of the reasons he had lunged at her when she spoke of bed, and precipitated her flight into the street, was his terror that the little girls thumping around in their playroom would hear their father so indecently traduced. It seemed they had not. For that he was thankful.

But it was clear to him that Penny must go. He bent once more to his list.

Locks ?? check P's key here or not?

He wondered for a moment where she was. Not round at the Harrisons', surely; even the renowned kindliness of Sheila Harrison must stop at that. A thought struck him, and in his socks the big man padded out across the yard to the outhouse. Sure enough, the caravan key was gone. Ha! He wished them joy of it. The battery, he knew for a fact, was on the way out, so they could do whatever they did in the dark tonight, God rot them. He liked the expression 'God rot them'. It was robust. He should have had a different kind of wife. Solid. More like Poppy, or

Sheila. His mind flitted back wistfully to the dark, amused beauty of Alaia Markeen, but he shook his head with gentle regret. Couldn't handle one of those. Would only make a muck of it, like he had with Penny.

To banish the thought that the muck was partly his responsibility, he finished his list briskly, and was re-reading it when Simon Harrison knocked tentatively at the front door. He opened it and regarded the rat-figure with distaste.

'You'll have come for her things,' he said. 'Help yourself. But you can tell her the locks will be changed by the end of tomorrow, unless I find her key here, and that she'll hear from my solicitor this week.'

'I think we ought to talk about it,' said Simon. 'It's not what you think.'

'I think you've been having an affair with her, and nobody's denied it, have they? So as far as I am concerned you can keep her. You won't,' the large man spoke with some malice, 'find her cheap to run, believe me.'

'You should talk to her,' burst out Simon. 'I'm not sure she wants to leave.'

'Tried to talk to her. All last night. Given up now. Game over, old sport. Really. You can have her.'

'The children—'

'I am not a monster,' said Alan Tranmere. 'The girls can see all they like of her. But this is their home, and Janet from the council estate knows them bloody much as well as their mother ever did, and she'll be only too glad to give us more time. Might even live in. Nice woman. When you and Penelope have some sort of proper establishment, we can talk about dividing the kids' time formally. But she needn't think I'm going to keep her in luxury, because I'm not. And I won't hand over the girls just so she

131

can claim the house, so you needn't think that. Either of you.'

Simon, who had always thought of Alan Tranmere as an amiable Yacht Club buffoon, a wobbler on windsurfers and prodigal stander of rounds, suddenly and horribly remembered that his adversary was in real life a very effective and decisive businessman.

'I have not,' he bleated, 'made any decision about leaving Sheila. This is all very premature.'

Alan Tranmere glanced at his watch and said, 'Are you going upstairs to collect her things or not?'

So Simon went.

Sheila, left alone in her kitchen, sat down for once at the table and cupped her hands round a mug of hot coffee. All was in order. Anansi was on one of her walks, the boys had collected their gear and gone sailing, and there was sunlight and tidiness and silence all around her. Experimentally, she took a deep breath, then a deeper one. The third breath exhaled in a massive, relaxing sigh. Something was missing from the air of the house: Simon's silent, irritable criticism. Gone. Evaporated.

Sheila began to think of how it would be if it never came back again.

Harry and Anansi climbed onto the varnished boat together, taking a wide step from the muddy ladder and then hauling themselves back out until they were afloat. Together they fixed the brown sail to the mast, and to the end of the wooden boom ('It's all cracked!' said Anansi. 'Strong enough for what it does,' said Harry). Together they hoisted it, pulling the hairy rope hand over hand as the bundle of baggy nylon rose and took a graceful shape above their heads. Then they lowered it again, and Anansi pulled it up a second time alone. She had a moment's trouble balancing on the little boat's wobbling floorboards, and as she sat down abruptly on the thwart, Harry asked, 'What happened to your foot?'

'Got kicked,' she said, beyond subterfuge or embarrassment now. 'I reckon my dad kicked it when I was little. I get a dream about it. Blokes do stuff like that, when they're pissed. He was a cook in the army, my mum said, and they're always pissed.'

'Are they? Gosh, that would explain some of the food,' said Harry. The child giggled. He stooped to look at her ankle, and for the first time in her life Anansi did not try to hide it.

'Hummm. It looks as if it wasn't set right. Do you remember if you went to hospital?'

'Don't think I did. Mum said I did, but I don't remember. It never comes into the dream.'

'It looks just like the kind of badly set injuries we saw after the war in Angola,' said Harry. 'It's quite possible that it could be re-set now. Though the muscles would take a while to adjust, and it could be painful. We sorted out a few kids that way, through a charity I was involved with in the seventies.'

Anansi turned to him with sudden passion, her eyes bright against the shade of the sail. 'You mean when I grow up I could get it fixed?'

'Possibly. Better sooner than later, though. The bigger you grow, the more problems. Now, put the rope round that peg, so, and bring it back, and then we flip it over and drop it over the top. It's called a jamming turn.'

Later, over Sunday lunch, Harry Glanville said to his wife,

'The kid. That foot of hers could be fixed. I'm almost certain of it.'

'Surely it would have been done, if it could be, dear? The health visitor or someone would have put things in motion.'

'I'm not persuaded,' said Harry, spearing a piece of roast beef, 'that things always work so well for kids in homes like that. Not when it isn't life-threatening. She's had half a dozen moves in her life, as far as I can see, run away from a couple of homes, and today she told me that when she was six she lost her grandmother, who seems to have been the only steady one in the family. Now her mother is in prison for drug dealing.'

'Any *father*?' inquired his wife, still with a shade of censure in her voice.

'Not heard of for years. Cook in the army, she says, not an African chief like she tells the other kids. Anyway, she reckons he's the one who lamed her. Madge, honestly, it's not the sort of household we're used to. Even with your social work in the county . . . I don't think you can assume anything will be all right, just of its own accord.'

'No,' said Marion, more thoughtfully. 'But do you really think – I mean, with the Health Service these days – do you think there's anything that hasn't been done?'

'Yes,' said Harry. 'I've tried thinking that. But simple things get very complicated when people are so poor. Seen it abroad. No reason it shouldn't be as bad here.'

'I thought,' said Marion, spooning more peas onto his plate, 'that drug dealers were terribly *rich*. Some of the ones I meet in prison-visiting are very cocky about what they made.'

'I think not if they actually take the drugs as well. Running to catch up with themselves, you'd imagine.'

'Ah,' said Marion. 'Poor child. What happens to her now, with the Harrisons in trouble?'

Harry hesitated, looking across at his neat, bright-eyed, white-haired little wife.

'I thought . . . could we volunteer to help? If Sheila won't keep her on? Have her here? Sort of grandchild, great-niece, basis?'

Marion pursed her lips. 'It isn't like ordinary children, dear. That I do know. If she *was* a relative, nobody would raise an eyebrow. But we're too old. Too old-fashioned. You know what they'd say, in the social service place. What's that word they use? *Inappropriate*. Especially as you're the one she's made friends with, and you're a man. You know how people's minds work.'

Marion, practical as always, had been wanting to deliver such a warning ever since her husband began coming home from Coker's Quay with accounts of his new young friend. She was grateful for the opportunity. People had horrid minds. She knew that from a lifetime in WIs and Officers' Wives Groups, and voluntary work in their retirement. Harry was an old-fashioned romantic innocent in some ways, for all his soldiering. Perhaps because of the soldiering. He thought you were allowed to just pick up English children and help them as if they were Angolans or Croats or whatever. She softened the remark, though, with a smile and a shake of her pretty white hair.

Harry began to eat, his face gloomy. 'Right,' he said. 'You're right. I wish we could do something, though.'

'Well,' said Marion, 'as long as it isn't you and her together, you could teach her to sail, like you promised. Take another child as chaperone. God knows there's plenty of them, running round the town like mice while their parents idle the day away. And another thing, you know

what an old sleuth you are. You could start by finding this
father of hers and seeing if *he's* prepared to take a bit of
responsibility.'

'He won't be,' said Harry, but his eyes gleamed. 'My
God, though, if anyone can get at the records, old Spike
could – remember Spike at the MoD? The chess chap? He's
retiring at Christmas, but he still might . . .'

'Well, then,' said Marion. 'Go on, make a few calls.
Tell Spike to riffle through his filing cabinets and break
the Official Secrets Act. Enjoy yourself.'

She whisked away his empty plate and trotted through
to the scullery for the trifle.

Sheila was a good packer. She made up a suitcase for
Simon, and explained when he arrived that this was to
save him time, since he would need to sort out his current
working papers himself. His winter clothes, of course, could
stay for the moment, but she was assuming that he would
prefer to be out of the house and with Penny. She was
bright and brittle, unreproachful and matter-of-fact. She
hoped that he would drop in as often as possible during
the holidays to see the boys – perhaps Saturday suppers *en
famille* would be civilized? No, of course, Fridays, because
Saturdays were junior disco nights.

Simon, who had come back in the hope of lunch since
Penny was still asleep, took the suitcase in silence, threw
in a few papers and his laptop for form's sake, and slunk
away. As he walked awkwardly down the High Street
with the two heavy cases, his and Penny's, he saw the
Tranmeres' cheerful baby-sitter Janet, from St Andrew's
estate, wheeling her bike with a tartan holdall slung over
the handlebars.

Simon was not a man to notice other people's domestic

staff; only when she confidently pulled out her key and let herself into the tall Tranmere house did he realize with a sinking heart who she was, and who she was replacing.

So it was that twenty-four hours after Anansi's declaration on the beach, two domestic landscapes were altered. Three, if you counted the newly created household down on Abbey Farm Marshes. Of them all, this was the least satisfactory. The marshes were lower than the town, and the early mist often lay over the caravan site like an inland sea until mid-morning. The grass beneath the vans stayed wet; the plywood veneer of cupboards and bunks warped gently through nine months of the year, and annoyed the holidaymaking occupants for the other three. Penny was woken from her uneasy slumber by a cupboard in the kitchenette swinging open with a bang; the others followed it, and an uneasy creaking pervaded the wooden inner shell of the elderly caravan. When she turned over, the flap on the top of the wardrobe fell open with a hollow bang. The mattress smelt gently of mould and of generations of children with imperfect nocturnal bladder control.

When she was no longer tired enough to sleep through these torments, Penny sat up, ran her hands through her hair, and wondered which of her women friends, this Sunday afternoon, would be faithful enough to give her a shower and the loan of some proper clothes. Susannah would probably be willing, if only for the gossip value, but she was staying at her mother-in-law's, and Penny could imagine all too well how fast the story of her public shaming would have circulated at the church door. Poppy had made her feelings clear, and certainly could not be approached. Nadine Carter and the Ward-Williamses were still in London. With a rush of joy, she realized that she had the key to the Carters' holiday cottage. With a rush of despair, she realized that it was hanging up inside her own house, guarded by Alan.

As she pondered the problem, she realized that she would very soon have to have a wee. Gingerly, she eased her feet into the pair of old espadrilles Simon had brought – Sheila's! Disgusting! – and went to the blockhouse. She had never found public lavatories other than an ordeal, and the bleak stained paperless sight before her served to harden her resolve. The showers were even bleaker. Not one night would she stay in this place, Simon or no Simon. Well, perhaps one night. It was already four o'clock, afer all. She quailed at the task before her: the task of rebuilding, re-establishing, raising herself again to the chic and status that were as necessary to her as oxygen.

Her mood was not improved by her lover's arrival with a suitcase, particularly since it was his own suitcase. He had, he said, accidentally left her case in the Crown and Anchor when he stopped for fortification. By the time he had remembered, the pub was closed. Blythney pubs still closed for the afternoon on quiet days. It was that sort of town.

They did make love that evening, though. After an hour of shrewish recrimination, and Simon's glum return to the pub when it reopened at six, Penny looked at her face in the crazed mirror over the slimy little sink, and was so horrified by its pinched and aged expression that she softened. Men's attentions were, in her experience, the fastest way to make oneself feel pretty again. So with skill and determination she solicited Simon's. It was not a satisfactory interlude; but it was, at least, horizontal. And afterwards they both found sleep.

*　　*　　*

Sheila rose early on Monday morning. The boys were back from the Cottens, crashed in sleep on their own beds and smelling, she thought as she peered round each door, rather strongly of beer. She must do something about this, especially about Douai, who was after all only twelve. The new sense of lightness was still with her, and she concluded in some astonishment that the reason she had never dealt firmly with the drinking before was because of Simon's presence. It was a discipline a father should impose on a son, and his failure to bother had rendered her, in turn, impotent. Now that he was not here it would be easier.

Stepping out into the yard, she opened the shed door and moved Douai's bike. Behind it, under a sack, lay three six-packs of Foster's lager. She took them and put them in the larder with the rest of the family provisions and, still light-heartedly, wrote on a Post-It note the words: 'I have counted these! One per boy per night only. S. Harrison (Mrs).' Smiling, she fixed it to the topmost box.

Anansi had appeared like a shadow behind her. Sheila turned and said, 'Breakfast?' It was a good approximation of her usual blithe manner, although less verbose.

Anansi said gravely, 'I oughter say sorry about what I said. At the picnic. I was out of order. I shouldn't have said that. You did all the work for the picnic, an' the boat an' all.'

'Well,' said Sheila, looking at the child for the first time as a person rather than a social work project, 'it might be all for the best, you know.'

She was surprised by her own words. Tentatively, as if it were a broken tooth she was probing with her tongue, she tested her feelings about Simon having rough sex in the Martello with pretty Penny Tranmere. Astonishingly, the feelings were almost entirely numb. All that mattered was this new peace and clarity she felt. Somewhere, an intolerable noise had been switched off. For years she had been prattling brightly against it, trying to drown it out with burbling fun and optimism, and now it seemed that few and simple words would do.

'Don't worry,' she said to the child. 'We've got your life to organize now. Miss Archenlaw and someone from Deptford social services are coming down to talk to us this morning. I'll send the boys out. Dondie and Alison aren't here either, they stayed on the floor at Bethie's.'

'Thanks,' said Anansi. And shyly, 'If the social say I can stay, that's all right.'

But before the London pair could arrive, before Anansi had even finished her cereal and bananas, Harry Glanville was on the doorstep.

Chapter Twelve

On some days, the brown river looked blue. When the light fell a certain way and the observer's distance was right, the great sweep of the Grend took on a pale silvery metallic sheen like the wing of a kingfisher. Harry had woken with the dawn that Monday morning, and stepped outside to breathe deeply on his mole-spotted front lawn. He gazed for a long moment at the blueness of the river and the pink fingers of dawn in the sky beyond the sea wall.

The early air was intoxicating, salt-marsh and heathland smells mingling with the honeysuckle on the wall in cold, fresh sweetness. He remembered a boyhood story about the land of the Heroes, where every breath a mere mortal took brought him nearer to becoming a giant and a hero.

On a morning like this, no problem was insoluble, no grief inconsolable. His eyes misted a little; beyond this view, this dawn and this river, there hung some intangible, enormous truth and illimitable goodness. Ever since early childhood Harry had felt such moments of conviction: a bay, a flower, a horse, a poem, a curving sail or a laughing child could set it off. Enormous truth, abundant goodness.

Any small good he could achieve would flow, like a marshy creek, into this ocean of beauty. He, and the river, and the honeysuckle, and dead Maurice, and the fluttering sails and the dark troubled child on the quay were all in a great dance, moving together to some ultimate unity.

He did not speak of such feelings to Marion, that steady, kindly churchgoer; but the feeling did not divide him from her either. It led, after all, to salvation by good works, and this sat comfortably enough with her Anglican pragmatism. But on such rare mornings as these, the Godliness of the whole landscape moved him simultaneously both to tears and to action.

So while Marion was still making toast in her frilly pink wrapper, Harry walked down the rutted track to the centre of Blythney and cut past the chip shop to knock on the door of Seafret. Sheila opened it with an expression of surprise.

'Uncle *Harry*!' she said. 'You're an early bird! The boys aren't up yet. And where's the dog?' He sometimes took Vincent and Douai rabbiting.

'Not come for the boys,' he said. 'Dog's at home. Bloody nuisance in other people's houses. Kettle on?'

Sheila saw him in. Anansi, at the kitchen table, looked startled and not entirely pleased. She felt uneasy at seeing him without the river and the quay.

Harry said to her, 'Do me a favour, Nancy? I left the boat on the mud overnight, with water up to the second plank. Wanted to see about a leak. If you go down now, tide'll be out; just tell me if the water's visibly dripping down the starboard side of the bow, near the waterline.'

Anansi nodded wordlessly, and quick as an eel slipped from the room.

'She won't know words like starboard and bow,' objected Sheila, amused in spite of herself by this swift obedience.

'She will, so,' said Harry. 'Picks things up very fast. Anyway, I've already checked the boat, so it doesn't particularly matter. Wanted a word with you on your own. Better hurry, or the boys will be up.'

Sheila poured his tea and sat down opposite him.

'So, are you keeping her then? Your little social terrorist?' he said.

'On Saturday,' said Sheila, 'I thought not. I thought for the boys' sake, and for the sake of Blythney in general, it would be better if she left. God knows what else she might have seen.' She laughed with a nervous coarseness that only rarely surfaced in her.

Harry nodded, and said, 'I don't think she'd do it again, even if she did catch half the town with its trousers down. It was a desperate defensive manoeuvre in a tight corner. What she thought was a tight corner.'

'But I was trying to be so *nice* to her,' said Sheila plaintively. 'I do my best by these poor mites.' Something of the old self-righteousness was visible in her broad face.

Harry sipped his tea and said, 'Quite.'

'What do you mean?'

'She's not a poor mite. She carries her own colours.'

Sheila remembered the expression from childhood, when young, bold Uncle Harry's visits came as a welcome relief from the querulous anxiety of her grandparents' domestic regime. She stiffened her back with mock military solemnity. 'Carries her own colours, commands her own regiment?'

'Indeed. Plenty of dash—'

'And not much judgement,' finished Sheila. She smiled.

'You said that to me once, when I tried to row through the creeks on a falling tide.'

'You were nine or so. A mutinous little pirate.'

'Oh, Uncle Harry,' said Sheila. 'Why don't we see more of you?'

He looked at her with fondness, perfectly understanding the question. 'Little Sheila. What becomes of us all in this life?'

'Some of us marry Simon,' said Sheila. 'Do you know, I have been feeling twenty years old ever since he moved out?'

'Won't do, though, will it? The boys.'

'Oh, sod the boys,' said Sheila, startlingly. 'They can make do with you for a while, like I had to. Fathers are very overrated, in my view.'

Harry then sat with his niece at the kitchen table, and unfolded to her certain plans and intentions. If Sheila would let Anansi stay and square the officialdom, he would keep the child amused with the boat and the river, and encourage friendships with the other children of the town. 'She's taken against your Dow. No point throwing them together.' Meanwhile he would sound out medical friends about her foot. He did not mention the search for her father. That was altogether too private a dream. Rational though he was, it was too much tied up in his mind with a knightly quest; with one of the stories he used to read as a boy, alive with giants' and heroes' breath.

'You can't go sailing with her alone,' objected Sheila. 'There's all sorts of rules. Children Act. Anti-molesting. You're the wrong gender for one-to-one care of a girl of eleven, a non-relative from a difficult background. It's for your own protection. Some of these children make accusations. People's lives get wrecked.'

'Not a fool,' nodded Harry. 'I don't think it of her, but some might make trouble. No, Marion had a brilliant idea. That skinny little kid of Jonny Markeen's, Marta. Jonny asked me weeks ago to give her sailing lessons in the Whitecap. He hasn't got one, but he likes the idea of her racing and doesn't think she's learning any damn thing from pretending to crew that Mirror dinghy with the blonde giggly one. I could take the two girls together.'

'Wouldn't it be rather hard graft for you? Two kids to look after?'

'Not look after. *Train*. Remember, a couple of years back I taught the Cotten cousins when their dad had his arm in plaster. Two weeks and they were fine.'

'Do you think Jonny would let you teach Marta with Anansi? He doesn't think Marta would get corrupted by – well, the sort of things she says?' Sheila was doubtful. 'You know her mother's in prison, and you know how choosy Alaia has always been about the company Marta keeps.'

'I raised that with Jonny. He said he'd square Alaia. Marta, apparently, has developed a Little Match Girl complex about your Anansi. Wants to adopt her, like Becky the servant girl in *A Little Princess*, whatever that is. Jonny said it was either that or else have the Tranmere brats round all day long playing dolls' house. Marta is quite the little mother.'

'So it all falls into place,' said Sheila wonderingly. 'Well, as I said, I'll keep Anansi for the summer. If they sanction it. The only thing is that I ought to talk to—'

Before she could say 'the boys', Douai, who had been standing in the doorway for longer than they knew, said in an awful voice, 'We're not keeping that stupid little bitch here. No way. If she stays, I go. Right?'

Uncle and niece stared at one another, open-mouthed, their plans crumbling. The front door slammed.

'It can't all crumble,' said Harry desperately a full half-hour later. 'Not just because of one child's views.'

'But he's my son,' said Sheila. 'I know I said sod the boys, but I didn't mean it. He's twelve years old, and he's heard his father humiliated, sexually, in front of his own peers and most of the adults he knows. Now his father's vanished off to the goddamn caravan site with another woman, and we expect him to sit down to meals all holidays with the child who came into his house and did this thing to him.'

Harry said, weakly, 'He's at a Catholic school, isn't he? Could we say forgive your enemies? Turn the other cheek, all that?'

Sheila said nothing, but turned her mug round in her hands.

'Might Vincent help?' Harry went on. 'Nice boy, Vince.'

'I can't,' said Sheila flatly. 'Douai's lost his father – lost his interest years ago, if truth be told. Simon's hardly spoken to him all his life. He never wanted a third baby and he blamed me because of the Catholic thing. Though God knows I was trying hard enough not to get pregnant. Now, if I welcome this cuckoo in the nest, Douai will feel as if his mother's putting him last as well. I should have thought of that. It was only the look on his face just now that made me see it.'

'But if you let them take Anansi back *now*,' said Harry in agony, 'they'll put her in a children's home, and God knows what happens to girls that age in care in this benighted country – and she'll run off anyway, and probably end up on the bloody *streets*. Or dead with a needle in her.'

Sheila broke out, her face puckering in distress, shouting at him, 'You can't do this to me. No! No! It's blackmail!' She pounded the table with her fist. 'It is absolutely not possible to say that we, a pack of strangers, living a hundred miles away from where she belongs, that we are the only thing standing between this child and a wrecked life.'

'It might be true,' said Harry. 'She trusts us. Trusts me. It happened by accident, through a few conversations on Coker's, but it is true. She trusts me. She's ready to learn something real, and if she manages that, it could open the door to her learning all sorts of other things. That's what I think, anyway.'

'She's resilient. You said yourself. A fighter. No harm will come to her even if she does go straight back to London.'

'Some things a child can't fight. Like when that bastard lamed her foot. Sheila, she can't even *walk* a hundred per cent properly. What the hell sort of chance does she have in the sort of world you say she "belongs" in?'

Sheila, tears in her eyes, kept her head down. 'It can't all depend on us,' she said. 'It can't!'

The train pulled out of London, crawling through the smoky suburbs, gathering speed as the land grew greener. In a second-class non-smoking carriage, Janice Archenlaw of CHA talked confidentially, leaning over the plastic table, to a prematurely grey-haired and remarkably thin young man called Mark Hinton. This skeletal, irritable figure was the case worker assigned to both Kyra and Anansi Cowper. It was unusual for him to travel outside his grey patch of south-east London, but the peculiar embarrassment of the circumstances – child on holiday, mother remanded in custody, middle-class hostess landed with a jailbird's progeny, no care place available for the child – had persuaded him to appear in Blythney and judge the situation for himself. You did not turn your nose up at a willing foster home. It was not as if it was adoption.

He did not look forward to the visit, though. Mark had strong theories about the role of his profession, and felt passionately about the need for what, in seminars, he called 'evenness and rational systematology in the care environment'. He despised irregular and idiosyncratic solutions to systemic social problems, and had a particularly strong aversion to what he decried as the 'Famous Five' world into which the CHA transported its children.

Never mind that most of them seemed to like it, at least at the time. To Mark, the whole thing smelt of cultural imperialism. By what right did these smug middle-Englanders think that their own hearty pursuits of tennis and sailing and rounders and horse riding (a particularly distasteful negation of animal rights) were any better than the native street life, community solidarity and sophisticated urban perspective of his clients? By what right did they patronize poor children, show them expensive pastimes and then throw them back into an envious and hostile peer group and family? How dare they play Lady Bountiful? If rural life was so healthy, why couldn't these children be sent to properly run communal camps with their peers? Mark had spent two formative years on a kibbutz in the 1970s and revered the experience still.

More pragmatic colleagues laughed at him and said, 'Middle-class guilt is a resource, Marco. Let's mine it.' He was unmoved. To him, what had been done to Anansi Cowper by the CHA was effectively worse than what had been done to her by her own parents.

He did not even much like ordinary fostering, redolent

as it was of a restrictive fascist idea of the 'family'. He had a romantic sense of the solidarity of the deprived, and would ideally have liked to place Anansi right now not only in a mixed-race Home, but in one where she would be certain to meet other children whose single parent was in prison for drug dealing. What use could bloody pampered middle-class children be to her, other than to lower her self-esteem?

He listened now to Janice Archenlaw with barely controlled hostility. She was, as planned, spending the journey persuading him that to leave Anansi with the Harrisons as temporary foster parents was the perfect solution. Once or twice he broke into her eager flow.

'If there was a possibility of long-term fostering, in an appropriate setting and family—'

'Well, there might be,' she cut him off. 'Mrs Harrison has sometimes talked of full foster care. There is a good school with a bus service from her little town—'

'Has she any experience with mixed-race issues?'

'She's had a lot of our younger children.'

'But she isn't in a multiracial family group. How can she prepare a child for the experience of racism? And what about access for the parents? How do you justify placing a child a hundred miles from its mother and sister?'

'The mother,' said Miss Archenlaw, 'is not likely to be out of jail for at least eighteen months. Not with her record, and the amount of stuff she was dealing. We also have reason to think she neglects Anansi very much indeed. The half-sister is in a care home where, as well you know, there is no room and a long waiting list.'

'There are other foster families. Out of area.'

'Where?'

He consulted his papers. 'One in Milton Keynes, specializing in mixed race. One in Newcastle.'

'Well,' said Miss Archenlaw triumphantly, 'that's even further away. Be reasonable. We have done a full police check on the Harrisons.'

Mark Hinton glared at her. 'I will come to my own conclusions about the Harrisons.' He already had. He hated the very idea of them.

At the moment this spiky conversation ended, Sheila Harrison was sitting at her kitchen table with her uncle, saying, 'No. No.' Douai was kicking an empty lager can along the prom, pretending it was Anansi. And Anansi, divining that she would do well to be out of the way for as long as possible, was swinging her legs on Coker's Quay, watching the water dribble unmistakably out of the loose seam on the side of the Whitecap dinghy, and enjoying a warm irrational conviction that at last, things were going to go right for her.

Chapter Thirteen

If the eight-thirty train out of Liverpool Street had not missed its connection with the Lowestoft branch line (points failure at Witham) a whole skein of lives would have been different. As it was, it was nearer one o'clock than the planned ten thirty when Mr Hinton and Miss Archenlaw, each in a separate cocoon of bad temper, arrived from Darsham station by taxi and made their way along the Edwardian seafront to the Harrisons' front door.

Mark was by this time almost speechless with irritation. During the short walk two people had been clearly heard by him to say 'Yah, super', and he had seen numerous women with sunglasses pushed up like Alice bands on their straight blonde bobs. Most were wearing white or pink pedal pushers, and sailing smocks with very white shirt collars poking up from them. All had an insufferable air of diffident assurance; not rich-bitch precisely, he thought, but rich-wife. These were girls who had been sent to hearty boarding schools, had taken footling little jobs for a while, and then married men with money who would keep them in clothes and country cottages for as long as they turned out a good *boeuf en daube* behind the kitchen knicker-blinds and raised the children with accents suitable to members of the master race. If they had jobs now, they would be to do with flowers, or estate agency, or art galleries.

One whose haughtily chic demeanour especially annoyed him was in fact Penny Tranmere, now thankfully reunited with her proper clothes and making her way to Bethie Cotten's house for sympathy and a shower. Mark took a particular dislike to her, even though her dark glasses were on her nose and not the top of her head. He put her down as a real bitch, a candidate for the ducking stool if even there was one. He could not have guessed the turmoil beneath the smooth blonde cap of hair or known how much of the arrogant tilt of her head was purely defensive.

The delay to the train, however, allowed two useful things to happen. The first was that Mark's irritation rose so high that it overwhelmed his soberer judgement. Until the long delay at Witham, his hardened preference had been for this Cowper child to be rescued from these predatory Lady Bountifuls and returned to a more relevant and suitable environment among her peers. Miss Archenlaw must be routed, as he surely had the authority to do. By the time the train had crawled on through Colchester to Ipswich, it began to seem equally important that he get himself clear of Miss Archenlaw's conversation and presence before he did her an injury.

A period of mutual silence in the Lemon Tree Cafe on Ipswich station was followed by a painfully quaint rattle northwards on the branch line (how *dare* there be green fields and chocolate-box cottages when there were slums and council flats and underpasses? thought Mark. How *dare* women in husky jackets stand laughing fatly on the platform?). These, followed by a taxi ride with a wheezy rustic 'mustn't grumble' character from a sentimental Ealing comedy, eventually brought him to the point where his only remaining desire was that this day should be over and he safe back in London with the book closed on this shaming, irritating case.

The other thing which happened during the delay was that Sheila, once she had been telephoned from Ipswich about the revised arrival time, took a walk up the town to calm her nerves. It was so unusual for her to leave the house without a definite bustling purpose that she found she had lost the art of strolling or straying. She stood for a moment irresolute, then – suddenly aware of a pitying gaze from an acquaintance outside the fish shop – turned up another alley. It led into a flight of narrow steps and connected with the top of the town where the Catholic church was. Few of her contemporaries were Catholics; those who were would certainly not be here on a Monday.

It was an unremarkable church, built in the 1950s of biscuit-coloured brick with stone lintels. The pale oak pews were modern and uncomfortable, and only a small panel of stained glass enlivened the tall white window behind the altar. Sheila genuflected and slipped into a pew, not for guidance but out of the merest habit. Her religion was, in fact, mainly a matter of habit: the legacy of the convent school where, at her dead Catholic mother's request, she had spent her teenage years. Her grandparents had very much wanted to send her to Benenden, and it was Harry who had told his parents squarely that Maurice himself would have wanted his wife's religion to be honoured. 'More than he would want his daughter brought up in his *own* faith, dear?' said Grandma Glanville doubtfully, and Harry, thinking of the anguished

153

lack of any belief in Maurice's last years, had said, 'Yes, much more.'

So Sheila went to New Hall, and became a Catholic schoolgirl. She always, secretly, rather liked the way that this set her apart from the other Glanvilles, and indeed from Simon the scornful atheist. It was all she had ever known of her mother, this allegiance and this school with its strange, rustling, glowing, numinous world of religiosity. Perhaps this accounted for the defiant naming of Douai, the baby his father so keenly did not want. Douai had been an abbey in exile, romantic to her from school history. So Douai would be her boy and only hers, the child of her emotional exile from Simon. The priest had jibbed at this, and insisted on the more conventional middle name of Xavier. But he had few enough parishioners in Protestant Blythney and did not like to alienate one.

Kneeling now in the pew, her eyes on the faint red light by the altar, Sheila let her mind go blank. This was the luxury of church to her: forgetting for an hour the duties and lists and arrangements of the day. She rarely paid much attention to the words and rites of the Mass, attending Communion automatically and frankly shutting out the sermon. She went to confession twice a year, and spoke only the easy formulae for achieving a generalized absolution. It was the church *mood*, remembered from the school chapel, that counted. It was peace that she came for.

There was nobody else in the church, only the flickering red light and the bulky form of Sheila, on her knees, head resting on her loosely clasped hands. Into the space of her mind floated fragments of church words. This was usual, not unnerving. Today, though, one phrase kept recurring. *Only begotten Son. Only begotten Son.* She frowned. *Gave his*

Only begotten Son. Why those words? *Gave.* She blinked, and more words came. *Abraham and Isaac. Gave his Only Begotten Son.*

She did not have an only begotten son. She had two. *Beloved Son, in whom I am well pleased.* Angrily, as if she suspected someone of interfering with her mind, Sheila shook her head. This time an image came: a pietà, the Virgin sorrowing over the body of her sacrificed Jesus. Then a picture in Harry's house, an artistically-minded newspaper photographer's image of an Italian mother near Naples in the war, her dead son in her arms, her pose echoing the pietà. The war: all those sons, sacrificed. All those mothers, weeping. Something else, a higher imperative, put before the protection of the only beloved son.

Sheila was really angry now. She rose from the pew, and turned her back on the sanctuary without genuflecting or making a sign of the cross. It seemed to her that her whole life had been a sacrifice already. She had put her husband before herself, her children before herself. She had sacrificed her own convenience and pleasure for the charity's children, for neighbours' children, for starving African children, for meals on wheels pensioners, disabled children – all of them had come first. For years she, Sheila, had come last. She had grown stout and (she knew in her heart) rather ludicrous and a little boring because of all this putting herself last.

Now some – *thing* – was suggesting that virtuous self-abnegation was not enough. It was demanding that she even give up the right to organize the pecking order of her own virtuous deeds. It demanded, quite explicitly, that she put Anansi Cowper's welfare before her own youngest son's. *Only beloved Son's.* Sheila was deeply, painfully angry. She stood with her back to the sanctuary, and her hands rose to plant themselves defiantly on her hips.

It seemed to her that the red lamp bored into her back like the point of a hateful little drill, or a laser scoring a hole through her body. She was impaled on it. She stood still, and then dropped her hands and began to walk away.

She had not reached the church door before she capitulated. Swinging back towards the altar (at just about the moment that the little train pulled into Darsham), Sheila said aloud, 'All right, you – you *bastard*. But if anything bad comes of it . . .'

On the way back home she slipped into the telephone box at the bottom of the town steps and rang Harry to say that she would, after all, offer Anansi shelter for as long as they would let her.

Chapter Fourteen

Anansi dawdled by the river, and arrived back when the meeting about her was nearly over.

Sheila looked up from the kitchen table, and gave her a quick, tight smile. Miss Archenlaw greeted her in measured fashion, saying that she had heard that Anansi was getting lots of lovely fresh air and seeing the sights. A quick, scared glance from the child at this point made Janice fleetingly wonder whether there was something not being spoken of, but she pushed the idea resolutely aside. It had become an article of faith with her that anything – especially anything involving clean country air, table manners and a halfway normal family life – was better than committing this child to the kind of 'Home' that would be able to take her.

Mark Hinton asked to speak to Anansi alone, and was shown into the chaotic front room, where oars leaned against picture frames and lifejackets served as sofa cushions. He left the door ajar, and sat down on the scuffed and faded armchair while Anansi perched restlessly on the arm of the sofa. Cursorily, he asked her views and recorded them in a notebook. He did not look up at her face while she spoke but made rapid notes.

Yes, she did want to stay on for a while. No, there were no problems. Yes, the family were treating her well. Yes, Mr Harrison seemed fine but no, she did not see very much of him. Yes, she had met other children her own age. Yes, she liked being near the sea.

Anansi was quick to divine that Sheila had not mentioned Simon's defection (in fact, she had said he was 'at work', and Miss Archenlaw had given her a quick puzzled glance but refrained from reminding the social worker that he wrote at home full-time). Anansi in her turn said nothing about Simon's move. When Mark Hinton pressed her a little about him (foster fathers were a sore point in his office, after certain high-profile accusations), she understood perfectly what filth he was fishing for, and merely said, with vague hauteur, that she never saw him for very long because of his work.

Finally Mark asked her whether she wanted to be taken on a visit to the prison to see her mother.

Anansi hesitated, then said, 'Nah. I don't think I should go. Is she gonna be able to see Kyra, though?'

'Well, it's thought to be too upsetting for a young child.' Mindful of his training, Mark left a silence and then said, 'What do you think?'

'Mum's really gone on Kyra,' said Anansi. 'She'd want to see *her*.' There was a shadow of emphasis on the pronoun which made the social worker look up, for the first time seeing properly the impassive little face opposite him.

'She'd be glad to see *you*,' he said, with a faint interrogative tone.

'Nah,' said Anansi. Her face was now quite shuttered. 'Little babies are different, with mums. Ain't they?'

Mark closed his notebook. 'Well,' he said. 'If you're happy staying here, until the new term starts, we can make plans a bit later on. I will liaise with the authority over schools in case we extend the placement. Meanwhile, enjoy your summer.'

'Yeh' said Anansi. She was looking away now, out of the window towards the grey sea. 'C'n I go out now?'

Mark followed her glance towards the window, and shivered. It did not look at all an attractive prospect to him, but he said, resignedly, 'Yes. Tell Mrs Harrison where you're going.'

Mark had been surprised by Sheila Harrison. She was upper-middle class, all right, and countrified and tweedily jolly and assured, everything he most loathed in principle; but he had to admit that she was very different from the chic, mewing, Alice-banded women who had focused his dislike as he walked through the town. Indeed her slightly curly fair hair was frankly dishevelled, and unashamedly streaked with grey, and her generous bosom and bulging midriff would not have been out of place on one of his council-house clients. He was less antagonistic now to the idea of leaving the child with her, not because he felt she would be any better for Anansi but because he unwillingly absolved her of the more unpleasant kind of patronage. She was just a big motherly being who liked looking after people; harmless enough, all right for a short-term placement in a difficult summer. The child seemed to have no objection to her, although she showed no noticeable warmth for her hostess either. But that child, he thought, never showed much warmth; a chilly little being, with a sour twist to her mouth. You could not know what she was thinking.

He was faintly uneasy at having to take Simon Harrison on trust, but Janice Archenlaw spoke for the man and appeared to know him well. He also knew that he should have interviewed both Harrison siblings. But the last viable train from Darsham was growing closer, and Douai was still at large in the town. Vincent, sprawled at the kitchen table, had said Anansi's staying was Fine By Him, and that he would tell Dow when he saw him, 'if he was interested'. Then he slouched off without elaborating. Vincent privately thought that his brother was being pretty stupid, not at all grown-up; moreover he enjoyed the sense of his own quasi-adult complicity with Harry and Sheila. The thought of his father troubled him slightly, but several of his friends had adulterous and separated parents, and the general wisdom at school was that one had to be 'cool' about it. Like he was cool about Anansi. Hardly noticed her.

Thus by nightfall Anansi was formally in the care of Sheila Harrison and Simon Harrison (who was on his hands and knees half a mile away, trying to reconnect the battery leads on the caravan). Miss Archenlaw was reporting success by phone to the director of the CHA, and Mark Hinton was safe back in London, shuddering slightly at the company he had been keeping. Still, it was sorted now. Several months' grace. Even the foster payments had been waived, thanks to the generosity of the Country Hosts Association. He sent a note of his doings to Suffolk social services, and put Anansi Cowper firmly from his mind.

Douai did not reappear for supper. A few telephone calls from his mother revealed that he was eating pizza with Alison and Dondie at the Cottens'. It was common for Blythney summer children to treat several houses as their own, and Sheila maintained a bright pretence that nothing was amiss. Vincent, however, left their reduced supper table with his treacle tart still clutched in his fist, observing to his mother that he would 'bring Dow home by ten, no sweat'. Sheila glanced her gratitude at him, and returned to the business of pressing more pudding on Anansi.

'We've never had a slice left over yet! Not of my treacle tart! Come on, now!'

Anansi, by now, could recognize a nervous reflex in Sheila when she saw one. Making people eat puddings, she perceived, was one of her hostess's tools for coping with difficult moments in life. Graciously, remembering her promise to Harry, she managed to say, 'Thanks. I never had any dessert as good as this in my life. Even in school dinners.'

Later, kneeling at her bedroom window, Anansi saw the dim shapes of the two boys making their way along the seafront, followed at a distance by the giggling duo of Alison and Dondie Cotten. Douai was feeling his way by the concrete wall, and Vincent half dragging him by the other arm. Anansi knew enough of life to see immediately that Douai was drunk. His thin growling voice rose as he approached, and his words became intelligible.

'Black – bitch – bloody – *bitch*.'

Then Vincent, shushing him, then the drunken half-human growl again.

'Bloody – black – bitch – bloody.'

She shrank back from the windowsill, and climbed into bed. Hauling up all her reserves of determination, she blotted out the sound and the thought of Douai and replaced it with that of Harry. When she had seen him, this afternoon, walking out towards Coker's Quay, he had given her a thumbs-up, paused to listen to her account of the leak and said, 'Well done, Nancy.'

She called up the echo of it, and with his 'Well done' she drowned out the growl from the street, the slam of the front door and the rising sussuration of argument and remonstration from the room below.

Half a mile away, Simon lay on his back on the narrower of the two caravan bunks, longing for a cigarette. Penny was unconscious; she had returned from Bethie Cotten's with a sachet of herbal tea and two sleeping pills in a twist of tinfoil, but he did not dare risk waking her with the loathed smell of smoke. Besides, there were only two fags left in the packet, and the precariousness of his immediate financial position had been bearing down on him with increasing weight throughout the day.

There was the joint account, fed by Sheila's dividends and interest and providing for the bills and tax on Seafret; but by mischance his chequebook on that account had run out. In any case a certain shame gripped him at the idea of using it. Sheila did not maintain a separate, private account but he did; it was currently useless, though, being overdrawn by eight hundred and twenty-two pounds on a limit of seven hundred and fifty. Alan Tranmere had made it brutally clear that anything his wife got from him would come only via the tightly clenched fists of solicitors; she had only minute earnings of her own from her work for Jonny Markeen. Yet Penny's last words as she turned over on the hard caravan mattress had been, 'Tomorrow, I'm going round the estate agents. Even in July, there must be a flat or a cottage. To buy, if necessary.' Had he given her the wrong impression about his income from writing?

Simon put his thumb in his mouth, as the nearest

comfort to a cigarette. Gazing into the darkness, he allowed his mind for the first time to focus on the inescapable fact that he did not want to set up home with Penny Tranmere anyway. Never had wanted to, never would, never *could* want to live with her. Let alone with her children. She would fight to get them back. Obviously. Women always did. The words 'Oh God!' formed on his lips, and to his surprise sounded aloud. Too loud, echoing in the fibreglass box. Guiltily, he glanced at Penny, but she slept on, her little pointed weasel face sideways on the horrid foam pillow, her mouth slightly agape.

'Oh God,' he said more quietly. 'Get me out of this.'

Sheila and Vincent hauled Douai to bed and laid him carefully on his side, with a basin close at hand for the inevitable nausea. Vincent dragged the cushions off his brother's sofa, as they did for visitors, and brought in his own duvet.

'I'll sleep here,' he said briefly to his mother. 'Make sure he doesn't choke when he chucks up.'

'Are you sure you know what to do?' asked his mother, overcome for a moment by a sense of helpless exclusion from this boys' world. She had bent over Douai, her heart expecting the sweet-skinned smell of his babyhood, and her nostrils had been assailed instead by a stale, foul pub breath. This affronted and upset her at a joltingly deep level. Some line from a jazz song went irrelevantly through her head: *my baby smells of booze.* 'Will he be all right?'

'I know all about it. I got my St John's three-star, didn' I?' said Vincent impatiently. 'I'm going to be a doctor, aren't I? I might as well practise. He's only pissed. There's no drugs involved. So be cool, OK?'

'Well,' said Sheila, groping for the remnants of her

maternal authority, 'call me straightaway if there's a problem. Have you got some water for him?'

'Yes. Don't flap. I'm across it. I've looked after blokes at school. I told you, he's only pissed.'

Douai rolled suddenly, flopping half off the bed, and growled, 'Bitch!'

Vincent rolled him expertly back, then turned to his mother. 'You know why he's doing this?'

'Yes. Anansi.'

'He really, really doesn't want her here. He went on and on about it at the Cottens'. It was their whisky he drank, while Mrs Cotten went up the road for something. That's what did it. He wouldn't be out of it like this if he was just on lager.'

Sheila looked at her tall, impatient elder son, hesitated and asked with unaccustomed diffidence:

'What do you think? About Anansi staying?'

'I think he's being a dickhead. But he really means it. When I told him, he went ape. Said he'd told you it was her or him, and you'd obviously made your mind up pretty quick.'

Sheila pressed her lips together, to avoid crying. *Only beloved Son.* There was not a shred of self-satisfaction in her now, no credit availing from her strange surrender in the church. This was a mess, and she had made it. Her baby, her youngest, sweetest, gurgling child, lay degraded before her, reeking of whisky and beer and feral boy sweat. Even in his sleep he growled 'Bitch!'

And she had done this. She, with her do-goodery and her imperialist desire to be the whole world's little mother. She had been an unsatisfactory enough wife to chase his father into the arms of another woman, and now she had made his home a battlefield. She reached down and touched Douai's cheek, trying not to breathe in too deeply.

'Baby,' she said. 'My poor baby.'

'Uohhh,' growled Douai, and from his mouth came a thin, disgusting stream of vomit. His mother, despite herself, jumped back.

'Good,' said Vincent briskly. '*Excellente!* I'll mop that up and he probably won't do it again. Mum, go. I'm *trained*. In six years or so I'll be a *doctor*.'

Sheila retired and lay for a long time sleepless, dreading the breakfast table.

In the morning, though, it was Anansi who solved the immediate social problem in the house. She got up early and alone, helped herself to cereal, rinsed the bowl and slipped out of the front door. The sun was rising and the low mist lying over the sea; she stood for a moment entranced by the drifting pink mystery of it. The sea was flat, the only movement tiny ripples at the bottom of the steep pebbled beach. The ripples, too, were pink, shading to gold. It would be a hot day.

Emboldened by solitude, she clambered over the concrete wall and began to crunch down the pebbles towards the water. There was a narrow strip of damp sand at the edge of the ripples, and she kicked off her sandals and experimentally let the water come over her feet.

It was cold, and smooth and – 'sweet', she thought surprisedly. Sweet, like ice cream. How could you know sweet, through your *feet*? Especially when it had to be salt, really. But you could. She looked down, grimacing at the distortion of the twisted right ankle beneath her, and watched the water bubbling and sliding over her feet, then retreating and returning again, merry and sweet. The pink edges just showed where her toes and insteps curled under, pale and bright against the darkness of her skin. No wonder the little kids paddled all day with their buckets and spades. She had watched them from the prom all last week but never come down here herself. Never paddled, not ever, not anywhere. Well, not in sea. In the recreation ground pool once, but it was dirty, with condoms in. And they laughed at her foot, and Nanna shouted to her to come back to the bench.

For a moment, with a detachment beyond her years, Anansi thought about the small children who paddled at Blythney, and wondered how it would be to have such heady experiences when you were really, really small. Kyra should paddle. At the thought of her half-sister, the desolate place opened inside her. Abruptly she stepped back from the water and shucked on her sandals. When she had climbed back up the pebbles to the wall, she saw that Simon was standing behind it, watching her.

'Hello,' he said, in a more ingratiating tone than she had ever heard. 'You're up early.'

'Yuh,' said Anansi. She waited, her eyes shifting away from him.

'Is Sheila up yet?' continued Sheila's husband, humbly.

'I s'pose. She was walkin' round when I left. Upstairs, like.'

'Good. I'll, er . . .' He turned towards the house door, and Anansi watched him go in. It was not locked; it was hardly ever locked, so he did not need to use his key.

Chapter Fifteen

Sheila was in the kitchen. Her thoughts were so pre-occupied with Douai and what to say to him when he woke that when Simon came in she temporarily forgot what lay between them.

'Oh, hello,' she said absently, cutting bread. 'Have you had your breakfast?'

Simon started. This was not what he had expected. 'Er, no,' he said. 'But I didn't – I mean, I'll probably go along to the Bosun's Bite . . .'

Sheila focused on him properly, with a touch of bewilderment. 'Oh hell,' she said. 'Gosh, I actually forgot – oh well, never mind. What do you want, anyway?'

This was nearer to the script that Simon had written in his head. It was a script that he would have scorned to use in one of his novels, and would have excoriated in a television play as unrealistic, gutless Aga-Saga nonsense. Nonetheless, it was the only script he could imagine for this hard situation, so he went ahead and delivered it.

'I think,' he began, 'that we ought to talk.'

'Oh?' said Sheila. 'And about what?'

'About what happened.' He ploughed on, desperately, 'It was all such a shock to all of us, the other day – I don't think we were thinking properly, and with Alan's reaction on top of it all . . . well, we haven't exactly coped with it in a civilized way, have we?' He hated himself for saying 'civilized'. He had written reams of scorn about the very concept, setting it against the brave, cruel rawness of life as he liked to think of it: street life, hard life, unsentimental modern life.

But Sheila did not notice him wince, or reflect on how far he had travelled from his usual poised scornfulness. Her swirling worry about Douai concentrated itself suddenly into a single point of irritation against her husband. She had not raised her voice to him in ten years, but she raised it now.

'Coped with *it*?' she said. '*It* was a shock to all of us, was *it*? Are you trying to turn your voluntary, calculated infidelity into some sort of neutral It which happened to all of us, like a – a – *freak tide* or something?' She took a deep, shaking breath, shocked by the fire she was spitting at him, and equally shocked by his passivity. He was just standing there. Hanging his head, almost. Usually he would flare up and snap at her for infinitely smaller defiances than this. His silence all but disarmed her, and she continued after a moment a little more quietly.

'*It* didn't happen. *You two* bloody happened, you and Penny. You chose to happen. Any coping that has to be done is being done, as per usual, by me. And your sons.'

'It wasn't supposed to be like this,' said Simon. 'I didn't put an end to our marriage.'

At this point he had imagined Sheila turning aside, her bulky profile abashed in tearful gratitude, glancing shyly sideways at him with dawning hope of his return to the marital hearth. Not that he had decided to return, but it would have helped the decision if she had shown signs of yearning humbly for such a reprieve. Yet he looked at her now and she was neither bashful nor visibly moved at all. She was standing four square, looking at him.

'Are you saying you want to come back?' She regarded him with narrow, appraising eyes. 'Split up with her already, have you?'

Simon was silent. Sheila felt strange, as if somewhere within her another woman, accustomed to years of anxious, bright, marital conciliation, was looking on in amazed revulsion at this new spitfire energy.

'Has she found out you don't have any money, then?'

This was too much. Simon raised his head and looked straight back at her. 'You've never reproached me with that before,' he said levelly. 'I suppose I asked for it, though.'

Sheila subsided, her rage spent. 'No,' she said, and in a sudden healing moment the old anxious Sheila and the new defiant one were reconciled, both accepting an identical code of fairness. 'I shouldn't have said that. If I was going to nag you about money I should have done it long ago. Anyway, if you and Penny are in love you'll have to make a new life for yourselves. Do some kind of job. But I promise I won't start dunning you for child support or anything.'

'No,' said Simon. 'I didn't mean all that. Sheel, there is something – about Penny – I have to say. I think you might have got the wrong idea.'

A thud and a slam, far overhead, made both husband and wife start and glance upward, realizing that their time for private conversation was running out.

Hurriedly, Simon went on, 'She and I are not *necessarily*, er, a long-term item. We haven't discussed it.'

Sheila folded her arms and stared at him. 'So?'

'So,' he shrugged, a boyish mannerism which Sheila had long ago found endearing, 'so . . . look, I shouldn't have gone to the caravan. Left you on your own.'

'I like it on my own,' said Sheila. 'No, honestly. I do. The only thing is the London child. Anansi. There's something I need to say to you quickly, now, before Dow gets down.'

'Who? The charity kid? What about her?' He was not pleased at this change of subject.

'Her mum's in prison. I'm now her official fosterer until September. At least, we are. You're on the paperwork. They think you're living here. Stable nuclear family, all that. I would be grateful if you would please not rock the boat. There's an inspection sort of thing in a month. I'd like you here.'

Simon was shaken by how much more animated and engaged Sheila was about this child's residence than about his own. He swallowed. A beautiful idea occurred to him.

'Had I better come back now?' he asked disingenuously. 'For the child's sake, and all that?'

'God, no,' said Sheila, startled. 'No, no, no. You carry on as you are. I only need you back for one afternoon, when the social worker comes. But keep us posted where you're staying, when you leave the caravan, and the boys can come visiting.'

A dishevelled figure appeared in the doorway. It was Vincent.

'Mum,' he said. 'Dow wants some water and a bit of bread to chew. I told him that was better than coffee, because of the dehydration. He's been sick again, but I reckon it's the last time.'

'OK,' said Sheila briskly, running the tap. 'It's OK, Simon, you'd better push off now, and not complicate things. He's only hung over. I'm dealing with it. Come to supper, if you want. But not Penny, I think.'

She left the kitchen, glass and crust in either hand. Simon stood for a moment irresolute, then went to the untidy letter rack on the dresser and pulled out a thick brown envelope with his name on it. Alleluia. A new chequebook, at least. He trudged back to the caravan, and to the still sleeping Penny.

Anansi, loitering on the promenade, saw him leave and slipped indoors. From above her head were sounds of movement, and Douai's squeaky growl. Vincent appeared round the door.

'Oh, hi,' he said. 'Look, are you going out?'

'Yeah,' said Anansi. 'I just came in to say. To Shei— to your mum. I'll take a walk, OK?'

'Look,' said Vincent, fishing in his trouser pocket. 'Do us a favour? Eat your lunch – I mean, dinner, you probably say – from the chip shop or somewhere. Here's three – no, four quid. Just so Mum can sort out Douai.'

'OK,' said Anansi, taking the money in the practical spirit in which it was given. 'Thanks.' She smiled at him. Vincent had never seen her smile properly, and the sight of it – a dark, white-toothed, beautiful, lightening smile – thawed his cool hostility. She was even asking: 'Is Douai OK now?'

'Did you hear him, last night?' asked Vincent. His neck was reddening, Anansi noticed with detached interest.

'Yeah.'

'He doesn't mean it. He got a bit overdone.'

'Pissed, yeah?'

'Very. He shouldn't have said what he said, out in the road there.'

'They say I gotter stay,' said Anansi. 'Here. For a bit.'

'Yeah,' said Vincent. 'Well. He'll have to get used to the idea, won't he?'

'Will he?'

'Have to,' said Vincent unemotionally. 'We're kids, aren't we? We don't have much choice. Any of us. They just fix things up and we have to lump it.'

Anansi nodded, pocketed her money and slipped from the kitchen like a dark wraith.

The old man was on the quay, in the bright sunshine, and was not alone. Walking cautiously towards the group, Anansi saw the short, vivid figure of Jonny Markeen, his long hair dark against a red polo shirt, with Marta at his side in pink shorts and a white vest which showed her tummy. She had two lifejackets, one blue and white and the other an old-fashioned orange kind filled with kapok. When she saw Anansi she leapt up and down, flapping the lifejackets like unruly wings.

'A-nan-see! We're going sailing! We were going to *fetch* you, but now you're here we can go straightaway!'

Anansi stopped. Jonny Markeen smiled at her, his scar crinkling oddly up his cheek.

'Not me,' he said. 'Harry as skipper, you two mutinous dogs as crew.'

'Not crew,' said Harry severely. 'Not yet. Cadets. Trainees.'

Both men seemed to be in excellent spirits, and comfortable with one another in a way that Anansi had not expected. The children of the town seemed to flow everywhere, belonging equally in the streets and alleyways and chip shops and Yacht Club and kitchens, but the most vivid of the adults still seemed to fall into separate categories, like species caged apart in a zoo. In her mind Harry belonged to the solitude of his slimy and ruinous quay, and Mr Markeen to the rarefied silence of the gallery, among pictures and spotlights.

It had been enough of a shock to find Harry in Sheila's kitchen. Now, seeing Jonny in grubby sailing shoes on the quay, she had to rearrange these people: just as Sheila had become a daughter and a niece, Harry an uncle, now Jonny became a friend of the older man's and of the river's. They had been laughing together, like two boys, before Marta's shouting and flapping began. They were all joined together, these people. Like kids in a school. A week before, she would have added to herself 'joined together against me!' but not now. Her rapport with Harry could now, she dimly but happily apprehended, make her easy with Mr Markeen. Abruptly, she smiled at him, a broad beautiful smile directed entirely at the little art dealer. He responded with a monkey grin of delight. All for her. Anansi wondered, for a dizzying moment, whether it was possible that these people actually liked her.

All the time Marta was waving the lifejackets and shouting, 'All aboard! Swallows and Amazons for ever!' and similar gibberish.

Her father put a restraining hand on the bouncing child's shoulder and said, 'Pipe *down*. Now, Harry, are you sure you can cope with both of them?'

'Nancy's got enough sense for both, I would say.'

'Why do you call her *Nancy*!' shouted Marta. 'She's called Anansi, and it's African, because her father was a chieftain in the wide wild jungle.'

There was neither mockery nor disbelief in her tone. Marta liked stories, and Anansi had spun a good one, and the fact that Douai didn't believe it was neither here nor there. Douai was a spiteful spitecat, as she would have said, and Bum to him.

'I'm sorry,' said Harry. 'It's just that I like the name Nancy, and it sort of fitted. But you're right, Marta; shouldn't give nicknames till you're invited to. Bad manners.'

'I like it,' said Anansi. This time she smiled at Harry. The sun flickered on the rising tide, and threw darts of blinding happiness up into all their faces.

Jonny clapped his hand on his daughter's back and said, 'OK. I'm off. Don't drown.'

'If not duffers, won't drown!' said Marta, beginning to bounce and flap again.

'One more quotation from Arthur Ransome,' said Harry, glowering at her, 'and this lesson is off. I am not Captain bloody Flint.'

Anansi did not understand the reference but laughed as much as Marta. Silly word. Flint! Like Clint, crossed with floppy. 'Flint!' she said. 'Flaptain Flint!' Marta crowed and whirled around like a top, hitting them both with the lifejackets in her outstretched hands.

It was a day that Anansi never forgot, all her life. They hauled the brown dinghy to the quay and boarded it, the two girls first while Harry watched. Anansi, after some fumbling with knots and experimental tugging of halyards, showed Marta how the sail went up. She had forgotten nothing of the previous day's lesson, and Harry again said, 'Well done.' Then he stepped aboard and pulled up the small sail at the front, and tightened up the halyards until, when Anansi reached out to touch them, they felt like iron bars standing away from the wooden mast. Harry fiddled with some more ropes then, leaning over the stern, fitted the rudder on its pintles. The boat tipped backwards while he did it, and Anansi's hand tightened on the gunwale in momentary fear; but the fear evaporated as fast as it had come, for Harry had said that it was the helm who was responsible for not tipping a boat over, and he was the helm now, and he was to be trusted.

But when the mooring had been dropped and the rough ropes pulled tight to catch the wind, the boat had not been moving through the water for a minute before he said, 'Right. Marta, sit for'ard more. Nancy, back here on the helm.'

'I don't know how.'

'Which is why you're learning. Back here. On the seat. Hold the tiller. Keep it where it is. Feel it.'

'It's – moving,' said Anansi. 'Like a *animal*.'

'I think it feels like a rabbit, shivering,' said Marta poetically. 'I steer Dad's boat sometimes.'

'What do I *do*?' squealed the older girl as a push on the tiller made the sail begin to flap above her head.

'Pull it towards you,' said Harry, and miraculously the sail filled again and the boat leapt forward, cutting a clean foaming wake under its square stern. 'Now, do it again. Make the sail flap, then stop it. Small movements. Experiment.'

'Whee!' said Marta, as Anansi caught a gust. 'Whee-yip!'

'Trim the jib, pest,' said Harry. 'And don't interfere. Nancy's got a nice light hand. Go on. Find the wind, then lose it, then find it again.'

After a while, Anansi frowned at the red flag which fluttered at the masthead.

'Does that show where the wind is blowing from?' she asked.

Ahead, too close, a moored yacht loomed suddenly. 'Oh shit!' Without thinking, Anansi pushed the tiller violently away from her, and the dark boom with its thousand cracks full of varnish whipped over her head, narrowly missing Harry as he ducked. Ahead of her the jib flapped violently, and she was about to cry out when she saw that Marta, unfazed, was undoing one of its sheets and making the other one fast.

'You tacked!' she said. 'I've only tacked when I've been crewing. I've never tacked at the *helm*. She tacked, didn't she?'

'She did,' said Harry admiringly. 'Now, find the new wind. Up a bit – back . . . there you are.'

'We aren't going the same way,' said Anansi. 'What do I do?'

'Tack again, in a minute,' said Harry. 'Then point at the Viking burial trees.'

He had not touched the tiller since she first took it, but he was holding the mainsheet and now, as they reached the corner, he paid out more of it and the boat came upright. With a growing sense of power, in a light south-westerly breeze, Anansi carried on upstream until it was time to turn left and open up another new vista of the sliding Grend.

'Is the Grend called after the monster Grendel?' asked Marta.

'Possibly,' said Harry. 'More than possibly. Nancy, are you expected back for lunch?'

'No. Vincent – I mean I got money for chips,' said Anansi.

'Good,' said Harry. 'We shall have chips in Catley.'

'Right up past the *bridge*?' squeaked Marta (who, Anansi privately thought, acted more like five than ten sometimes).

'I've never ever been past the bridge! Not in a boat. That's further than Miserley beach.'

'Your daddy's mast doesn't come down as easily as mine,' said Harry.

'Except when he breaks it.'

'Horses for courses. He's a racing man.'

Anansi steered all the way upriver, with a soldier's wind to help her. Near the bridge they moored to the bank for a moment while Harry took the mast down; then kneeling upright, each in a puddle of muddy salt water, the two girls paddled the old boat under the dripping span of the road bridge, ducking and squealing as cold dirty droplets fell in their hair.

By the time they tied up at the village staithe below Catley, it was two o'clock and all were famished. Harry sat with his back to a wall on the green, waiting for the tide to slacken, while the girls ate their chips and then began to play.

They had found an old dog's rubber ball in the grass, and improvised a game, throwing and catching the damp, pitted thing as if it were a shuttle weaving strong gay threads between them. Harry looked on, thoughtful and pleased. Good things, he thought, could still happen in a sorrowful world. A river's flow away from the social constraints of Blythney, the fey bookish Marta and the wary, sullen Anansi were binding themselves together, unselfconscious in the moment. He watched them quietly, playing in their temporary Eden, smelt the honeysuckle on the warm wall, and rejoiced in this latest movement of the dance.

Douai had never felt so ill. Not with his childhood jaundice or chickenpox, not in the school infirmary in

177

the great flu epidemic. His head throbbed, his mouth seemed to be crawling with filthy insects, and his throat burned with bile. He would be sick again, surely. He gave an experimental moan; the last such moan, a couple of hours ago, had brought Vincent with a glass of cold water. He pressed his eyes shut and willed it to happen again.

After a moment he opened them. His mother was standing over the bed, blocking out the cruel brightness from the window. She did not have a glass of water with her.

'How are you feeling?' she asked.

'Rough.' The word was torn from him; he did not really want to enter into a conversation on the subject, not at all, certainly not with her. 'Water.'

'I'll bring some in a minute. Now you know the effect of alcohol poisoning, perhaps you won't do it again.'

'Doohhhh!'

'Water coming up. And some bread.'

'I had bread. It made me honk.'

'That's the point. Otherwise you honk empty, and it hurts.'

'Hurts anyway. My head.'

'I'll bring some Nurofen.'

Douai lay back on the pillow, examining the unease he felt. His mother was not as sympathetic as she usually was when he was ill. He did not like the difference. Vincent had been more sympathetic than that. Suddenly he remembered what it had all been about. When Sheila returned with the bread and water and pills, he was sitting upright, flushed and aggressive again.

'Where is she?'

Sheila did not pretend not to know what he meant. 'On

the river, with Uncle Harry and Marta. Having a sailing lesson, Jonny says.'

'In what boat?'

'Harry's Whitecap, I suppose.'

After a moment he said, 'So she's staying here? After what she did?'

'She mainly did it to me and Daddy and the Tranmeres. And Daddy and I agree she ought to stay, and it's not a lot to do with the Tranmeres. So there we go.'

Douai considered. He had said 'She goes, or I do', but in his weakened state he quailed at the thought of walking out of the house with nowhere to go. Remembering how strong and invincible the drink had made him feel at the time, he was filled with wonder at how weak it had made him now. Perhaps that was the system: a sort of exchange, like being overdrawn on your school account. Using the next lot of strength before you were due for it, and having to pay back later. He groaned again, theatrically, to postpone comment on this new situation.

'She's out for lunchtime. You know what Blythney's like in summer. You've got enough friends to avoid her if you really want to, except for the odd family supper. She might make friends of her own. Girls.'

Douai said, grudgingly, 'So if I don't make a fuss now, what?'

Sheila knew that she should offer no bribe, nor capitulate to her son's sullen disapproval in any way. But maternal feelings have been softening the will and the reason of womankind ever since Eden.

'You can ring up *Yachts and Yachting* about those Laser Twos on sale,' she said. 'We'll see how Granny's investments are doing.'

'Cool,' said Douai. A deal had been struck.

Sheila went downstairs, relieved but obscurely dissatisfied. She preferred, on the whole, a more honourable kind of truce.

Chapter Sixteen

Penny was at Bethie Cotten's house again, envying her the solidity and space and blissfully uncaravanlike comfort of it. She was not happy. Bethie, who was struggling to untangle washing from the elderly machine in the holiday kitchen, was having to hear about this unhappiness, chapter and verse.

'He is a Victorian. No other word for it. Victorian!' said Penny viciously. 'Do you know what he said to me when I went to the house today? Do you know?'

'No,' said Bethie, who by now did not much care. 'What?' Her natural gossip's curiosity about the state of the Tranmere marriage had been so flattened and sated by a morning of ranting from her friend that she could hardly bear to utter even this much encouragement. But 'What happened, Pen?' she added, pricked by guilt at the harshness of her first response. She coughed to excuse it, and vented her frustration by tugging fruitlessly at a pair of jeans tangled round a damp grey sweatshirt of Hugo's.

'Alan said,' Penny continued, all but oblivious of Bethie's reluctance, 'that he wouldn't take off the stop he's put on my credit cards, and won't pay me a penny. Not as long as he has the children, because it's only the children who have rights now, and, get this, "The man who is enjoying my favours should pay for the privilege!" Did you ever hear anything like it? *Enjoying my favours!*'

Bethie was glad that her face was turned to the open mouth of the washing machine, because all of a sudden she was no longer bored but giggling. 'How awful,' she said. 'That is a pretty archaic turn of phrase, isn'it it?'

'Told you. Victorian!' said Penny. 'And what am I supposed to live on?'

'Simon—' began her friend, but Penny cut her off angrily.

'Simon is hardly any better. I wouldn't ask him for money. Even if he had any. You know Sheila's always held the purse strings.' She paused, and glanced rather slyly at Bethie. 'Well, no, I didn't really know to what extent they actually *did* live on Sheila's money. Not until he said so. It seems she's never wanted him to contribute. Likes it all her own way.'

Bethie made a noncommittal noise. None of the Blythney wives were truly close to Sheila Harrison, whose façade of bustling good will had always served as a curious deterrent to intimacy; but she, as a good listener and essentially kindly soul, was closer than Penny had ever been. It was no news to her that Sheila's late grandmother's money subsidized Simon's faltering literary career. Sheila had let drop the occasional worry on this score, when the investments seemed to be doing worse than usual. As an unwilling reader of any book more contemporary than Georgette Heyer, Bethie had her own astringent views on Simon's novels, and held even more corrosive opinions about men who would not or could not support their families. She felt disinclined to go into any of these views with Penny Tranmere.

'Anyway, he's broke,' continued Penny. 'Flatter than flat. And so am I, because the bit I've been earning from Jonny Markeen for the print research all went straight into the overdraft after Easter shopping. And anyway, Simon and I . . .'

This time, quite uncharacteristically, Penny stopped of her own accord, and stared out of the window with eyes which, Bethie saw with dismay, were beginning to brim with tears more real and more affecting than any of her previous outrage. Bethie pulled herself upright, noting ruefully that her knees did not seem to unbend as readily as they had five years earlier, and went across to the slight blonde figure who stood, in a tragic attitude, by the bow window.

'Isn't it going well, you two?' she asked, as neutrally as possible. Her hand crept, tentatively, to Penny's thin shoulder.

'I think it's more or less over, actually,' said Penny in a low, expressionless voice.

'But it's only just beg—' Bethie could have kicked herself for the tactless phrasing of this. 'I mean, what went wrong?'

'These last few days he's been different. I think he has a problem . . .' Penny hesitated. 'I think he has a problem with commitment.' Then her tone lightened as she grasped at a comforting cliché. 'It's not about me, it's about him.'

For some reason, the tone and the phrase brought Bethie's irritation crashing back like a returning wave on a harsh shingle shore. Everything married, everything maternal, everything that liked a quiet and cheerful life grated and rattled within her. Before she could stop herself she said, 'Commitment-phobic? That's odd, considering he's been married for nearly twenty years. Commitment there, all right. Are you sure it isn't just that he's opting to go back to Sheila and the children?'

Penny glared at her. 'I've got children too,' she said, answering the meaning rather than the words. 'Do you think I'm not suffering?'

'Well,' said Bethie, still ruffled and grated-upon, 'you did leave—'

'I did *not*!' shrieked Penny. 'I was chased out of the bloody house by an impotent bloody Victorian! And do me justice, Beth, he isn't pining for Sheila, either. I mean, just look at her! Would he?'

Moments later, she was gone, taking her towel and wash bag. Bethie knelt down again in front of the washing machine, trembling with an unexpected anger, and continued untangling the hard-knotted, sordidly entangled symbols of her own family life.

The tide began to ebb at Catley Bridge, and Harry made the girls pull up the sail and get the dinghy ready for the water again. The wind had turned lighter and become fair for the downriver journey; they glided along gently, with laughter and companionable silences, until the low square shape of Coker's Quay appeared round a wide bend. Anansi was startled; she had not expected it yet. Marta, erratically steering and humming, began a new flow of chatter.

'See, we're home. From a great voyage of exploration, like Magellan. Do you know about Magellan? He was even before Columbus. Columbus found America, but he didn't know it was, and it isn't even named after him but after another man called Amerigo. Imagine having a whole continent named after you. Anansia would be a good name for a continent, wouldn't it? Or Harrope, like Europe, for Uncle Harry—'

'Are you *her* uncle as well?' asked Anansi fiercely.

Harry, seated opposite Marta in the stern, said, 'Certainly not. No relation of mine talks that much, or steers with her feet.'

'Mummy says it's polite to call grown-up men Uncle, unless you're going to call them Mister something,' said Marta, putting her foot back on the floor of the dinghy and straightening the tiller.

'That is weird,' said Anansi crushingly. 'Saying everyone's your uncle. Innit weird, Harry?'

She had never called him by his name before, and something twisted in her stomach in fear that he would reject it. But Harry only said, 'Yes, do you know, I think it is a bit weird. Ask your mother why, some time, Marta.'

'She will say it is a traditional English thing to do,' said Marta in a sing-song voice, her little black brows snapping together in a mock frown. 'It comes of not being English really at all. Daddy isn't either. Mummy says he's like Mr Salteena, not quite a gentleman.'

Harry laughed. 'Jonny's good enough. But he isn't English by birth, that's true.' He was watching Anansi, aware of the oddity of this conversation to her unaccustomed ears.

Marta rattled on. 'I am English, though. Through and through.'

'Yes,' said Harry. 'If you insist. One sort of English, anyway. The national characteristics of reticence and modesty need a bit of working on.'

Anansi, to his delight, understood this and giggled.

'Anansi is another sort, yah?' said Marta. 'A town sort? A brown town sort?'

'Yes,' said Harry. 'But you both have exotic hybrid vigour. You both bring new blood to old shores.'

'Sometimes, in my school, right, the white kids shout at me to go home where I came from,' volunteered Anansi.

'Stupid,' said Harry. 'Pay no attention.'

'I don't give a fuck about what they say,' she said shortly.

'Good,' said Harry, recognizing the test she had set his friendship with the word, and passing it with insouciance.

'I have exotic *tastes*,' said Marta. 'I like truffles and caviar. I've had them both.'

Her steering was becoming erratic again, and Harry took the tiller from her as they came level with the quay and prepared to turn into the wind and glide up to the buoy. He watched the tide run past the mooring, judging his approach.

Anansi's eye travelled up the quay and suddenly she said, 'Your dog's come!'

The brown lurcher was looking down from the quay, its whole body shaken with an intensity of wagging. Harry looked more alarmed than pleased.

'Damn!' he said, lunging for the buoy. 'Marion must have let him out. Blast and damn. Hold the rope, Nancy, tie it on the bow ring, lots of knots—'

Before the girls could know the reason for his alarm, the dog demonstrated. From the quay's edge it took a flying leap towards the boat and its master, and inevitably fell short and landed on the uncovering mud by the steps. For a moment the animal seemed to stand still, knee-deep in the ooze, and then began, rather horribly, to change shape. Anansi thought for one wild moment that the dog was shrinking, but then she saw that in fact it was sinking. Its legs shortened in proportion to its body as the deep, sticky, slimy mud rose round it. When its lean belly was resting on the mud and the sinking had temporarily arrested, it shook off its paralyzed surprise and began to struggle. Anansi could see the muscles in its chest working as if the forelegs were running, but there were neither fore nor hind legs to be seen. As the animal writhed and struggled, it seemed to sink deeper. It stretched its neck to keep the mud from nose and mouth, its back humping and glistening with vain effort.

With cries of alarm, she and Marta flung themselves to the side of the dinghy nearest to the exposed mud, but then as it lurched, they were caught by a fear that the same might happen to them. Helpless, they stared at the struggling dog. It gave a couple of alarmed barks, and then began whimpering.

'Oh, help him!' shouted Marta, and Anansi, voiceless, stared pale-faced at the sudden drama before her.

'Stay in the boat!' said Harry curtly. 'Trim it. Keep it level!' He was on the foredeck of the grounded boat, steadying himself with the taut painter he had been going to thread through the ring to the quay.

Anansi held the slack of it behind him and said, 'I got it.'

From the foredeck Harry lunged for the rope which hung from the quay, made a long step to the bottom of the quay staircase, ran up it and reappeared with the flat lid of his fish-box cart. He threw it down on the mud, then pushed it towards the trapped dog. The board slid gently over the glistening brown slime until its edge nudged the animal's chest. Harry had a rope knotted through its nearer edge, and as the dog gripped the flat board

187

between its teeth, he gently pulled it towards him. As the animal moved, the suction seemed to break; there was a horrid, quiet, sucking noise, then a 'woof' as with a wild muddy scrabble the lurcher brought its forequarters onto the board. Harry gently sledged it towards him. Finally the dog was entirely on the board, sitting up. Anansi saw with fascination that the board, with the dog's weight spread across its flatness, did not sink at all but glided over the ooze. The dog, unrecognizably matted and filthied, made a wild leap for safety as soon as it got close to the solid steps, and its master was left to haul the mud-coated board towards him and retrieve it.

The girls watched this from the dinghy. When it was over and Harry was busying himself with the mooring lines, Marta said in a small voice, 'Would Dobby have gone right under?'

'Might have,' said Harry, who spared nobody the truth. 'Depends how deep it is at a particular spot. But it's dangerous stuff, is mud, and you'd do well to remember it. A terrier was lost downriver at Heron Island last year. They struggle, that's the problem, and it makes them sink faster.'

'Could it swallow a person?' asked Anansi. 'Could you drown? In mud?'

'Not here. It only goes down three feet or so till you get to shingle. Dobson might have got himself out, in the end. But there are places downriver, at low water, where it could get a short person under. Not often been known, though. Biggest danger would be the cold while you were stuck. You'd need someone tall, or a board, to come along pretty quick!'

More subdued than they had been all day, the two girls tidied the boat and got themselves ashore. As the trio trudged across the marsh towards the top of the town, Harry felt a momentary qualm; he did not want to have scared them off the river with this affair of the dog in the mud. Tentatively he asked, 'Want another sailing lesson tomorrow, then? There's a good forecast.'

The spell of fear broken, both turned glad faces towards him, one pale and black-browed, one dark and intense.

'Yeah!' said Anansi. 'I mean, all right, OK?'

'Oh yep!' said Marta. 'You mean we can go every day? Not once a week like ballet?'

'I am not a ballet teacher,' said Harry. And, to prove it, he executed a few clumsy chassées on the rough marsh, and made his followers crow with renewed delight. Marta, graceful as a swallow, began her own small dance and Anansi, for once, walked on serenely with her lame foot and did not think to resent the younger child's agility. She was, after all, as Harry had said, a better helm.

She would get a lot better still. Better than Douai. A small, involuntary attempt at a skip came into her halting gait. A new age of mastery lay ahead of her, shining like the river itself.

Chapter Seventeen

The sun shone on day after day; the tides moved onward, their flux of high water through rushes and mudbanks growing later each afternoon. The sailing lessons continued to take the same route, upriver to Catley Bridge and the green, until by the end of the week the tide's later turning meant that Marta and Anansi were getting home only just in time for their suppers. After the first evening, they took to eating these companionably together at the Markeens' house before Alaia drove Anansi down to Seafret for the night.

'It makes all kinds of sense,' she said to Sheila on the second day of this arrangement, 'if it keeps her away from Douai while he settles down. She and Marta get on tremendously, even with nearly two years between them.'

'Are you *sure*?' asked Sheila doubtfully. 'Anansi's language, the life she's led, her table manners even . . . I mean, we're used to it, after years of Country Hosts children. But you've always been so careful with Marta.' She heard herself say this, and bit her lip with unaccustomed vexation. Had that sounded tactless? Was she seeming to accuse the other woman of being a snob? But Alaia smiled, and for the first time Sheila noticed that her smile was almost as dry and crooked as her husband's.

'Bulls-eye. Yes, I did *flinch*,' she said. 'Once or twice. I admit it. But Jonny says I wrap Marta in cotton wool. At her age he was already doing a paper round and getting in fights.'

'There's nothing wrong with being careful,' said Sheila, anxious to soften what she had said. Only a week before, she would not have felt any such compunction, and indeed had sometimes said sharp things, in the neighbourhood, about the Markeens' serene isolation from Blythney life and the difficulty of entangling them in her clubs and tennis leagues and children's drama groups and social work. But the landscape was different now, and stoutly Sheila said, 'Nothing wrong at all. Especially with a little girl.'

Alaia smiled again. 'Jonny thinks otherwise,' she said lightly. 'And actually, when you come down to it, there's no problem. Anansi did try us out with a couple of fucks and cunts, and some stuff about all policemen being pigs and only snobs drinking wine. But we didn't rise to it, and now the poor child has gone astonishingly demure. I gather she had a granny who took a firm line on effing and blinding and knives and forks.'

Sheila sighed. 'I know very little about what goes on in her head, really,' she confessed. 'I feel bad about it, but things here have been difficult this last week or so.'

Alaia looked at her, noticing the changes in the bigger woman's bearing and manner and thinking that this new, hesitant Sheila was rather more to her taste than the exuberantly bossy earth-mother of yore. The two women were standing in the hallway, talking in low voices. Anansi had gone immediately to her own room overhead, and could be heard moving around there.

'Difficult,' Sheila said again, almost pleadingly. 'With Simon, and the boys ... Douai especially, it's a difficult age.'

'God, yes,' said Alaia, thinking of the pallid sullenness of Douai Harrison and suppressing a shudder. 'But really, don't worry about the suppers. I couldn't be more pleased to put a bit of variety in Marta's social life. I eavesdrop on the pair of them a bit, but all they seem to talk about is sailing and war.'

'War?'

'Harry Glanville, I suppose. Anansi was asking Jonny all sorts of things about coastal assault forces, about which he knows naff all. I suppose she thought it was the sort of thing men always know. He did pull out some Ardizzone prints to show her. Anyway, both of the girls have great battle fantasies. They had the fort out yesterday.'

'Marta has a fort?' Sheila was momentarily diverted. 'But she's so feminine! I had her down as a porcelain-doll girl!'

'Jonny bought it when I was pregnant. That loopy astrologer woman from Bungay who does the zodiac paintings told him, in an atmosphere suggesting ululation and ectoplasm, that his unborn child would sure-lee, sure-lee be a boy.'

'How extraordinary,' said Sheila. 'Simon had an agent once who read people's auras, and she told him he would father only girls because his life stream was strong and true and boys are a corrupt and lesser version of the Female Principle.' She hesitated, because the image of Douai's contorted, dissipated face the other night came into her mind. Then, shyly, she said, 'It's not so late – would you like a coffee?'

And so in the Seafret kitchen, with the boys wandering complainingly in and out looking for lost garments for their evening out, and the tribe of Cotten children watching cartoons in the next room, the plump, homely, slightly ludicrous Sheila Harrison and the elegant, cool Alaia Markeen – neighbours for years but friends never – sat together and laughed about the vagaries of their husbands' clairvoyant acquaintances. They further shared the rumour that Susannah Rattray had been to see a medium in Diss while she was trying to get pregnant, expressed each in their own way a powerful appreciation of Harry Glanville, and generally wove a loose skein of comfortable gossip.

At last Alaia glanced at her watch and said, 'Must go. You know, Anansi could stay over with us, one night.'

Sheila grimaced. 'I'm not sure what the rules are. Fostering. All that. It might not be allowed.'

'Well, Harry definitely wants them to camp on Heron Island and take the early tide up the creek. Says I have to go as chaperone, and sleep in a damn *tent*. Needless to say the children are both wild for it.'

'Oh dear,' said Sheila. 'I suppose the fostering rules will say that I have to be there, wherever she sleeps overnight. I'd better let you off that, and sleep in the tent myself, hadn't I?'

Alaia smiled, liking the fact that it had never occurred to Sheila simply to rule that Anansi could not go camping.

'No,' she said. 'That would be very unfair. We'll both go, and take Li-los and a proper big duvet and a bottle of port and a box of Belgian chocs. Jonny can sail us down in the big boat.'

'Done!' said Sheila. They struck their hands aloft on the bargain and Alaia departed, laughing.

That night, alone in her bedroom, Sheila closed her eyes and re-created, with infinite care and comfort, the crooked smile and raised eyebrow of her new friend at that moment of accord. As she fell asleep, she could feel the imprint where their hands had touched.

On Sunday, Harry was to go with Marion to a lunch party on the other side of the county and could not sail with the girls. The Markeens were expected to a buffet lunch in Blythney with London friends who had arrived for the summer, and despite all Marta's begging and Alaia's gentle encouragement, Anansi refused to join them.

'But I'll be *bored* at the Ward-Williamses without you,' moaned Marta after Saturday supper. 'They're all *babies*, and they make you go off and play stupid games with the au pair. Mum, if Anansi came we could *escape*.'

'Leave her alone, Mart,' said Jonny Markeen from the depths of the *Art Newspaper*. 'She doesn't have to come, and good luck to her. I wish I didn't. I wanted to do the practice race.'

'The Ward-Williamses bring us a lot of customers,' said Alaia severely. 'And they're very kind hosts.'

Jonny grunted and since Marta rarely defied her father, the heat was taken off Anansi. Covertly, from his newspaper, Jonny watched her as the children resumed their fort game. The face which had struck him as beautiful a fortnight ago was even more so now; more animated, less watchful, filled out with proper food. The child was, he saw with pleasure, wearing a sweater of Alaia's; just the right one too, old enough not to be an embarrassing gift but still beautiful. It was a red silk-and-cotton knit

195

with a finely rolled neck which blazed against the child's dark skin. Alaia, with her exuberant Slavonic instincts of generosity, had talked to him in bed about her plans to buy Marta's new friend an entire wardrobe of clothes to replace her cheap frayed nylons. Jonny had forcefully dissuaded her.

'That is a disastrous idea. Just lend-give her some old stuff of Marta's, casually, when her own clothes get muddy.'

'Marta's half her size!'

'Well, yours then, skinny. Just don't bring money into it. I'm warning you, Ali – don't play dolls and Little Princesses with her.'

So Anansi had acquired a couple of sweaters and T-shirts, also a green swimsuit and a fetching pair of pale pink cycle shorts which Alaia said had been left at the house by some visitor 'yonks ago' and put in the dressing-up hamper. Both had, in fact, been bought by her in Ipswich specifically for Anansi, and secretly washed and creased for verisimilitude.

'People leave their things everywhere in this benighted town in summer,' said the artful donor. 'Just look in the lost property box at the Yacht Club. There are enough towels there to start a hair salon, if you didn't mind a hair salon smelling of boys' feet.' And both girls laughed, and in the laughter the awkward moment of donation passed.

But even new-clad, Anansi would not go out to lunch with the Markeens and their unknown, alarming, double-barrelled friends.

On the Sunday morning, though, waking in her bed at Seafret, she felt a dreadful sinking in her heart: no river, no Harry, no Marta, no sailing. Harry had said that soon she would be good enough to go out without him, but the moment had not yet come. She lay in bed for another hour, staring at the ceiling, her mind blank. At last she got up, pulled on her clothes and splashed cold water on her face before creeping soundlessly downstairs.

Hearing Douai and Vincent's voices growling in the kitchen, and Dondie Cotten's from the far door, she did not attempt to find breakfast but stepped outside instead. It was barely gone nine o'clock, but in the blazing sunshine the stony beach was already sprouting bright parasols and windbreaks. Mothers were rubbing suncream on small children's shoulders, and fathers crunching down the pebbles as they carried out cool-boxes. From the Hamptons' house next door came ear-splitting shouts as Grania fought with her cousin Alison over some disputed garment. Sheila, Anansi knew, would not be back from church for a while yet.

She turned her back on it all and limped alone along the sunny seafront, making for the track towards Grenden Quay. The tide was half down, and running out fast; along each edge of the river was a popping, sucking, glistening ribbon of mud. From the sea wall she watched it, almost hypnotized by the changes in the river from minute to minute. Lively wavelets lapped around the quay, hitting a different place each time, leaving random patches of dampness which grew lower every minute as the weed above the new tide line became paler. Out on the water, a few boats were already moving across its sliding surface, sailing straight but making long diagonals as the fast tide took them downstream. A patient small child in a nutshell of a boat – an *Optimist*, thought Anansi, secretly proud of her new knowledge of boats – was trying to tack upriver, encouraged by a mother who stood on the end of the quay shouting, 'Weight *forward*, darling, and get her drawing as soon as you can on the new tack.' Anansi sat down by a lump of concrete sea defence, hidden from the path, and looked downriver. Shading her eyes, she cupped her fingers exaggeratedly to block out the ruined Martello tower as well as the glare of the sun.

After a while, seeing Douai and Vincent cycling below her on the track, she slipped down onto the beach side of the sea wall and walked back, unseen by them, to find a late breakfast.

Sheila was back from church, rolling pastry in the kitchen. She greeted her guest with a smile.

'Day off?' she said. 'I should think you need a rest from the river. Harry's working you two pretty hard, I gather.'

Anansi said nothing.

Sheila rattled on, 'I was thinking of a picnic, but I don't know. I might just sit here quietly, and look at the sea. You can have enough of picnicking.'

Anansi, remembering Sheila's gleeful picnic preparations before the disaster at Miserley beach, looked at her feet. A question, however, burned strongly in her and after a moment's silence she said, 'We went up past that beach, in Harry's boat. To Catley, the grass an' that.'

'Yes, it's lovely up there, but you need the high tide, don't you? Wouldn't do today. You'd be on the mud before you even passed the bridge.'

'If you go the other way,' persisted Anansi, 'if you sail past the – tower thing . . .' Embarrassment suffused her and she stopped, and glared at her ill-matched feet in their damp, scuffed plimsolls.

Sheila looked at her, grasped the reason for her embarrassment, and calmly answered, 'Oh yes, downstream. Past Martello. Yes, you can sail down with the tide as well. About four miles, and you get to Heron Island, and then the river splits in two. There's a long muddy creek which goes about three miles to a pub, and then the main River Blyne which goes on two miles before you reach the sea. It's a very difficult entrance, with the channel changing sides twice a year – even worse than the Alde or the Deben. That's why we hardly ever get yachts in the river. Or big horrible motorboats. It's the saving of our river, really, if you think about it.'

Anansi, reassured by Sheila's return to the old rattling mode of delivering too much information, extracted from this the nugget that she wanted. 'So you can sail down? Is that where Heron Island is? Where people sleep in tents?'

Sheila looked at the child with a more personal good will than she had felt since her arrival. She remembered, with a pang of sweet loss, how she herself had once looked forward to her first night under canvas on the coot-haunted Heron Island.

She had tried taking Country Hosts children there for the night a couple of times, but they had always hated it and complained at the discomfort. Too young, perhaps. Her sons were fond enough of their excursions to the island, and indeed had demanded the tents for later in the week when the low tides would serve; but they now regarded camping as a masculine rite and pointedly excluded her from any planning or – heaven forfend! – participation. The simple blaze in this child's eyes at the thought of an island camp warmed all Sheila's own memories back into happy life.

'Yes,' she said fondly. 'I'm sure Harry will start taking you downriver this week.'

Harry did. The upriver days were over for a while; as low water grew nearer to midday, he had the two girls sail the Whitecap downstream, leaving the winding shallow Grend for the straighter, deeper waters of the Blyne. Here they sailed round the island, admiring it and planning their camp site; once they saw fast keelboats racing in a midweek series, Dragons and Swallows bending round their marks and flinging up bright spinnakers on the turn. The shouts of the crew, the creaks of rigging and high, ringing, ratchety sound of the winches carried across the water to the spellbound children in the varnished brown dinghy. For half an hour they hung on to a mooring buoy, just to watch the shashing, thundering, flapping, flying progress of the race.

When it had passed, Harry made the two of them practise round the marker buoys themselves, turning sharply, ducking the boom, handling the jib until they were perfect. He himself left his watchful post opposite the helm and sat near the mast, perched in the centre facing aft. His role became more passive as the days went by and the children took responsibility; or at least Anansi did, for Marta was only too happy to take the older girl's orders. After three days of this practising they found one morning that new, clean ropes had appeared on the mast, passed through a block at its head; on the side deck was fixed a chipped pole with snap fastenings at its ends, and a mildewed sailbag was tucked under the bow.

'Whassat?' asked Anansi, conducting her usual morning baling and inspection of the boat.

'Spinnaker,' said Harry. 'Don't fiddle. It's packed ready to go up.'

So later, heading back upstream in a sharp southerly, with shouts of 'Wheel!' from Marta and 'Cool!' from Anansi and Harry steady on the helm, they pulled up the sail and watched it bulge and flower in a triumphant red-and-yellow curve ahead of the skimming boat. Looking astern, Anansi saw to her wonderment how fast the wake was being left. The Whitecap flew across the water. After a few minutes Harry motioned to her to take the helm and learn to hold the spinnaker steady and full of air.

'There was a bit too much wind for the old kite, really,' said Harry later to Marion. 'But I couldn't resist it. You should have seen the crews' faces.'

Marion was finishing the crinkled edge of a fish pie. 'Are they going to sail in the junior regatta?' she asked.

'Probably,' said Harry. 'Nancy's around for the whole of August now. She almost remembers the racing rules already.'

'When do you go up to London, about the other thing?'

Harry began to pace up and down the kitchen. 'I had a letter,' he said.

'Yes,' said Marion. 'I do know an MoD envelope when I see one, after all this time. *Two days ago* you had that letter.'

'I was going to tell you.'

'Yes, I know,' said Marion, unruffled. She gave the piecrust a final tweak and put it aside under a mesh cover. 'And since you haven't told me anything at all, I presumed there were complications you needed to think about before I gave an opinion you wouldn't like.'

'Yes,' said Harry. 'Spot on.' He continued to pace. 'Spike shouldn't have used Ministry stationery, or even written, come to that. I gave him the fax number, silly beggar. Risking his pension, passing on that sort of thing.'

'What sort of thing?'

'Well, about Private Cowper.'

'So he *is* still in the army! You found him! Are you sure it's the right one?'

'Well, *was* in the army. Catering Corps. And yes, it has to be the right one. Being black – there still aren't that many, you know. The cook thing. She said he was a cook. The wife's name, Tracey – they were married, you know, all regular. The child's year of birth, the separation when she was small, recorded in his personnel file. He was posted to Travemünde and she didn't go. It all fits. Even . . .' he hesitated. 'Madge, he sent a photocopy of the ID picture in the file, and even that fits. It's her face, only darker. Same brow. Same mouth. Been looking at her in the boat for days. It can't be the wrong man.'

'You said he *was* in the army,' said Marion. 'Discharged?' He was silent. She looked at his face. 'Oh no, not killed?'

'No,' said Harry. 'In prison. Just like the bloody mother. Theft of government property. Some food racket. Would you believe it?'

Chapter Eighteen

'How,' said Marion after a while, 'do we find out which prison?'

This time it was Harry's turn to be startled. 'Why?' he asked. 'Oh, I see. But I rather figured that was the end of it. Both parents inside, poor little devil. She's on her own.'

'Well,' said Marion consideringly, wiping her fingers on a tea cloth and throwing it down on the worktop with less than her usual care. 'A racketeer is better than nothing, surely? It's not as if it's violence. And it can't be that long a sentence. Not these days, with all these parole rules and the prisons full up. When did he go down?'

Marion Glanville had been an intermittent prison visitor, and before that a formidable confidante to the families of other ranks. Her fragile white-haired prettiness and taste for domesticity often made even her own husband temporarily forget this. Harry shook his head in silent tribute to her resilience, and pulled the letter out of his jacket pocket.

'Spike says nineteen ninety-four,' he said. 'Dishonourable discharge, civilian trial. Whatever the ramp was, he was obviously too efficient at it for them just to sling him out quietly.'

'Well,' said Marion, 'he must be pretty nearly out by now. Would Spike have known if he was free?'

'Yes, apparently. Some parole rule – they have to let the defrauded service know, in case the chap picks up his old contacts when he comes out.'

'Well then, still inside. Which prison?'

'Home Office matter. They probably wouldn't tell us.'

'They probably would tell Spike. If he made up some MoD reason for knowing.'

'It's too much to ask him,' said Harry.

'Rubbish!' said Marion. 'I will, if you won't. Anyway, I bet he's carried on sleuthing off his own bat. You know how *bored* they get, in the Ministry. A bit of human interest would set him up nicely.'

She was stringing and slicing beans now. Watching her capable hard fingers flying through the green stuff, economical and ruthless, Harry felt a wave of love: for Marion, for Anansi, for the man in prison, for bored Spike among his grey filing cabinets on Whitehall, for the whole cockeyed world.

'You think we should go on? Speak to him about the child?'

Marion stopped slicing, and turned to face him. 'Of course we should. I wouldn't say so if he was in for rape or armed robbery, but he must have brains, to run a racket inside the army – especially since he's black and therefore always an automatic suspect in those circles, dear, don't deny it.' She resumed chopping. 'Anyone that bright must have the brains to think of some way of making it up to his own daughter.'

'But I've been thinking about that too,' said Harry. 'In

the interest of finding him I almost forgot. She thinks he kicked her when she was little. Lamed her. Perhaps I should have let sleeping dogs lie.'

'Perhaps he was drunk,' said Marion tranquilly. 'Perhaps he's had nightmares about it ever since. Perhaps he's a nice man, even if he is a thief. Perhaps she remembers wrong. Whatever the truth is, we're too close now to ignore it. I think one of us should speak to him. Or Jonny Markeen. He's taken an interest in her. Or even Sheila could go. Perhaps we should have a meeting about it.'

Harry shook his head wonderingly. 'Look at us all. Poking our noses in. All because of this child.'

'You know what Hillary Clinton says,' observed Marion surprisingly. 'It takes a village to raise a child. Not many villages any more, certainly not where Anansi comes from, so I suppose we're it. And it's as plain as the nose on your face that the child needs to know who and what her father is. He might know about other relatives, from his side. The child might have grandparents. Even if they're dead, they'll have a history. She'd be happier with a proper history. The black side might be better than the white side. That would be useful for her to know, wouldn't it?'

'We could tell the social service chappie,' said Harry, doubtfully.

'Useless!' said Marion. 'Go on, ring Spike at home tonight. Tell him to find out which prison. I hope it isn't up north somewhere. If it is, it'll have to be Jonny who goes, in his big car.'

Anansi, oblivious of this plotting, was back at the big house with Marta. For the first time a shadow had fallen across their easy companionship; the spinnaker run had got them home an hour earlier than usual, so that Alaia was still out shopping and calling on Sheila. The pair of them were left under the loose supervision of Karen the cleaner, who was pottering in the big kitchen with more than half her attention on a television quiz show.

Until now their friendship had grown in the context of the river, the boat, the swimming pool, light-hearted family meals with tactful parents and fort games on the rose-coloured carpet. Now, however, the girls were in Marta's room, and the hostess was busily pulling books from the shelves.

'Let's have a story,' she said. '*The Little Match Girl*. It's about a poor girl who lives on the streets and sells matches, and she looks into the rich houses and sees it all warm.'

Anansi glared. Books were something that she did not like; they reproached her, speaking only of failure and the abrasions of school. Nor did the subject matter of *The Little Match Girl* appeal to her. She could see the personal subtext all too clearly.

'Or *A Little Princess*,' said Marta. 'It's about a rich little girl who looks after a poor kitchenmaid, only then she loses all her money and her father dies, but even when she's poor she gives her last bun to another poor girl who's as hungry as a wolf in the snow. I could read it to you.' Even Marta knew, dimly, that she was treading on thin ice. Habitual fantasy and simple perversity drove her on. 'And in the end, the little Princess gets rich again and keeps poor Becky as her maid.'

'Yeah,' said Anansi, with the edge of a sneer. 'As if.'

'She's got a rich sort of uncle who turns out to live next door.'

'Prob'ly a pervert,' said Anansi. 'Fancies her.' She, too, knew herself to be on thin ice; around Marta, by instinct and delicacy, she had always moderated her words and attitudes. The two-year-old Kyra, she sometimes thought, knew more about life than Marta did.

'He's not a pervert!' said Marta angrily. The word did not mean much to her, but the tone did.

'How d'you know?'

'He's good! It says in the book!'

'Yeah?' Anansi was not happy now, not comfortable. But Marta's obvious self-elevation to Princess status had grated on her, and the only way she could remove herself from being cast as a match girl or grateful kitchenmaid was to be actively nasty. 'Bet he is.'

'Read it! You'll *see*!' said Marta. She was younger, no match for Anansi in this mood, and she flung the book down on the bed between them. Anansi picked it up and began to flip pages. The prickly, tight-packed print danced before her eyes and an old panic rose.

Marta watched her, eyes narrowed, breathing heavily. 'You're not *reading*! You're pretending,' she said.

Anansi threw the book down. She was glad to have the noisome thing out of her hands, and rubbed them on her shorts.

'He's a pervert,' she said. 'Puts his hands up girls' skirts, tries to shaft them down the alley. That's why he gives her the money. She's a prozzie.'

Marta's white face became whiter, her lips pinched together and her nostrils flared with heavy breaths.

'I hate you!' she said, inadequately.

'I don't care,' lied Anansi. Suddenly, appalled at herself even as she did it, she spat on the floor. A gobbet of saliva shone briefly on Marta's fluffy blue carpet. Then she turned, and left.

Alaia met her on the drive as she got out of the car. Anansi brushed past, not saying a word, and walked through the gate in the wavy red brick wall to turn left, down towards the town. Marta's mother stood irresolute for a moment, wondering whether to run after her; but at the last, she turned and went indoors to find her own daughter.

The Seafret suppers which Anansi was missing had, as often as not, included Simon. He came ostensibly to see the boys, but they stayed only long enough to eat before leaving on their evening pursuits. When they were alone, he and Sheila talked, in an ever less stilted fashion, about the family and the future. He generally left about nine o'clock to return to the caravan.

Penny got back even later, usually having seen her daughters for an hour under the watchful eye of Janet, who now called herself their nanny, and then supped either at the pub with Susannah Rattray or with the Ward-Williamses, affluent Londoners who were only newly arrived at their holiday house and had not yet quite grasped the Tranmere-Harrison situation.

On the night before Anansi's quarrel with Marta, Simon had had a particularly satisfactory supper with Sheila. The boys had left early, followed by injunctions from Sheila not to go drinking, and in the ensuing parental conversation he had almost got to the point of proposing that he return to the marital roof to see how things went.

'I don't know,' Sheila said to Alaia Markeen when she dropped in the next afternoon. 'He is going to ask if he can come back. Tonight. I know it. And I really don't know the right thing to do.'

'Do the thing you want to do,' said Alaia lightly. 'It's about time you did something on a personal whim.'

They had become companionable very fast; Alaia's

kindly, witty cynicism filled a real need in Sheila, whose clumsy honesty and good will amused and touched the other woman in turn. Sometimes it seemed to Sheila that all her years of arranging mass outings and carnivals and picnics had been a substitute for such real and easy companionship as this. But at the thought of whims, she demurred.

'It isn't just what I want. It's what's best for the boys. They need their father, surely?'

'What did he do for them when he was here?'

'Ignored them, mostly. Or shouted. But he knows that now. He's looked at himself. He wants to be a better father.'

'Sheila,' said Alaia with bonhomous brutality, 'he's broke. He's living in a crap caravan with the bimbo from Hell, and he wants to get his feet back under the table. That's all. If you let him back, at least do it with your eyes open.'

'He's my husband,' said Sheila with simple dignity. 'I married him. If I had been nicer to him, and nicer about his career, he might not have got off with Penny. I'm responsible.'

Alaia was silent. The reference to Simon's work touched her. She thought of Jonny, how dependent he was on her approval, how anxious to wake her up when he came home from an art fair or a buying trip. If even that mature and worldly man relied on a wife's applause, why should not a weakling like Simon?

At last she said, 'Yes, I see that. But be careful, huh? Make him give up Penny and promise no more Pennies. Lay down some ground rules. Don't sleep with him until you're sure. He could hurt you again.'

'The awful thing,' said Sheila slowly, 'and the reason

I feel I should give him a chance, is that although I was embarrassed by the public thing at the beach, I wasn't all that hurt. About the sex, I mean. We hadn't bothered much for a few years, to be honest. I sort of knew he probably went elsewhere for it, and I didn't mind. I suppose getting so fat helped. A sort of barrier. An excuse. I shut him out.'

Alaia had been on the verge of saying, 'You're not fat!' but restrained herself. Instead she said, 'A lot of men like a bit of weight, actually. Alan Tranmere said to Jonny the other day at the Yacht Club that he rather fancied you these days.'

The two began to giggle. Sheila said, 'I know. He said much the same to me!'

'Talk about out of the frying pan,' said Alaia. 'Oh, go on. Go on, Sheila. Wipe Simon's eye. Kip with Alan Tranmere, *then* let him come back!'

'That,' said Sheila, 'is the most obscene suggestion anybody has ever made to me. I would rather . . .'

A silence fell, odd after the giggling moment. Both women knew what Sheila had been going to say. It hung between them, unsaid: 'Rather turn lesbian.' But in both of them, far below the conventional and maternal surface, wriggled a small serpent holding precisely that possibility.

They met one another's eyes and laughed again; this time ruefully, caught up together in the joke of it. Then Alaia reached out deliberately and took Sheila's smooth, soft, plump hand. The nails, she saw with surprise, were unvarnished but beautifully kept and polished. Who would have thought Sheila had such small vanities? She stifled an urge to lift the hand to her lips and kiss it. Instead she held it, steadily.

'You're right,' she said. 'Nothing, absolutely nothing, good has ever come from random frantic couplings down at the Martello tower. Think of it – fifteen minutes' fun, and then years of chaos and lawyers and caravan sites and puzzled children.'

Sheila twisted her palm uppermost and held Alaia's hand between both of hers, then deliberately released it with a light pat of dismissal.

'I'm not sure,' she said, 'that I would even rely on Alan Tranmere for the full fifteen minutes' fun.'

It was on getting home after this encounter that Alaia, still inwardly laughing and wondering how much to tell Jonny, met Anansi limping furiously down the drive. Only later, after comforting a tearful Marta, did it occur to her that this of all nights was the wrong one for Anansi to turn up for supper at Seafret.

When Alaia left, Sheila laid the table carefully, and on an impulse cut three roses from the branch above the back porch and put them in a small, round, cut-glass vase in the centre of the table, lighting the tall kitchen candle so that the heavy shadows of the roses fell on the scrubbed wood. Then she went upstairs, collected a copy of *Against* from Simon's row of author copies, and settled in her rocking chair to try and read it. The casserole was in the oven, the potatoes ready; the silence of the house was broken only by the weary footsteps and subdued chatter of families walking along the promenade after a day at the beach.

Simon arrived first, read all the signals of the table and then, amazedly, the even clearer signal of the book.

'You don't have to pretend to like it,' he said humbly. 'Not everyone does.'

'No,' said Sheila. 'But I ought to try and understand it.'

211

'Thank you,' said Simon, and meant it.

Once, she would have got up and given him a drink. Now she merely said, 'Bottle of wine open, if you fancy,' and returned to her reading.

Then Vincent appeared, and behind him Douai. Glancing up, Sheila saw their faces when they spotted Simon with the bottle, and noted the tentative half-smile on Douai's, and the open grin of pleasure that Vincent gave. There could not be much doubt, now, that he was as good as back. She wanted to sigh, but disguised it as a cough. Then she said something bright and inarticulate, and got up to pull the stew and potatoes out of the oven.

The boys sat down and Simon stood behind them, a hand on each one's shoulder, smiling across at his wife with triumphant relief. It was a pretty family tableau, and Anansi, standing in the open front door, saw it in time to step back out of sight and take herself off to sit on the sea wall alone, supperless and heartsore.

Chapter Nineteen

The next day, a day of small white scudding clouds and tempting breezes, Harry waited on Coker's Quay for half an hour past the appointed time. At last he saw Anansi, limping alone up the track from the seaward direction. Generally she called for Marta and came across the marsh with her; he felt a premonition of ill, and watched the child's approach in silence.

Spike had taken no time at all to provide, from his murky network of civil service friends, the Home Office information on the whereabouts of Charles Darwin Cowper, aged 31, felon. In Harry's pocket was the fax which had arrived just as he left the house. He liked faxes; the shabby curl of the paper reminded him of teleprinter messages, long ago and far away, when he, too, was On Her Majesty's Service. Mostly, the machine was only used for getting weather forecasts, and a boyish part of him always enjoyed the adventure of a real message. It said:

Thought you'd ask, so checked yestreen. An open prison, no less, and in your very neck of the woods. Willington.

First possible release date 12 September. Yours in cloak and dagger, G. Smiley jnr.

Marion had seen it, and announced her intention of ringing the governor that very morning. 'He's new. I met him at Maggie Marsh's family conciliation fund do. Nice man, lisps.'

Harry had no intention of telling Anansi, still less Marta what he had discovered: the romantic and disturbing proximity of a lost father in a penitentiary a mere two rivers along the coast. But he had brought the fax in his pocket for the satisfaction and the secret of it.

But now here was Anansi alone. And dragging that foot – worse, he thought, than usual. He stood up and put down the rope he had been splicing, and waited until she was close enough to hear him.

'Where's Marta? Not ill, I hope.'

'Dunno.' She stood on the path, not stepping onto the stone quay. He saw that she carried her lifejacket, but that her face was set in the old, sullen lines of their first meeting.

'Have you two had a fight?'

'Uh.'

'Anything worth fighting about?'

'Get outta my *face*,' said the child crossly.

'That is a very good expression, I always think,' said Harry lightly. 'As good as "get off my case", which Vincent and Douai favour. But seriously, if you have had a cat fight, you'd better make it up. You need a crew. She needs a skipper. You are two parts of one whole.'

'I can come on my own,' said Anansi. 'You could give me a lesson without Marta, see?'

'Can't. Rules. Chaperonage. More than my reputation's worth. You know the score. One man, two kids minimum.'

'You think I'd pull the rape scam?' she said, with scorn.

'No,' said Harry. 'But I promised Sheila. Queen's Regulations.'

'Huh,' said Anansi, scowling at the mention of Sheila. She had got her own breakfast, hungry from lack of supper, and wolfed it outdoors on the promenade wall. None of the Harrisons were up when she put the bowl in the sink and left for the morning; but she knew, clearly enough, that there were once again four of them in residence. A threatening majority. She had no intention of meeting them until she had to.

At this point Harry glanced sideways and saw the figure of the Markeens' cleaner, Karen, stumping with an air of unwillingness along the marsh path from the top houses.

'Uh-oh. Trouble,' he said. He walked fast to meet her and save her the extra distance; Anansi, sitting on the fish-box, watched gloomily as the two spoke, nodded, gestured, and parted again each in their own direction.

When he got back to the quay and the still figure of the child, Harry said, 'Must have been a bad fight, then. It seems that Marta has opted to go out with Grania Hampton in the Mirror dinghy. Just for today.'

'Huh,' said Anansi again. 'So I can't sail, then?'

'Not with me,' said Harry. He eyed her, speculatively. 'The safety boat's out till twelve, though. Take a spin on your own. No reason not to.'

The girl's eyes blazed with sudden passion. 'On my own? Sail the boat?'

'As skipper. Master under God. Yes. I think you can manage the jib from the helm.'

'I could, yeah.'

'Stay in sight of Grenden Quay. OK? Keep turning upriver so the tide doesn't take you off. It's ebbing till three at least.'

'OK.' She was down the steps, hauling at the line to pull the dinghy close, scrambling aboard.

'Just for an hour or so. If you do well enough, I'll buy you lunch in the Yacht Club.'

Anansi was barely listening. With a fervour that amused but slightly disturbed Harry, she was unloosing the ties on the mainsail, hanking on the jib, and preparing the boat for sailing. He had taught many children to sail during his retirement years, but never known one – certainly not a girl – so headlong in her anxiety to get afloat alone. A misgiving pricked him, despite the gentle wind and innocent sunny sparkle of the river.

'Take it steady,' he warned from the quay. 'Just down to Grenden, then tack upriver. Test the tide. It's only been running an hour, so it'll get stronger.'

Anansi looked up at him. She had both sails up now, and the boat tugged at the mooring as they slatted to and fro above her head. She did not answer his warning, but said simply, 'Thanks. I'll be careful of the boat, OK?'

'It isn't the boat,' began Harry.

Again premonition stirred in him. In boyhood he had fallen under the spell of falconry for a while; this, he thought, was how he had felt when as an impatient thirteen-year-old he loosed a hawk from his wrist without entire confidence that it would return. Anansi, however, was so nearly loose now that he could not tug at her restraint. As she dropped the mooring, hauled in the

mainsheet and inexpertly grabbed the line to back the
flapping jib and veer the boat into midstream, he raised
his voice and said, 'I'll watch from Grenden. Stay round
there. When you've had enough, beach the boat by the
club and I'll bring her back and moor her up later.'

She was gone, the small boat dwindling against the
far bank; he stood a moment and watched her gybe
neatly, change sides, and head purposefully downstream
round the wide shining bend, steering easily between the
moored keelboats. Then he half-walked, half-ran to a better
observation point on Grenden Quay.

It was nearly ten o'clock. Sheila woke with a start from a
dream in which she was in a tent with Alaia, playing chess
by candlelight while night gathered on the saltings around
them. Glancing over at the other bed, she saw Simon's
sleeping form. Glancing down at the unusual disarray of
her own, she remembered the night before. She closed
her eyes again, thinking to recapture the dream. It must
be, she thought vaguely, all of ten years since she had lain
in bed so late. But everything was out of joint, was it not?
Soon, she slept again.

Half a mile away, Penny Tranmere woke alone in the
comfortless caravan, shook off the mists induced by her
sleeping pill, and realized that Simon had not been back
all night. Like Sheila, she tried closing her eyes to the
reality of the day, but for her sleep did not return. She
knew where he would be.

Everyone, she thought morosely, would know soon.
Plump, mumsy Bethie Cotten would think it was for
the best, 'for the children'. That flat-chested bitch Poppy
Hampton would think it served her right. In every shop
in the High Street, from East Anglian Electrical to Barker's

Blythney Bakery, the assistants would know what had happened to her and give sly glances with her change.

Even if she and Alan could live together again, with the children, the events of the past ten days would hang around her for ever, a grimily exotic miasma. Everyone, always and everywhere in her small daily world, would know the lot. *Up against the wall, in the old Martello. Down the road with only a towel on. Hiding in Markeens' gallery. Lived on the caravan site, for a while. He went back to his wife, the novelty obviously wore off.*

A connoisseur of scurrilous gossip herself, she had enjoyed many other such stories in the past (for Blythney, for all its Enid Blyton charm, was not a notably chaste society, particularly in the dull, cold Suffolk winters). Now she would be the joke herself. Damn and blast small-town life.

This, Penny decided at that moment, eyes still closed against the squalor of the little caravan, was the end of Blythney for her. She should never have let Alan bring her to this horrible time warp, chasing the stupid dream of his stupid childhood. She should have made him stay in London where you could get on with your life without every shopgirl tittering. She would go back there herself, take the Ward-Williams' basement flat in St Charles' Square – they grumbled endlessly about their short-let foreign students, after all. They would be glad of such a like-minded tenant. They might even waive a few months' rent to have her. She would move the girls up there, and get some research work for the London galleries. Jonny might give her some. Eventually she would take holidays, not in Suffolk but in Tuscany or Provence. She would not, absolutely not, stay here to be pointed at by every old cat in Blythney. No, no, no.

Penny was too wide awake to keep her eyes closed now. The sun streamed in through the dirty plastic windows, and she hauled the pillow over her head to defy it. She would speak to Nigel Ward-Williams today. She would wear her pink striped sweater to do it. She would get herself out of this, showing a prompt, ruthless efficiency that would take their breaths away. Alan's, Simon's, Sheila's, everybody's.

Douai and Vincent were in the kitchen at Seafret, munching cold Pop Tarts rather than bother to put them in the toaster. Flabby crumbs and gouts of fruit filling fell on the scrubbed table, disregarded. Vincent was reading *Loaded*, without much apparent understanding or pleasure, and caressing what he was smugly convinced was an incipient moustache. Douai had finished scanning *Yachts and Yachting* for likely second-hand boats and now was looking at a tide table.

'Vince?' he said after a moment.

'Uh,' said Vince, his hand in the Pop Tart packet and his mouth still full of crumbs.

'You know Mum's getting me a Laser Two?'

'Uh.'

'Well, are you sailing today?'

'Nope,' said Vincent. 'Tennis. With,' he blushed beneath his ghostly moustache, 'Janie Cotten.' The tone of his voice defied his brother to make capital of this breathtaking development.

Douai paused for a moment, tempted, but sought the greater advantage instead. 'So can I take the Flying Frog out?'

'Who'd crew?' asked Vincent suspiciously.

'Mark,' said Douai promptly. ''Cos Grania's helming the Mirror every morning in the practise week.'

'He'll have to crew for her, then,' said Vincent, and returned with an air of finality to his magazine.

'Bet he won't,' said Douai. 'Oh, go on. Tell you what, we won't use the spinnie at all. Otherwise,' he added artfully, 'I'll have nothing to do but come down and watch the tennis.'

Vincent started at this unappealing possibility. He and Janie were to play doubles against a completely unknown brother and sister from London, all of them sophisticates together; the penetrating gaze of a younger brother behind the mesh could seriously affect his showy new service.

'Well,' he said, 'only if you get Mark. Or Maurrie. I'm not having some dork on the wire. Or Dondie, with his big flat feet. And you definitely can't use the spinnaker.'

'Thanks,' said Douai. Without ceremony he crossed to the kitchen door and bellowed up the stairs 'Mu-um! Going sailing, OK?'

'OK,' came faintly from the parental bedroom. 'Safety boat cover till twelve thirty. Be back by then.' Even in half-sleep Sheila knew the workings of the Blythney summer. She had sat on the committee which resolved to pay the club boatman overtime to provide the children with cover for their practices on the Wednesday to Friday before the junior regatta. Upstairs, she turned over and fell back into a third sleep. Simon, newly reborn to the comfort of a sprung bed, had not stirred even once.

Alaia Markeen wondered often in after years what would have happened to them all if she had not been soft enough, on that bright morning, to ring round the sailing set and find Marta another boat to crew in. She knew, even as she did this, that it would have been wiser to confront the fact of the two girls' quarrel and attempt some kind of reconciliation. But she hated to argue, and her daughter's peaked, unhappy white face touched her so painfully that she could not bring herself to challenge it. It would pass, whatever it was. They were children. Part of her mind murmured that Anansi was not quite the usual kind of Blythney summer child, and that this fight might bear some adult intervention, but she pushed the thought away.

'I'm not going on the river with *her* and Harry today,' was all Marta had said, with tremulous haughtiness. Pressed gently on whether it was the river itself she rejected, she had said firmly, 'No. I want to go sailing, just not with *her*.'

Whereon soft-hearted Alaia rang first the Cottens – who were committed to tennis – then the Hamptons, asking lightly whether any crew were needed. Grania Hampton, who would have sailed with Adolf Hitler rather than her elder brother, shouted with glee in the background to the second call and neatly solved the problem. Alaia was vague about the skills and experience of the rabble of summer Yacht Club children, all so similar in their rubber suits and lifejackets and mousy fair hair and freckles. When efficient Poppy Hampton said, 'Oh yes, there's rescue-boat cover all morning, and Grania's tremendously responsible,' that settled it. Karen was dispatched across the marsh with a message to Harry before she had a chance to take off her outdoor shoes.

It was all as easy and undoubtful as that. Alaia's main concern was to rub sunblock on the pale little face and legs, slip five pounds in the zip pocket of her daughter's shorts, and settle that the Cottens would leave Marta at the club to be picked up after her lunchtime burger and chips. She did not think again about the breach with Anansi. Children were like that. It would be something and nothing. It would sort itself out. Perhaps

Anansi could be asked, formally, to tea. Yes. That would be nice.

By eleven o'clock Harry had decided that he need not have worried about his pupil's solo excursion. In the light steady wind, Anansi had mastered the Whitecap perfectly. She skimmed downstream, turned abreast of the Martello tower, and tacked up against the tide with decorous neatness, only missing stays once and almost being blown back onto the uncovering mud. She recovered the situation, spun round with much flapping, and returned to the right course. She did him credit. Perhaps, he thought sentimentally, fingering the fax in his pocket, before long she would be telling her father that she could sail, alone. Maybe – Harry was a romantic – she would take him a modest regatta trophy; not a cup yet, but a fourth or fifth place trophy. An engraved shot glass, or a club coaster with the crest on. The kind of things that he had won here sixty years ago as Junior Whitecap Class Captain. The kind of reassuring prideful trophy whose nature had not really changed, any more than the river had. He had armed her with a skill, a mastery. It was a good beginning.

Eventually he signalled to her to beach the boat, and she stepped from it onto the slipway, glowing.

'You did tremendously well,' he said. 'Deserves a drink.' Together, they walked up to the clubhouse, and as he was providing her with a fizzy orange, Marion walked in.

'There you are! Allie Markeen said you weren't teaching – it's a mercy. We could . . .' she glanced at Anansi. 'Finished, dear? Jolly good. I thought it was you I saw single-handing. Well done!'

Anansi sidled away with her drink. Marion leaned across to Harry and said something.

'Now?' he said, loud enough for Anansi to hear. 'Today? Steady on!' He was rattled. He did not feel ready to lose the imaginary prisoner in his mind, the sad-eyed King Leontes waiting for his long-lost Perdita. He knew that the reality of the man at Willington, where Marion now precipitately wanted to drive him in her Mini Metro, was unlikely to live up to his imagined figure of Charles Darwin Cowper. He felt annoyed with his wife for suggesting it, but as usual she had sweet reason on her side.

'The governor says there is no visiting for four days after today, because of staffing or something. He said we could come today and be issued with an order at the gate. Take it or leave it, he said.'

'Next week—' began Harry.

'Next week as you know I have the carnival committee and all the jobs—'

'Give me a minute,' he said, defeated.

Anansi watched this conversation from the corner of the bar, her eyes narrowed. She thought how little it suited the masterful, mysterious, warrior Harry, the man of the riverbank, to be pushed along so briskly by this white-headed little woman. When he came back to her and slipped her three pounds for a chip lunch, she said nothing.

'I've left a message for the boatman to tow the White-cap back when he gets in from the rescue boat,' he said. 'So don't worry. Tide's going down till three, so she won't float off the beach. See you tomorrow morning?'

'Uh,' said Anansi, sullen again.

'And Marta?'

'S'pose.'

Harry put his hand momentarily on her thin shoulder. He wished he could tell her where he was going. But he could not, and after the briefest moment of acquiescence, she shrugged his hand away.

Chapter Twenty

Douai reached the Yacht Club just as Harry left it. He was in the Hamptons' car with Mark and Grania. Grania, still halfway through a voluble quarrel with her brother, broke off at the sight of Marta and Alaia waiting on the sea wall above the dinghy park.

'God, we're so *late*,' she mourned. 'Marta's *changed*. It's your fault for not getting up, Mark.'

'You could have come on your bike,' said her brother.

'Not carrying the *centreboard*,' his sister grumbled. 'We had it home to fix the chipped bit, right? The one *you* and Maurrie did, banging into the sill at Heron pier. Now we're *late*, and we've only got an hour.'

'Ah, bollocks,' said Douai. 'We're going downriver anyway. Got all afternoon.'

'There won't be a safety boat,' said Grania primly. 'No cover after twelve thirty or downstream of Martello. Says on the board.'

'Safety shmafety,' said Mark. 'You babies can stay here and practise if you want. We're going downstream. Down to Heron. The tide turns at three, then we can get back up by teatime.'

Scornful of the girl's doubt, Douai added, 'It's only force two anyway.'

Marta had appeared, leaving her mother on the sea wall. She took Grania's arm and said, 'Let's us go to Heron Island too.'

Douai looked doubtful. 'You might not be up to it.'

'We are, so!' flared Marta. 'I've done lessons with Uncle Harry all week. We went to Heron Island *three times*. We went round the island.'

'Race you!' said Mark, his round pink face beaming. 'Mirror versus Laser, give you ten minutes' start as a handicap. And we aren't using the spinnaker. That's fair.'

The girls glanced at one another.

'We could,' said Grania doubtfully. 'They didn't say we couldn't. If the boys were there. It's only force two.'

'Force two,' agreed Marta, with a serious meteorologist's nod of the head.

'Would Vince mind?' said Mark. 'Nah, he goes downriver on his own, doesn't he?'

'Yeah. Even singlehanding. 'S no sweat,' said Douai.

The girls, seized with the idea of a voyage, were rigging the Mirror dinghy with more haste than care. Glancing away from the mast for a moment Grania saw the dark figure of Anansi loitering a few yards away beyond some keelboats on their tall trolleys.

'Hey,' she said. 'There's Anansi. I thought you said she was on a lesson with Mr Glanville.'

Marta looked up, startled, and found herself meeting her former friend's eyes.

Anansi had come to make peace, but had no idea of how it might be achieved. Aside from the confused enmities of school, her only experience of quarrelling had been with her mother, and Tracey never apologized or made overtures of reconciliation. They would merely glower around one another for a day or so, and then grudgingly resume normal relations, with nothing ever said. Now, all that Tracey's daughter could do was to stand stupidly, looking at Marta, and wish that she had not found her in such a tight little knot of tow-haired, deadpan, identically lifejacketed Blythney compeers.

The three others stared at her in silence, and Marta – who was, after all, by far the youngest of the group – picked up their coldness and said in an unnaturally high voice, 'Did Uncle Harry cancel the lesson?'

'Nah,' said Anansi. 'He said I didn't need the lesson. So I went out for a bit on my own.'

Marta was hugely impressed, and began a smile which could have changed everything. But before she could respond, Douai cut in, with whiplash venom, 'As if! She's telling porkers again. Like about her African chief dad. Uncle Harry wouldn't have let her go out on her own.'

'He did!' said Anansi furiously. 'I beached the Whitecap over there. Look!'

The children looked at the familiar brown boat, heeling gently on the muddy shingle near the slipway.

'And that's *proof*?'

'Loads of people saw. I went single-handed, OK?'

'Yeah, right.' He nodded in mock agreement. 'All the way to Africa to see your dad, I s'pose.'

Grania had moved away from them to pull the Mirror on its trolley towards the water. She was a good-natured child, and Douai was being poisonous beyond her experience of him. She did not understand what lay behind it, and sensed a trouble too dark and deep for her taste.

'Come on, Mart. We'll get our start. Ten minutes, boys, on your honour.'

'Give you fifteen. We'll still beat you.' Douai had entirely switched his attention away from Anansi now, redoubling the insult by acting as if she was no longer even visible. 'Come on, Mark. Let's rig.'

Anansi turned from them, and limped stiffly away along the waterfront. When she reached the stranded Whitecap she hesitated for a moment, looked round for the club boatman, and when she saw that he was nowhere near, began to pull the sails up with furtive haste. The drinkers on the terrace paid no attention; another child, another set of sails flapping upward. The scene was too ordinary even to register.

When she had got the boat ready, she moved round to the bow and began to push it towards the water. The tide had gone down by a couple of feet since she landed, and for a horrid moment she thought that it would not move. She threw all her weight onto it, bent her knees and then straightened them, pushing hard and steadily. The boat moved. She had never launched from a beach before, and had a moment's panic about how to put the rudder overboard in the shallow water before jumping in; at the last minute she remembered that by releasing a thin line Harry had cleated to the tiller, she could allow the blade to fold upwards. She put it on, and with a final push she had the boat floating. Soaked to her waist but not caring, she stood beside it in the water for a moment then clambered awkwardly in, her bent ankle twisting painfully as she landed on the floor boards.

The dinghy began to drift downstream, but luckily blew away from the first obstruction, the long floating jetty which the rescue boat used. Within a few moments she had achieved some sort of control, hauling in the mainsail and lowering the rudder again. Next she stiffened the jib, and suddenly was tearing across the river on a playful gust, heading for the reeds on the far side. She would have to gybe, to bring the sail across, in order to head downriver. Gritting her teeth she swung the helm over and ducked as the wooden boom whistled over her head.

A great exhilaration filled her. She had known what to do, and done it. Now she was pointing downriver, and with most of the club children tidying their boats ashore, she was one of only few boats on the river this weekday lunchtime. She was also gaining rapidly on the little Mirror dinghy. Glancing towards the slipway, she could see Mark and Douai, pointing and gesticulating towards her.

'Catch me now, you fuckers!' she said, and hauling in the sail to tame its flapping, she drove the boat hard downstream, the tiller thrumming under her hand. Minutes later she passed Marta and Grania in the Mirror dinghy, without so much as a glance.

'Are you crying?' said Grania to her pale, black-browed little crew with incredulity. 'What's the matter?'

'Nothing,' said Marta with a sniff. 'Catch up with her! Beat her!'

It took barely half an hour to reach the lonely penitentiary on the peninsula, known locally as 'The Colony' from its Victorian foundations. Marion drove, with Harry beside her mainly silent but sometimes voicing doubts which she brushed aside.

'Suppose he's real trouble? Suppose he's nuts? We ought not to let him know where she is.'

'Successful con men are rarely nuts,' said Marion tranquilly. 'And he won't cause trouble while he's on parole, will he?'

'But a lost daughter . . . we're playing with fire. Oh,

maybe not. Maybe not. But Madge, suppose he wants to see her, and she really doesn't want to see him? Suppose she's scared, because of the kicking, all that?'

'I wouldn't have her down as a nervy child. Would you?' said Marion, swerving onto the verge of the narrow lane to let a van past. 'More of a seeker after bald truth, I should say. That's probably why she quarrelled with Little Miss Fantasy.' Marion had never really taken to Marta Markeen.

Harry said, 'And that's another thing. I wish we adults had moved in and made the kids sort that one out. They were such good friends all week.'

'Pish and tush!' said Marion briskly, slowing down for the prison gatehouse. 'Grown-ups can't direct children's lives as if they were amateur dramatics. Blythney's full of interfering people with set ideas. Like Sheila. It does no good.'

'Well, we're interfering,' said Harry.

'No we're not. We're researching. We're getting all the facts, and offering them to her, so she can decide what to do.'

'She's not twelve yet!'

'And what's so special about twelve?'

'Oh God,' said Harry, looking at the glum façade of the prison. 'We should have got some professionals involved.' The army officer within him cringed in horror at the unofficial and unapproved nature of their quest

'Rubbish!' said Marion. And with deadly, wifely perception, 'You just want a rubber stamp, don't you, to confirm you're doing right? Come *on*, dear.' She had swung her legs out of the car and was changing from her flat scuffed driving shoes to smarter ones. Followed by her husband, she clicked briskly towards the prison.

*   *   *

The sail down to Heron Island was one which Anansi never forgot. River and sun and wind came together in rare perfection; the banks shone in palest greens and browns, lines of warm wind ran through the meadow grass, and overhead hung a bowl of pale blue sky rippled with thin cloud. At the horizon it fell behind distant stands of trees and the crouched shape of the Viking hill.

The straight, austere lines of the Blyne made the downstream river less conventionally pretty than the winding Grend; here were no miniature beaches or wide shining bends. But Anansi, watching the bow wave chuckling past the varnished sides of the little boat, thought it all entirely beautiful. This afternoon it was her boat, her journey, her choice. The smallest push on the tiller altered the course, at her will and hers alone. She could slow the boat by letting the sails flap, speed it up by hauling in and shifting her own weight forwards.

For a while, with a fair wind and tide pushing her onward and the banks rushing past at gratifying speed, she experimented with all these things. The Mirror dinghy was behind her on the far side of the river, Marta's dark head and Grania's fair one just distinguishable against the red sail.

The tide, Harry had told her, was faster in midstream; she took the Whitecap on a long diagonal until she was an equal distance from each bank, watching the banks and markers as she did so. When she had found the speed she wanted, she glanced back; the Mirror was well astern. The point was made. Suddenly a cold feeling came over her: this boat belonged to Harry! This was wrong. She must go back.

With brief horror, she imagined him angry: cold, dismissive, like those bitch teachers who thought she was scum. The image softened; he would, she thought tentatively, perhaps understand that she had to do it. To show Douai that she could do it, that she was not lying, that she had learnt.

He would see that, if she turned back now. Hauling in the sails, manoeuvring awkwardly with her lame foot, she steered experimentally across the river. Cross here, tack round, head upstream for the Martello tower – still just visible – a few more tacks and then she could beach the boat again, just where it was.

Her tack, though, took her dismayingly far downstream as she crossed the river; the tide was flowing at full strength. When did it turn? He had said – what? Three o'clock. Day after day in the boat he had talked to her and Marta about the workings of the tides. It would change round earlier at the bottom of the river. Or was it later? Earlier, surely.

But before that you could cheat, by staying at the side of the river where the tide was weaker or even ran the other way. Eddies. That was it. Marta had made jokes about the name. 'Let's catch an Edward,' she had said when they had to leave Catley before the fair tide. 'Let's catch an Edwina.' Despite herself, Anansi smiled at the memory of Marta. But how could she catch an Edward if she had to keep tacking right through the middle of the fast, wrong-way tide? Zigzagging to and fro, making little ground against it, she tormented herself for five minutes with conflicting pictures of an angry and a sorrowful Harry.

Then the Mirror came past her, still sailing downstream. She could hear the two girls laughing together as they passed, fifty feet from where she was wrenching her little boat round into the wind again. Then, in the distance and moving fast towards her, she saw the Laser Two. Douai was going on downstream, to the island, to laugh at her with Marta and the others. It was beyond what she could stand. Angrily she pushed the tiller over, ducked under the boom, and caught a gust of the strengthening wind. She moved forward, reaching behind her to steer, and adjusted the jib.

Joyfully, released from its effortful beating, the little boat shot forward and within a few moments Anansi saw, to her delight, that not only was she past the girls again but that the racing boat with Douai at the helm had ceased to grow bigger in the distance. Harry had talked about speed, and she realized that although the Whitecap was technically slower, her own weight as crew was less than half that of the two big boys in their Laser. Carefully, all other thoughts forgotten, she trimmed her sails and willed the boat onward, faster, using every ounce of wind and tide.

Far astern of her, Douai shouted, 'Shit!'

Mark, holding on to a shroud and peering ahead, said admiringly, 'She's going well, the kid.'

Douai's face, pinched with anger, glared at him as he glanced back. 'Get the spinnaker ready!' he spat.

'I thought we weren't allowed,' said Mark.

'Get it!' Mark had never seen Douai so angry. 'She thinks she can just swan in and say things about my dad and pinch my Great-uncle Harry's boat and . . . and . . .'

Clumsily, Mark began to fix the spinnaker ready for hauling up. He was unpractised and it took time, all of that time filled with Douai's nervous, angry muttering. At last he said, 'Hoist!' and held the guy.

Douai yanked viciously at the line by his feet, and the

gossamer fabric rose, frivolously bright against the brown water. 'Yess!' he shouted.

Mark hauled in the sheet and the boat picked itself up and flew forwards; but only momentarily, because in his surprise and haste he had not fixed the halyard on properly. Less than a minute after the bellying sail began to draw, the top of it pulled right away from the mast, so that it flew ahead of the boat for a moment, parallel with the water, before flopping down under the slicing bow. There was a ripping, sickening sound as the boat sailed over its spinnaker.

'Shit! The little bitch, she made me, she made me . . .' Douai was gabbling now, murderous; he had let go of the tiller, flung himself forward and was scrabbling violently at the ripped sail. 'Come on, help me, *help* me.'

Between them, the boat drifting all the time downriver, they hauled the remains of the spinnaker up and squashed it into its bag. Mark was hit round the head by the boom, and Douai scratched his arm on a rigging pin, so that it bled on the floorboards and on his arm.

'Better fucking well go back,' he growled.

Mark stared at him in alarm. 'We *can't*,' he said. 'The girls. They're going to Heron because we are. If we don't, they'll be on their own.'

'Can't they cope?' said Douai. 'Shouldn't have gone, should they, if they can't manage.'

'I'm sorry,' said Mark stiffly, 'but Grania is my sister, and she's only just learnt to helm, and she only went because we were.'

They glared at each other for a moment, then Douai said, 'All right. We'll catch them and tell them to come back.'

'Fine,' said Mark.

They sailed on. The Mirror by now was out of sight round one of the few slight bends of the Blyne, the Whitecap even further ahead. When eventually the boys saw the girls' red sail, but no sign of the brown one, Mark said, 'Better tell your Anansi girl as well, hadn't we?'

Douai only growled.

Chapter Twenty-one

Ever since Simon's defection Poppy Hampton, who knew her duty as a Christian and a Yacht Club committee wife, had paid frequent calls on Sheila. Sometimes she loomed while Sheila was shaking out the doormat, and chatted brightly across the low wall. Sometimes – with or without a perfunctory knock on the door – she invited herself in for coffee.

Sheila, in her new detached mood, accepted this without protest but equally without enthusiasm. In the days since the friendship with Alaia had begun, she found herself strangely dissatisfied with the kind of bustling, practical conversations about carnival clothes and Cinema Club outings and litter patrols which had, hitherto, been the staple of her Blythney friendships. Now she tolerated Poppy's brisk stream of clichés, no more. Her vague replies, unexpected private smiles and *laissez-faire* attitude caused Poppy frequently to inform Andy, with a gusty sigh, that Sheila Harrison was 'still in shock, poor thing'.

On the day after Simon's night in, Poppy had a busy morning. Phone calls to make, tickets to organize for the summer theatre, a crisis with the firm supplying the Yacht Club ball marquee. Many of her bustling duties, it has to be said, were ones which Sheila would normally have taken over or initiated herself. On top of this there were two children to dispatch to the river with kit and lunch money, and reminders about tea with the de Benville children at the Country Club. So it was after noon when she finally got round to paying a visit to Seafret.

'Coo-ee! Hello-oh!' she shouted from the front door, left open by the departing boys.

'Here,' said a still sleepy voice.

Poppy stepped briskly into the kitchen, looking (thought Sheila with her new, detached eyes) like a glamorous transvestite deckhand in her narrow navy canvas slacks and white shirt, with her artfully cut brown locks just curling over the collar. Quite sexy, in a crisp-and-dry sort of way.

'Hi,' she said, and yawned.

Poppy's eyes widened like a very surprised deckhand indeed when she saw Sheila, fair hair not swept up as usual but cascading round her face, sitting barefoot in what looked like a dressing gown with No.24's wandering ginger cat on her lap.

'Nice morning,' said Sheila, noting with more amusement than embarrassment Poppy's surprise at her dishevelled appearance. 'I was going to go for a swim later, hence no clothes.'

'Are both boys out?' asked Poppy in a low, understanding voice.

One of the aspects of these pastoral visits which had been grating on Sheila was Poppy's insistence on parading her understanding of just how the boys must be feeling. Now she merely replied, with a brevity that unnerved her friend entirely, 'Yup. Tennis and river.'

'Well, I know Douai's sailing,' Poppy bridled a little at the idea that she might not know what was going on on any morning of the Blythney summer, 'because Mark's crewing. Obviously! But I thought you and Vincent might be having a *private* chat. As he's the eldest. I thought you probably needed some space, the two of you. That's why I haven't been round this morning. Give you time for a heart to heart.' Something, she could not say what, was forcing Poppy to fib. She was not a good liar, and reddened slightly as she spoke.

Sheila looked at her, and for the first time, she thought to herself with vague amazement, she perceived the ghoulishness of Poppy Hampton's sympathy. Ha! So she wanted to be in on the drama, did she? First with the news, queen of the details, all under the mask of caring supportiveness? Well, *fine*, thought Sheila to herself with a spurt of anger. Go for it! The woman wants red meat – give it to her.

She leaned further back in her chair, tweaked the cat's ginger ear, and said, 'No, Vince is playing tennis. He doesn't go in for heart to hearts much. Anyway, Simon came back last night. He's upstairs, snoring his head off right now.'

Poppy started. 'You mean—'

'Well,' said Sheila, tossing back her mane of hair – a heavy mane, suiting the face which, her friend suddenly saw, had grown thinner. No, not thinner, not really; just more animated, less bun-like, replacing its bland habitual smile with a rarer, sharper one. Sheila gave one of those new, unsettling smiles now. 'We slept together, if that's what you mean. First time in ages, actually. But I'm not at all sure he's going to be allowed to get his feet back under the table.'

'It always takes time,' said Poppy, the vicar's daughter,

239

with an air of unsurprised wisdom which took all her sparse acting skills to maintain. 'After what happened . . .'

'Actually I am grateful for what happened,' said Sheila. She paused, listening to the echo of these surprising words, and was pleased to find that she meant them. 'Simon and I were pretty well washed up. Penny was the symptom, not the disease. I made the effort last night, because I thought that for the boys' sake it was my job to cobble things up again. But I've decided it isn't.'

'Are *you sure*?' asked Poppy, with the accent accusingly on the last two words, as if addressing a small child prone to go wilfully astray. 'I thought you and I agreed that marriages shouldn't be thrown out lightly.'

Sheila looked at her, without favour or anger, and her hands were steady, stroking the cat's back. After a moment she said, 'Oh, piss off.'

A heavy tread on the stairs made Poppy Hampton turn, startled from two directions at once.

Simon came into the room, jibbed at the sight of her, and said with forced brightness, 'Morning, darling. Any coffee?'

'Make your own,' said Sheila. 'I'm going swimming.'

And, magnificent in her bare feet and voluminous dressing gown, she padded past both of them, flipped a towel from the chaotic hooks in the hallway, and vanished across the promenade and down the stony beach.

Julia Ward-Williams and Ellie de Benville, almost identically dressed in snow-white pedal pushers and tucked-in T shirts, were standing together, wreathed in bright talk. They paused to watch Sheila moving towards the sea, purposeful as a polar bear.

'It's a mystery to me,' said Julia, 'how that woman walks barefoot on pebbles.'

'Especially at her weight,' said trim Ellie, her hand unconsciously moving to her flat little stomach. 'Ooh look, there's Poppy! Hello-oh! Haven't seen you since we got down. How *are* things?'

Poppy, emerging slightly shaken from Seafret, moved gratefully towards them. She abhorred gossip, so she always said, and indeed was not a regular practitioner. But some instincts run too deep and strong to be resisted. She glanced back nervously at the door of Seafret, as if a new surprise might rocket out and knock her over.

'You won't believe this,' she began.

The three women put their heads together. Fifty feet away Sheila, by now kicking on her back in the cold, gently heaving North Sea, watched them serenely for a moment before rolling over and swimming lazily away.

Anansi was approaching Heron Island. The tide was two-thirds gone, and the rough grass and miniature cliffs of the islet were surrounded by a fringe of shining mud, ten foot wide and sloping so gently that she remembered Harry's lectures on what he called 'reading the foreshore' and steered further out than seemed immediately necessary. 'If the slope starts off gradual, where you can see it,' Harry had said, 'it very likely goes on in the same shape. So it's still shallow a long way out. If it's steep-to up at the edge where you can see it, the water usually gets deep quicker.'

There was, she knew from watching other boats, one low-water landing place on the islet. It lay just beyond its mid-point in the narrower of the two channels. Cautiously, she steered towards it, planning how to turn her boat into the wind and coast up to the short stretch of firm, slimy shingle. If the boat stopped, she could paddle. There was a paddle clipped under the bow deck.

Moving along the length of the island, looking at it with interest, she touched the mud once with her keel, distracted by what at first sight she took for a hut. It was, however, no more than a pile of half-overgrown planks, long ones and short ones. She remembered that Harry had said there was a plan to build a jetty for sailing club members' use, a plan delayed since last year by a dispute with a bird protection charity. You could use that wood to build a hut, she thought. Live here. Cool! The thought of Harry momentarily disturbed her conscience, but she shrugged it off. The moment was too good to waste: a first solitary landfall. A new land lay open to the invader from the river. The two boats behind her were almost forgotten.

Harry and Marion were waiting in a bare room of official dullness, enlivened only by a faded print of a sailing barge and a sign reminding them of the dire consequences awaiting any visitor who attempted to pass any object or substance to an inmate.

Harry stared for a while at the picture, then said, 'I wish I had one of those mobile phones. I'd like to make sure the boatman got my message about the dinghy.'

'He will have,' said Marion. 'It'll be tied up on your mooring by now.'

Harry was still uneasy but could not tell why.

A prison officer entered, keys jangling at his belt. 'The governor thought you might like a private interview room,' he said, 'given that you have family news for the inmate. Is that right?'

'That's very kind,' said Marion. And to Harry, 'Normally, it's all open plan, with the other poor creatures' children running everywhere.'

'Will we be alone?' asked Harry.

'They have to observe, silly,' said his more experienced wife. 'Because of the substances and objects, see?'

'That's correct. This way then, please.'

Their shoes clicked along the corridor outside. Glancing up at a high, barred window, Harry saw the sky. The clouds, he thought, were moving faster than when they came in.

The ripping of the spinnaker had delayed Douai and Mark for longer than they expected. By the time they came close to the Mirror's red sail, it was silhouetted against the near end of Heron Island.

'Shout!' said Mark. 'Call them back. We'll have to beat back anyway.'

Shouting had no effect. Either the girls could not hear it or interpreted it as a mere cry of defeat. Grania, her cheeks pink with effort and pleasure, said to Marta, 'We beat them! We beat them!'

'Anansi beat us,' said Marta. She shuddered briefly in her cotton sweater and lifejacket. 'Ugh, I'm cold.'

The thin cloud had covered the sun now and was thickening, greying the bright day. The pleasure of the outing was gone anyway for Marta; it had always been a sour desperate pleasure, a demonstration to Anansi that she had plenty of other friends, and boats, to spend her summer with. Now she was truly sorry for the quarrel, and had privately admitted to herself that it was wrong to talk about beggars and kitchenmaids to someone who, well, in the Olden Days, would have been one. An unfamiliar sense of shame gripped her, and made her shiver again.

'It's not that cold,' said Grania, annoyed at Marta's failure to recognize the skilful helmsmanship which in her view had won them the race. 'Let's go to the landing place.'

She had not had the benefit of Harry's lectures on 'reading the foreshore', and put her helm down, pointing the little dinghy confidently towards the landing inlet. In a moment it had struck the mud, stopping abruptly and throwing the two girls forward.

Recovering herself, Grania pulled the tiller over and said, 'Pull up the centreboard, Mart. We'll sail off.'

Marta had been lectured, often enough, by Harry Glanville on the unwisdom of pulling the plate up too quickly when you hit what he called 'the putty'. 'Always', he had told the girls, 'make absolutely sure that your bows have turned and you are truly going to sail straight off'. He had demonstrated, sitting on the grass at Catley, with his thumb to represent the centreplate and his hand as the boat. 'The thing that's sticking you to the bottom is also stopping you sailing any further up the putty, see? If you're not a hundred and ten per cent sure of sailing off in the right direction, don't unstick yourself. If you're in a hole, stop digging.'

Marta had heard this and understood it, at the time. But, cold and discontented and distracted by the sight of Anansi watching them silently from beside a heap of wood on the shore, she reached across unthinkingly and yanked the plate up in obedience to Grania's order. The little boat lurched forward, hit something harder than mud and stopped with a scraping noise. A gust caught the sail, and swivelled the boat round. Grania felt the tiller lifting under her hand, and realized that the rudder was aground on shingle.

'Uh,' she said. 'Sorry. I could get out and push us off.' She took her hand off the tiller for a moment and leaned back. As the boat rocked towards the stern, the rudder lifted right off the pintles which held it in place and slid away backwards with a faint splash. Grania lunged after it. Lazily, inexorably, the whole S-shaped assembly of rudder and tiller had turned on its side and was floating away downstream on the shallow running tide.

Marta looked at it in dismay, and after a moment said, 'On Uncle Harry's Whitecap, there's a little spring thing you push down when you put the rudder on. It stops that happening. Harry showed us.'

'It broke,' said Grania crossly. '*Mark* broke it.' Her frown cleared for a moment. 'Mark and Douai can give us a tow back! Or take us in their boat!'

Marta was looking at the shore again. Tentatively, the dark figure by the woodpile waved.

'Anansi could take us back,' she said thankfully. 'I'll go and ask her, when the ground's got drier. The tide's still going down, isn't it?'

The inner end of shingle spit on which the dinghy had grounded was almost uncovered now; it seemed to Marta an easy highway by which to gain the shore.

Grania, however, was looking upstream. 'Oh, here they come,' she said, relief mingling with resignation. In a minute, the Laser was speeding gracefully down the deep channel outside them.

'We called you to come back!' shouted Mark. 'Now look what you've done!'

'We lost the rudder,' said Grania.

'We tore Vince's spinnaker,' said Mark.

'We're hard aground and can't get off anyway,' said Grania.

'It's starting to rain,' said Mark.

Douai and Marta, each from their own viewpoint, tired rapidly of this competitive exchange.

Douai said, 'I suppose you want a lift back. Don't know if we can fit four, beating.'

'No, thank you,' said Marta. 'We've got the Whitecap. We'll go in that. I'm just going to tell Anansi.' She stood up in the boat, which wobbled. The water was visibly falling around its blue sides. 'Just getting the sail down first,' she said, and did so. Seeing Anansi had reminded her of Harry, and sailing lessons, and the comfortable feeling you got when you had tidied up a boat. She tied the sail neatly to the boom as he had taught her, and felt better. The rain was now making an impression, and she shuddered again.

'I'm going. You coming?'

Mark and Douai were jilling up and down in the narrow channel.

'Put a long rope on,' shouted Mark. 'When you're gone we can try and pull the Mirror off the mud.'

This made such good sense that Grania began fumbling for a long rope to tie to the regular short painter. Marta stepped gingerly out of the boat and dipped her foot into the water until she felt the firm but slimy surface of the shingle. She was glad her mother had bought her proper neoprene sailing bootees; the foot felt warm, although her bare leg above it registered that the water was chilly. When the second foot followed the first, Marta, still holding on to the mast, found that the shingle easily bore her weight. She let go of the mast and looked at the shore, some twenty feet away, and Anansi, who was still watching. She waded a few feet, and the water grew shallower.

Cupping her hands, Marta shouted, 'I'm coming!'

'No!' The cry was shrill, and made the wading child pause. 'Don't come that way!'

When she was not monosyllabic or silent, Anansi often spoke fast, in what was almost a patois: staccato, clipped

South London. Distorted by the need to shout, her words did not reach Marta's understanding in time.

'I can see from here – look, the stone bit stops – I fink it's all sloppy, like when the dog – don't walk on it!'

Marta stepped forward on the uncovering shingle. Ahead of her lay a long muddy beach not unlike the one all Blythney children were used to dragging their little boats over when the slipway was taken up by impatient adults. So she would get muddy legs; so what?

'I'm coming,' she shouted again. Behind her Grania was preoccupied by an attempt to throw the rope to Mark, who was hanging over the side of the Laser as Douai brought it past her down the channel.

'Owow ow!' she shouted, as the rope missed and flopped into the mud. 'Now I have to pull it in all *filthy* – why couldn't you get it?'

Marta took another step forward, felt the mud sucking at her boots and decided there was only one answer: to go as fast as possible. The shore was close. Anansi was there. She retrieved her foot, expecting it to be caked with mud but noticing with academic interest that the mud slid straight off, wetly, not balling under her feet at all like the sticky mud near the clubhouse.

Anansi, on the shore, saw the same thing, and yelled with new urgency, 'Don't! Get back to the boat!'

Marta took a big step forward, and sank.

Sheila finished her long swim, rubbed her wet hair down briskly with the towel, and left it to dry in its saltiness while she walked up the beach into the house and made herself a sandwich. The day, she observed, had clouded over. There might even be rain. Glancing at the kitchen clock, she saw that it was after one o'clock. Well, the juniors would be off the river by now, anyway. Pity if the rain spoiled Vince's tennis, though. She wondered whether Anansi and Marta would make a full day of it with Harry, or go back to the Markeens' house. She might walk up there and catch Alaia and see how they were getting on. There was no sign of Simon, for which she was grateful.

Sitting in the corner of the interview room at HM Prison, Willington, Officer Kevin Andrews looked at the three people at the table, whose conversation was all but inaudible to him. Not that he was much interested. He was an amateur photographer, though, in his blessed hours outside the prison, and what caught his attention was the extraordinary combination of good looks in the three people.

There was the old bloke, tall and straight like a soldier, with a face, thought Officer Andrews poetically, like something on a Roman coin. Then the old lady, all that white hair and wrinkles but still beautiful, like an old lady in a film, with those blue eyes. And Cowper – well, they all teased Cowper. Best looking nig— no, better not even to think that word, these days. Best looking bloke of any colour, even in a prison of fit young men. The bent ones all fancied him, not that there was any chance; but he had caught even straight cons, even screws, looking in amazed admiration at Cowper. The old governor, who fancied himself knowing about Africa, used to say he had classic Masai looks. Whatever a Masai was when it was at home. No wonder Cowper had got away with all his fiddles in the army. His face habitually wore an expression of beautiful, big-eyed, innocent melancholy, which was pretty enough for any picture. Today, although his back was three-quarters turned to the officer, a different face was visible in odd glimpses as he turned to and fro to look at the old couple each in turn. A radiant face, a joyful one, transfigured. It must, deduced Andrews laboriously, be good family news then. That made a change. Usually it was either the wife having run off, or a suicide. The officer yawned. Ten more minutes, they had, then he could take his break.

Chapter Twenty-two

'We need to ask you something,' said Marion, with a sideways glance at Harry. 'About the time when you were living at home with Tracey and Anansi.'

'Anansi,' said the man dreamily. 'My baby. I used to take her, right, for walks? She could walk damn good for a kid only jus' three years old. One day we walked right down to Greenwich. By the docks. She liked the ships. And the cranes. Then I bought her a ice-cream, an' she ate that so-o tidy. Like a princess, in her red ribbons.'

There had been a lot of this; it reassured Harry but tried Marion's patience a little. It was duty, above all, to which she had come to recall this man. Not sentiment. She had done enough prison visiting to mistrust sentiment in these circumstances. Emotional reunions were not enough; happy-ever-after seemed, in this case, less than likely. Nor did the sullen, complex, present-day Anansi sport red ribbons and a baby smile. Marion sighed.

'The child is lame,' she said baldly. 'An injury. She remembers a man kicking her. Her mother told her that you were responsible.'

The change in the atmosphere of the small room was sufficiently electric to make Officer Andrews suddenly stiffen. He thought the big man was going to rise from his seat. But Cowper contained himself after a moment with an icy dignity that impressed even Marion.

'I never have laid one finger on her,' he said. 'She was the only damn good thing that happened out of bein' married to that whore.'

'Not a finger, or a foot?' asked Harry. 'You never kicked her? We do have to ask, you know. She vaguely remembers a scene with a tall man kicking her, who was drunk. Are you a drinking man?'

'Some days,' said Cowper briefly. 'But when I drank, I didn't come home, did I? I drank an' stayed out because otherwise I would have hit *her*. Tracey. I'm tellin' you,' he leaned forward, as intensely as if he had not already told them this four or five times, 'that woman was one whore! Always shaggin' everything she saw. White men, black men, postmen.' He paused and looked at Harry, a frown creasing his smooth, beautiful brow. 'Did she say I kicked my kid?' he demanded. 'I'll kill her.'

'You will *not*,' said Marion with nursery sharpness. 'In fact, you will not get into any trouble any more. You have responsibilities. To see your daughter if she wishes, and if not, to put money towards her support, and above all to put her in contact with any relatives she has.'

'No, I won't kill Tracey,' said the big man affably. 'But I might find Win Brindley an' kill him.'

'Who is Win Brindley?'

'The guy, the last one, the big black bastard. The one that made me go to Travemünde camp an' say goodbye Tracey. There was a deal.'

'What deal?' Harry sat forward, wanting more than anything to believe what he thought he was hearing.

Cowper, tapping out every word with his big fingers on the table, said, 'Deal, OK? She says: this one is serious. She says: if I stay around and give her any grief over Win, she'll stop me ever seeing my daughter, an' tell lies to social services to make damn sure. So I go to Travemünde. Deal, see?'

Their faces were blank.

He tapped the table again and said, 'Deal: I let her play around with Win Brindley, marry him if she want. Keep out of the way, like. Two, three years I save enough money – pay, Germany allowances, rackets. Then I come home, get a business maybe, then Trace, she lets Anansi come an' live with her dad.' He leaned back, beaming, forgetting for a moment that the deal had never worked. Seeing disbelief on Marion's face, he added with a bitter twist of his fine mouth, 'She dun't like Anansi much anyway. She kep' saying she wanted a little girl with proper hair, blonde like, to dress. She said Anansi got wog hair.'

Harry moved as if to speak, but Marion tapped his hand warningly. She knew the value of silences. Into the silence, delicately, she poured just enough incredulity to make Cowper go on.

'No, mam. 'S all true. You think I shouldn't leave her with Trace, right? If Trace don't like her? But it was OK leavin' her, see. Because Tracey's mum, Beverley, she knew the deal. She's a good, good woman. She mostly looked after Anansi. She said when I come back, she might help me with the shop. Work there, look after my girl with me.'

'Without the child's mother?' said Marion.

'Beverley says there's all kinds of shapes of families,

an' you get what you get. Only she broke that deal, my lovely whore wife. When I come home on leave, everybody's moved. I never see them again. Social won't tell me nothing. So I stay in the Corps, don't I, and do the rackets. An' that's how I lost my daughter.'

The tale told, he exhaled deeply and leaned back. As he regarded his still doubtful audience, an idea struck him.

'You ask Beverley. Tracey's mum. She'll tell you, straight up. She prob'ly knows which bastard kicked my baby, an' all. Win Brindley. Yeah.'

On this reflection, he looked morose and threatening again for a moment; it was a look so familiar from his daughter's face that Harry almost laughed. Then Cowper repeated, 'Yeah, that's it. Ask Bev.'

'Oh, my dear,' said Marion sorrowfully. 'Anansi's grand-mother died years ago. A road accident. I'm so sorry.'

The man had not shed one tear when they had brought him, cautiously and tentatively, the news that his daughter was found. He had only moved in an instant from wary prison politeness to blazing joy and a torrent of reminiscence and optimism. But at this bald information he bent his head into his hands and began to weep.

Behind him, on the high skylight, raindrops began to patter. After a moment Marion stretched out a hand to hold Cowper's muscular forearm.

Raising his eyes to her he said simply, 'She was a good woman.'

Marion's own eyes filled with tears. It was Harry who spoke.

'I know she was,' he said. 'I can tell, from Anansi.'

When Alaia looked out of the window and saw Sheila's little car on her sweeping drive, she smiled, threw down

the curtain she was about to hang, and went to the front
door to greet her. On the way she called to the patient
Karen in the kitchen. 'Sheila's here. She'll probably have
Marta with her, so we'll all have that soup.'

A clang and a muffled assent met this, and Alaia skipped
to the door.

'Hi-yee!' she said, then, seeing Sheila alone, 'Oh, Mart
still down at the Hamptons', is she? They must be getting
on, those two. Last time they were in a boat together they
couldn't wait to see the last of each other. Remember?
Last summer? You gave Marta a lift up here because she
couldn't bear to be at the Hamptons' for another hour
waiting for me.'

With a faint prick of guilt, she remembered that day,
and the fact that then there had been no question of Sheila
getting out of the car on the immaculate Hall drive, let
alone being asked in for soup. Sheila, however, frowned
with puzzlement.

'I thought Marta was on the river with Harry and
Anansi.'

'No-wooh! They had a quarrel, and I reckoned a
cooling-off day would be a good thing. Marta was doing
the morning practise session with Grania Hampton.'

'Oh dear,' said Sheila, vaguely. 'Do you think Harry
took Anansi on his own? We had a talk about not doing
that because of the background and the social services and
all that.'

'Maybe she stayed ashore. Yah, must have. I thought I
saw Harry and Marion go out in the car earlier anyway.'

'I ought to go home and get Anansi some lunch then,'
said Sheila regretfully. 'But it's quite late, and there wasn't
any sign of her when I left.'

'Oh, you know these children. She'll be eating chips

somewhere,' said Alaia. 'Soup?' She smiled crookedly at Sheila, who returned the grin.

'Oh, twist my arm. Soup. God, look. It's raining.'

When Marta took her big stride onto the quaking mud, her front foot sank so far and so suddenly that she fell forward, throwing out an arm to protect herself from the surface which her eyes still told her was hard ground. The arm sank in also, so that her face was almost in the ooze; kicking with the other foot, she felt that it too, was sinking. Neither foot met anything hard; it was as if she were swimming, except that she could hardly move her legs beneath her.

Anansi was shouting again. 'Spread your arms! Like wings! Keep still!'

At the familiar voice, Marta looked up and saw Anansi, arms outstretched like an angel in a Nativity play. She understood through her panic, and copied the action. Trembling, cold, paralyzed, she realized that she was no longer sinking. Yet there was nothing under her feet. She swivelled her eyes downward, not liking to move her chin down into the horrible ooze; she saw that the mud was black where she had stirred it up, but glimmering brown on the surface, like some evil animal. Around her neck and chin little rivulets of water ran, and bubbles popped into little black sucking holes as the mud settled.

There was someone screaming. Grania. Marta, her eyes on Anansi and the shore, could not turn to see her. Anansi, remembering the fish-box top and its role in the dog rescue, thought for a moment then shouted, 'Grania! Get on the hard bit and push the centreboard out to her. You could pull her up.'

Grania, frozen with fear, could not make herself step

from the boat, even onto the hard shingle patch. Instead she took the wooden board, leaned over, and pushed it in the direction of Marta's visible head and arms. It skidded forward, missed by some distance, and lay useless on the surface. A gull landed on it, slithered, and squawked away.

In the Laser, the boys zagged to and fro in the squally rain. Mark lunged over the side as they came close to the bank where the Mirror was stranded, and managed to pick up the rope which Grania had dropped. The wind was blowing straight across the river now, sending gouts of rain splattering into their faces when they turned into it. But it meant that he could hang on to the rope from the stranded boat, and use it as an anchor.

When the Laser had steadied, Mark shouted, 'Can you get her?'

Grania began to cry, loudly and extravagantly. Among the weeping was the word 'No!' and the word 'Help!' Anansi, on the shore, seemed to have turned away and was doing something with the woodpile.

'It's her fault!' wept Grania, pointing. 'She told Marta to come over the mud!'

Douai never really understood what happened within him at that moment, but to the especial amazement of Mark, who had suffered his ranting all the way down the river, he shouted fiercely, 'No she didn't! That's a lie! Anansi told her *not* to!'

He had seen the moment when Marta fell and Anansi made angel wings with her arms. The fright had been extreme; of all the Blythney children Douai, the eldest, was the only one who had understood straightaway what could have happened in that moment. Marta could have disappeared entirely, under the brown surface. Anansi had seen it too, and she had prevented it. He understood that, and the fact set up some invisible cord between them. It did not, never could, resolve every reason that he hated her. But it made him give her justice in that moment.

Grania was sobbing hysterically now. 'Someone come! We're going to die!' Her little boat, hard aground, was a firm enough anchor for the boys' dinghy to stay steady.

Mark glanced at Douai and said, 'D'you think I ought to go and shut her up?' It was boy language, the only translation he could find for the process of comforting his sister.

'Yeah,' said Douai. He was even paler than usual, more pinched, his lips stiff. The last thing he wanted was for Grania to run into the mud in some kind of illogical female panic. 'Good idea. Can you get onto the hard bit?'

'Mm,' said Mark, and pulled the Laser in carefully until its bow grated on shingle. He stepped cautiously out into the knee-deep water and waded up to the Mirror dinghy. Then he climbed in and, self-conscious but determined, put an arm round his sister.

When he dropped the rope, Douai's boat drifted back and caught the wind. He hauled the mainsail and, letting the jib flap with a fusillade of noise, coasted along the island until he was near enough to shout to Anansi. She was still by the woodpile, dragging a long plank out and glancing up every few seconds at the immobile Marta, arms still outspread.

'I'm coming ashore,' he shouted. 'I'll help.'

Anansi straightened. 'No!' she said sharply. Then, seeing his face, 'Please, no. Sail back. Get help. Grown-ups. Quick. I got something to hold her up, for a bit.'

'I could stay,' shouted Douai. '*You* could sail for help.

In your boat. You're nearly as quick.' Even in the crisis, it cost him something to say it.

'No,' said Anansi. 'You're better. Faster.' That, too, cost something.

Douai swivelled his boat; the river channel now was so shallow that his board hit the mud and he had to bounce the boat off.

'I'm going,' he said. 'I'll get someone.'

'A grown-up,' said Anansi, 'would be tall enough to stand in that mud, Harry says. A tall grown-up.' Then, turning back to her woodpile, she added, 'Good luck.'

Douai barely heard. With all his concentration, and the blessed new shift of the wind he was flying upstream, both sail lines in one hand and sitting far out on the side of his boat. As Mark watched, arm round his trembling sister, he thought for a terrible moment that a gust was going to topple the Laser, but Douai threw himself backward, hiking out with all his strength, legs straight, and the boat came back level, picked up speed and began to plane. Mark returned his attention to Grania.

'It'll be OK,' he said gruffly. 'Look, I want to go and help Marta now.'

But Grania sobbed, and clung, with the rain running down her tearful face, and said, 'Don't leave me. I'll die, I'll fall in the mud.'

Mark tried to prise her fingers from his jumper, failed, and looked helplessly at Anansi who had dragged a wide plank from the heap and was trying to manoeuvre it down the bank to the mud beach. Her foot was obviously giving her trouble on the rough ground. At last, she knelt and shuffled on her knees, pulling the wood behind her. He admired her doggedness, and wondered fleetingly whether to slap his sister, as they had told him at school you had to slap hysterics. Nerve failed him there. She might, he told himself, throw herself in the mud too. Or push him in. So he held on, and watched.

When Sheila and Alaia had finished their soup and their gossip, Alaia glanced at the clock and said, 'I'll ring the Hamptons. See if Mart needs collecting.' She left the kitchen, and Sheila sat for a moment enjoying the golden oak tranquillity of the room.

Moments later Alaia was back, running her hands through her dark hair distractedly. 'They're not *back*!' she said. 'It's half past *two*!'

Sheila gaped. 'Is the boat back?'

'Poppy's just been down. It's not in its place. Or anywhere. She thought they might have gone off upriver, or down, I suppose. The boys aren't back yet either. No sign of your Laser.'

'Shit!' said Sheila with unladylike alarm. She, of all people, knew the times of safety-boat cover. That cover had expired two hours ago. The absence of the children from lunch was not a matter of concern; the circle of Blythney summer children used one another's houses almost indiscriminately as refuelling stations. The absence of the boats, however, worried her very much.

'What's Poppy doing?' she asked.

'Well, she reckons they've gone upriver. Pulled up on a beach, and maybe upended the boats to hide from the rain. She's going to send Andy up in the launch. Bloody children!'

Despite this attempt at robustness, it was obvious that Alaia was seriously frightened. Marta was nine, Grania not yet eleven, and new to command of her little blue boat.

Sheila attempted comfort. 'It hasn't been specially windy,

you know, today. They're not very likely to have capsized.'

A slap of rain and a gust of wind rattled the pane, and
the two women glanced towards it.

Alaia said, 'Shall we get down to the club?'

Sheila nodded. 'And Jonny?'

'Pick him up from the gallery. He can get the other
launch out. Try downstream.'

Anansi lay on her stomach, on the plank, and began to
wriggle forwards. It sank a little into the mud, but not far;
it was a good wide one, and she found that by pushing
with the sides of her feet, and paddling her arms in the
ooze, she could inch along it quite well. The first attempt
at plank rescue had failed; it depended on Marta clinging
to the plank and wriggling herself onto it, as Harry's lurcher
had done. But there seemed to be something wrong with
Marta; she was too terrified to move her outspread arms,
perhaps. So Anansi, after a moment's thought, took the
precaution of weighting the inner end of the plank, which
rested on hard, packed mud, with two concrete blocks to
keep it on the safe bit. Then she began to wriggle out
along it.

It took probably five minutes to reach the end of the
plank; to Anansi, it would always seem like a lifetime.
Long afterwards, when people asked her what was the
worst bit, she said, 'Going out. It was so frigging slow.'

'Not the wait? Holding Marta?' they would ask. 'You
must have been worried then, how long you could hang
on?'

'Nah,' she would say, and explain no further. 'That
was fine.'

The moment she touched Marta's hand, she knew

it would be fine. An unacknowledged part of her had begun to believe, from the frozen stillness of the child, that Marta was, mysteriously, already dead. The hand, however, clutched hers with convulsive gratitude, and she returned the pressure. The movement made Marta sink, slightly, and the shocked frozen look returned to her eyes. Anansi breathed in deeply, attempted a smile and said, 'I'm firm. I'm on a strong plank, see? It can't sink.'

Marta made an inarticulate, terrified sound.

'Nah, it can't. Remember the dog on the board, that Harry pulled in? Right. I'm going to put my arms under your arms. I'm on the plank, so I can't sink, right? Then you can't sink if I hold you, right? Then we stay here and they come and get us.'

In the stranded Mirror, Mark and the trembling Grania saw Anansi – with excruciating slowness and some heart-stopping lurches – manoeuvre her arms under Marta's armpits, and hold her encircled at the end of the plank. When the horrible squishing, mud-bubbling movements of this operation ended, Mark called to her, 'Are you going to try and pull her in to the shore?'

'No. Too sticky.'

'Shall I come and try and pull you onto the shingle? With the mast or something?' Mark's mind had been working, his eye running over the parts of the Mirror with panicky determination.

Anansi, holding Marta, considered this option. Marta was closest to Mark's shingle bank. Marta would panic. This she knew, with a sinking certainty. No rescue plan involving action from Marta could be considered. Strangely, this thought brought with it neither resentment nor contempt, but an all-encircling warmth of pure love. Marta depended on her, now. For her life.

The fact felt like a gift. Lying on the plank on the quivering expanse of slimy rottenness, with her arms encircling the younger child, Anansi felt a surge of gratitude. Harry said he had always wanted a chance to save someone, to pay back for the river sentry he shouldn't have shot. Now she had this gift. All hers, all alone, here by the merciless brown river. She smiled.

'OK, Marta?'

'OK,' came a thin, disembodied voice. 'Will they come soon?'

'Yeah. Oh yeah. Hang on.'

Chapter Twenty-three

The late lunchtime stragglers in the Yacht Club bar were
thrown into a buzz of sensational apprehension by the
arrival, out of breath and stony-faced, of Andy Hampton.

'I need the boat,' he snapped to the junior of the two
boatmen. 'The fast one. Kids gone missing.'

'Jake's got it,' said the boy, bewildered. 'Gone to
look for Mr Glanville's Whitecap. It was on the beach,
and someone's taken it, or put it adrift. He went ten
minutes ago.'

'Downstream or up?' snapped Andy.

'Well, I said it would have gone down, with the tide,
like. If some kid just pushed it off. But he said someone
saw it sailing round up past Coker's.'

'I'll take the little boat then,' said Andy. 'Downstream.'

'No petrol,' said the boy apologetically. 'Jake was taking
the van up to get some.'

'Oh, for God's sake!' Andy exploded. He ran back to
his car for a can, but on his return found that things
were worse even than anticipated. Before setting off in
search of the missing dinghy, the methodical Jake had

265

been stripping down the four-stroke engine on the smaller club launch in readiness for the weekend's racing. It was, Andy remembered bitterly, he himself who had complained about its erratic behaviour during Sunday's points racing. By the time they had reassembled and started it, Poppy had got back and was loudly expressing horror that they had not even set out. Alaia and Sheila appeared just as they cast off, having failed to find Jonny Markeen. Altogether, the scene was a disquieting combination of panic, resolution, and scalding anxiety. More sanguine spirits in the bar muttered that the kids must just be aground somewhere, as they themselves had been a hundred times in their own more carefree childhoods. Others, however, fully shared the parental unease. Grania in particular was regarded as a candidate for trouble. 'Featherbrained kid,' said Eric Rattray under his breath.

Alaia, who looked ill and, Andy critically thought, slightly mad, came to the waterside and said, 'Can I come with you?'

Poppy and Andy, long married and like-minded, glanced at one another with pure understanding.

Gently enough, Poppy said, 'There's not much room. I think it needs someone—' She did not know how to phrase it. Someone river-wise, someone seamanlike, someone level-headed, someone who would not be a liability. She had meant, on seeing Andy there, to go herself; but fear for her two children had burnt away all Poppy's self-importance and focused her practical mind, savingly, on the nearest need. Which was to stop Alaia going and getting hysterical in the launch. So she said, 'I think it needs a man. In case they're aground and need hauling off.'

To say this pained Poppy very much; she knew herself

to be the equal of most men on the river when it came to handling boats. However, the ruse worked. Alaia's eye fell on the nearest man, who was Simon Harrison. He had not been in the club for a few days, but today the coast was clear. Alan Tranmere was away at a conference in Nottingham, or so Penny had told him in her scalding farewell speech.

'Simon, will you come?' said Andy. The two had not spoken since the day of the fated picnic at Miserley beach.

Simon, who had been hovering indecisively, wondering whether to rig his own dinghy and sail in search of Douai, gratefully replied, 'Of course. You OK, Sheila?'

Sheila nodded, and took Alaia's arm. 'Come on,' she said. 'Come into the dry. As soon as the chaps are gone, they'll all come sailing round the corner from the opposite direction and everyone will have got wet and cross for nothing. You know how it is.'

Alaia held tightly to Sheila's arm as slowly they climbed the steps to the clubhouse.

'We can sit by the window,' she said querulously. 'We'll see, won't we? When they come?'

It seemed to Anansi, watching raindrops plipping mindlessly into the muddy surface around them, as if she and Marta were out in space, or a parallel universe. It was just the two of them, alone, their world reduced to one intense pinpoint of purpose. Life now was very simple: their only job was to keep their heads above the mud. Only out here in space it was hard. Her own body was changing, growing heavier by some strange interplanetary law of mass, and she felt an illusion that she was sinking.

The pins and needles in her arms had been at first

excruciating, and then vanished to be replaced by a cold numbness. She was interested and relieved to find that numb arms, arms she could no longer feel, still retained the shape and strength to hold Marta. She had locked her fingers together in the way a boy at school had once told her was stronger than anything; he had hurt her, in demonstrating, but now she was peacefully grateful to him.

The sense of sinking stopped. Early on, her head and torso, weighed down by Marta's increasingly limp weight, had indeed begun to sink; she remedied this by locking her feet behind her, twisting the insteps under the plank she lay on. Again with peaceful academic interest, she noted that the twisted foot was easier to keep locked on. Maybe, she thought, that was why it was twisted. Clever. Maybe the fuckilla man knew that when he did it. Her dad. Maybe he knew that one day she would need to lock it on a plank.

A great tremor went through her, and she jerked violently, so that Marta's eyes, an inch from hers, flew open in alarm. She had nearly fallen asleep. What a fucking stupid place to sleep! Mustn't. Could roll off the plank. Then what? She must not drift into dreams. Think of something. Harry. Think of Harry. War stories. Coming up the dark river, blowing up ships, losing his friends, killing the sentry. Wanting to save someone, to make up. That was her job now. Saving. One life. Then Harry could stop being upset about the sentry. It would make up for what she did, nicking his boat that he worked on every day, without permission, just to show off.

Well, here she was on the dark river – and with grey clouds gathered thick overhead, it was dark now. Bleak, too; a long way from the gay, fluttering, coloured river in the sunshine by the clubhouse. And there was no war, but you could still die. So she must stop Marta from that. And herself. Dimly, she now knew that she could not get back along the plank alone, not with the locked foot. But if they would just come, if Douai got them . . .

When the darkness threatened to close round her, she thought of Harry, doing it for Harry, paying it off for his sentry. A life for a life.

She did not sleep again, but there was a contraction of the circle that held her and Marta. A circle, ever smaller, of rain, and mud, and holding on, and keeping feet and legs taut round the plank. She did not hear Mark calling from the Mirror, where he had wrapped the sail round himself and the shivering Grania. She never heard his thin call: 'Anansi! Marta! Are you OK? I think . . . I think the tide's turned.'

'Tide's turned,' said Andy angrily. 'It's going to be bloody slow in this cow of a boat. I've told Alex to tell Jake to come down as fast as he can in the RIB if he hasn't spotted them upstream.'

Simon, standing in the bow of the open launch, was peering through the rain and mist, scanning first one bank and then the other.

'No sign yet,' he said. 'It's a big tide, isn't it? They could easily have gone on the mud.'

'We have to hope that,' said Andy, and his voice made Simon turn and stare at him.

'You really think something bad . . .' He could not control the tremor in his voice.

'I don't think anything,' said Andy toughly. 'But I've been an auxiliary coastguard long enough . . .'

'Douai,' said Simon, exhaling tremulously. 'I've hardly had anything to do with him. I am a rotten father.'

Libby Purves

Andy looked at him coldly. He did not approve of this kind of thing, from men. It was the reason you didn't bring mothers on rescue trips, not even stalwart Poppy. Nor did he approve, he suddenly remembered, of chaps having it off with other people's wives in the Martello tower.

'Time to think about all that when we've got them,' he said coldly. But unbidden there replayed in his mind the scene at breakfast when his effervescent gold-haired little Grania had been bitching about some sweater her cousin had borrowed. He had told her to stop whining and grow up.

Perhaps she wouldn't grow up. Perhaps it would be the last, ironic thing he ever said to her. He sniffed, and rubbed his face furiously on his sleeve. Luckily, Simon Harrison was looking ahead again and did not see his weakness.

In the bar, Susannah Rattray bearded Sheila. She had been in the Ladies', cumbersome with late pregnancy, and had not heard about the missing children. Settling on the bench beside the two taut-faced mothers, massaging her now vast belly, she said, 'Isn't your little London child doing well? I saw her sailing the Whitecap all on her own, very neatly.'

'This morning?' snapped Sheila. 'When? Think!'

Susannah blinked, hurt by the abruptness of her friend's response.

'Mm – no, I wasn't down till one-ish. It was on the beach, and she took it out. Looked like a private race, with one of the Mirrors.'

Sheila and Alaia exchanged horrified glances. After a moment, Sheila said, 'Oh, great. So we've lost her, as well. Where the hell is Uncle Harry in all this?'

'I met Marion,' offered Susannah. 'In the car park. She

said they were off somewhere for the afternoon. Shopping, perhaps?'

Leaving prisons, Harry thought, must always make the visitor's heart rise. They had been silent as they left, each wrapped in their own thoughts, but as they drove away from the gatehouse he ventured, 'What do you make of all that, then?'

Marion frowned, fiddling with the strap of her handbag. Harry had taken over the wheel, by tacit consent; they both knew that when she was thinking hard her driving suffered.

'I believed him,' she said finally. 'I don't believe everything I get told by prisoners, you know.'

'Mm,' said Harry, slowing for a bend in the deep leafy lane. 'That's the funny bit. We both believe it, and we think we shouldn't. I've been trying to pick holes . . .'

'Why couldn't he find her when he came home from Germany? Neighbours, social services, police?'

'People flit, don't they? And if the social services had been told something by the mother, they'd believe it. Big black chap, soldier, liked his drink. They probably fobbed him off. And I shouldn't think he'd go to the police.'

'But losing touch with a *child*! And one he loved! For what – eight years?'

Harry glanced at her. 'Mightn't seem long, do you think? Young chaps, eight years go by, they're busy, plenty of work, and his food rackets on top of that . . . he's not much over thirty, is he, even now?'

'Aren't we *old*!' said Marion suddenly. It was an uncharacteristic observation, but her husband understood perfectly. They drove on in silence for a while, then Harry suggested a stop for a cup of tea. That way, they could remain alone for longer in their strange bubble of astonishing knowledge, and work out how to use it.

Douai had never sailed so fast. Unaccustomed to the helm of the light racing boat, he found that without the weight of a crew it jittered and yawed around at the slightest tremor of his hand. He sat well forward, using the full stretch of the tiller extension. His arm ached, and the panicky trembling of his legs at first made it difficult to hike out. Early on, he very nearly capsized, and when he levelled the boat his heart was hammering and there were tears in his eyes. After that he worked the wind better; it was, he calculated, going to give him free fast sailing all the way to Martello. Visibility was getting worse in the rain, and he had to crane to see the line of the riverbanks and stay clear of them. But the contrary tide had gone; it was with him now.

He was glad of this for a few minutes, until the thought occurred to him that this also meant that around the rudderless Mirror and the trapped Marta, the same water would very soon be rising. Fast.

He wondered about Anansi's plank. He had seen the sense of what she was doing straightaway. It was a good wide plank, and quite light and thin, designed for the new pontoon. She might get Marta up onto it. They might be on the island by now, all of them, making a shelter from the rain out of the Whitecap sail. He tried to imagine this: a brown, comforting tent, and the four of them giggling and waiting for rescue. In his heart he thought it unlikely. He was glad, then, of the need for absolute concentration on the bucking boat beneath him.

Then he saw it: an open motorboat, white with a blue rim, looming towards him in the channel. He let go of the sheet and let the boat slow down, the boom flapping angrily in the wind.

'Hoy! Help!'

The boat nosed closer. In the bow a man stood. His father.

'Dad!' he cried, his voice half breaking. 'Down at Heron Island! Marta's in the deep mud!'

Andy Hampton offered up a brief exhalation of thanks that he had not brought Marta's mother.

'Can you show us where?' he shouted.

'Yes. Shall I come on board?' The vision of himself relaxed, on a seat in the motorboat, under the care of adults, was almost irresistible.

His father stretched out a hand to take a line from him, but then Douai said, 'No, it'll slow you down. I'll have a good reach back. Follow me!'

Before his father could object, he had gybed his boat round and was speeding back downriver, making as good progress against the flood tide as the motorboat could. Through the rain, against the tide, the men followed. Simon, in the bow with raindrops coursing down his face, allowed himself some tears. Against all odds, against all that he deserved, he had been given another chance. Guiltily, he suppressed his happiness. Other people's children were still out there.

Anansi was nearly asleep again but had found a way of pushing sleep aside before the moment of jerking panic could come. She talked to Harry, sometimes aloud. *Thanks for the sailing. Thanks for the stories. I'm hanging on, see? Like a soldier. Like a Viking.* Then she spoke to the girl in her arms. 'Come on, Marta, be that Princess you wanna be. Hold on. Stay awake. Like the Princess, OK?'

She did not like the cold, flat feeling of Marta in her arms. A fishlike feeling, horridly appropriate in the cold mud. But when by the feeling she knew that Marta had lost consciousness, the hot spinning focus of determination flared brighter in her own head. *It's me now. You watch, Harry. Watch me win!*

Douai turned his head. The engine in the motorboat astern of him had coughed, once. It coughed again, and he saw that the boat was no longer keeping pace with his sails. Gybing the boat round, he coasted up to it, sails flapping, and heard the engine finally fade. The bow was blown off course, so that the helpless launch lay broadside to the slowly flooding tide.

'Bitch!' Andy Hampton was saying as he wrested the cover off the engine. Simon knelt on the thwart and spoke urgently to Douai as he hung alongside, dismayed.

'Can you get on down there and tell them to hang on? Do you think they can hang on? The tide's still quite slow.'

Douai, the picture of Marta's awful descent still burning in his brain, said harshly, 'No. They can't. Come with me. It needs someone *tall*. Uncle Harry says the mud's not too deep for a tall grown-up down there. None of us is *tall* enough.'

Simon was weedy and stoop-shouldered, Andy Hampton athletic; but Simon stood six inches taller. Also, there was no chance of his fixing the engine. He stood up now, and awkwardly clambered across to the dinghy.

'OK, Andy?' he said over his shoulder. 'He's right. I have to go. Good luck with the engine.'

Andy looked up from his problem to watch them go. It was one of the bleakest moments of his happy, busy life so

274

far. He had loved the River Blyne and Grend all his life, and today he hated it like the most malevolent of enemies.

Douai shivered at the helm, torn between relief at having his father to deliver to the rescue site, and frustration that the boat went slower with an adult in it. The few minutes' journey to the bend above Heron Island seemed to take an age. Simon did not speak, just craned forward. His own son was safe now, and with him; the strength which had come over him at that knowledge seemed to ebb away now that he was setting out without tools or confidence or expertise to the rescue of these other children.

'There's the Mirror,' said Douai at last, with a squeak of exhaustion in his voice. It was still aground, but the water was lapping round it now at almost the depth at which it had first been stranded. 'There's a rope trailing off it.'

Simon peered ahead, wiping rain from his eyelashes. There were children in the boat – three? Four, even? No. Only two, huddled under the red sail. Two fair heads, the Hampton children. For a moment he could see nothing else, and felt his stomach plunge with fright at the sight of the smooth expanse of mud which might have swallowed and told no tale. Then, as they came closer, he saw the plank. Its far end, on the beach, was held by two concrete blocks which presumably had been rolled onto it for this purpose. The other end was invisible, shading into the mud. But there was a lumpy, small shape prone on the end of it, and he suddenly saw that it had two heads.

Douai understood faster. 'She's holding her up!' he said. 'Anansi's got Marta. Look!'

'What a—' Simon could not go on. He took hold of his emotions and stifled them violently. 'Get me off. Onto the shingle bar, near the Mirror,' he ordered.

Douai drove the bow of his dinghy hard aground not

far from the Mirror, and Simon jumped over the bow, up to his thighs in the swirling water, and held the boat a moment.

'Rope,' said Douai. His father saw it trailing from the Mirror's stern, understood, and passed it to Douai. Then Douai jumped out, fixed the rope to his mast, and hauled the Laser up hard onto the bank.

'Got about ten minutes, at least,' said Simon, 'before the tide floats the Mirror off. Let's go.'

He pulled the Laser's alloy spinnaker pole off its clips, and waded cautiously across the shingle, using the pole to test the depth. When he got to the mud, a few feet from the girls, he drove the pole in as hard and deep as he could. It was a long pole, taller than himself; he felt the soft resistance of mud going on and on, until it struck bottom convincingly with a good two feet sticking out. He threw his weight onto it; it did not move further. As he was preparing to step in, he glanced back at a sound and saw a figure wading towards him: little Mark Hampton. On his arm was a coil of thin rope, the mainsheet from the Mirror dinghy. He handed one end to Simon.

'Tie it on you,' he said. Simon nodded in silent approval, and Mark went back to the dinghy, where his sister was now crouched unmoving under the sail. He tied the other end of the rope round its mast. Then Simon stepped in and sank, steadying himself on the post; when the mud was high up his chest, he stopped sinking. Leaning forward into the stuff, he half walked, half swam against its wet resistance towards the spot where Anansi lay. The difficulty of the situation suddenly almost overwhelmed him. To Douai, on the hard shingle behind him, he said, 'We have to pull them in. The tide's coming up.'

'With the rope?' said Douai.

Anansi's lips, Simon saw, were blue and her eyes closed. But she opened both, and croaked an order:

'Put the rope on Marta.'

It was hard to see what was limbs, what rope, and what mud, but Simon made a rough noose, with a slip, and as an afterthought tied a stopper-knot to prevent the noose tightening too much round a fragile chest or neck. He passed it towards Anansi, then saw that she could not move her arms easily and waded another step, with difficulty. He knew that this was not the way to effect a mud rescue; that he might have done better pulling the Mirror dinghy across and using it as a platform, but it was too late. The posture and look of the children told him that although they had held on till now, defying fright and cold and shock, they did not have much longer. The sight of rescuers, he guessed, could push casualties either way. Some drew superhuman new strength from it, others gave up all attempt to help themselves. With great difficulty, he put the rope over Marta's stiff arms and gently tightened it. To Douai, on the shingle, he just said, 'Pull.'

Simon stood next to Marta, supporting her floppy head in case it was dragged under, and tried to ease her upward and out of the mud's grip. Then he began to wade. Several times he almost lost his footing; once, pushing the child up, he slipped so that his own head went under and his mouth and nose were filled with ooze. At last he felt the ground rising, and himself rose caked and shivering from the mud, to fall on his knees with the child draped in his arms. Douai let the rope go slack, and father and son looked at one another over the small slumped body.

'I'm going to put her in the Mirror. You get her warm.

Do anything. Make Grania and Mark cuddle up to her, and wrap them in all the sails you can find. Pull them off the Laser. Anything. Doesn't matter about floating off and getting home; the tide'll take us up, and Andy will get the bloody boat going. *Just get her warm.*' The cold feeling of Marta's body was terrifying him, and his voice cracked and ran up the scale.

When she was lying in the dinghy, he eased the rope off her and put it round his arm before heading back for the plank where Anansi still lay, her head now slumped forward on her numb arm. She seemed to be unconscious. He hoped she had an airway open.

'She'll be a bit heavier,' he warned Douai. 'But she isn't stuck in so hard.'

He moved towards her, with the nightmare slowness imposed by the mud. But when he got to her, in his eagerness to have the business over with he overreached himself, stumbled forwards, felt his foot slip on the invisible hardness underneath the swamp, and crashed into the fragile balance of plank and child.

Anansi rolled sideways, with a strange sound from her throat, and began to sink under the ooze. Simon, blinded by a faceful of it, struck out in panic to find her. It seemed to Douai, transfixed with horror on the edge, as if some malevolent force was pulling them both down beneath the smooth, brown, gleaming surface.

He opened his mouth to scream, but before he could do so a new and blessed noise cut through the panic. It was not the low chugging of the small launch, where presumably Andy Hampton still struggled with sparking plugs and spanners, but the high, demonic whining roar of the fast RIB. Douai watched his father's head reappear, gasp, then deliberately sink itself into the mud again in frantic search. He leapt up and down on the shingle, not screaming but shouting purposefully:

'Here! Here! Here! Quick!'

Chapter Twenty-four

'With one bound, he was free,' said Eric Rattray, passing a pint of beer along the bar to the head boatman, Jake. 'Sounds nasty. Well done, anyway.'

'Not a problem, with three of us and the floorboards out the Whitecap,' said Jake modestly. 'Pity the kids didn't think of that.'

'Are they all right? All of them?' Hugo Cotten, surrounded by a posse of his red-headed children and their cousins, had arrived at the club rather too late to see the shaken, filthy little group arriving in the RIB and being driven away by ambulance to Ipswich. Those who had been there were full of excited description: of how Simon Harrison leaned on his son and seemed to be crying; of the whites of his eyes showing bright and crazy through the black mud plastering his face; of the frighteningly inert figure of Marta and the way her mother had run to her. The more thoughtful also mentioned the oddity of Jonny Markeen, dapper in his town suit, running not to his own daughter but to the child Anansi and carrying her up the pontoon in his arms.

'Well,' said Ellie de Benville to Julia Ward-Williams, 'it does sound, from what little Mark says, very much as if the child saved Marta's life.'

Mark was the source of more information than the taciturn Jake; Grania Hampton had been taken straight home but Mark, at his strenuous insistence, had been merely looked over for cuts and scratches and allowed to stay at the club with the rescuers. His tale, told to the admiring circle of Maurrie and Jane and Alison and Dondie and assorted parents, grew better with every retelling.

'He may be exaggerating,' said Julia. 'From what I heard, little Douai Harrison was the hero of the hour, sailing to the rescue.'

Mark, bristling, overheard this and rudely interrupted Julia (who was his godmother, after all. He had a responsibility to prevent her talking nonsense).

'*Douai* went to get help,' he said. 'And *I* stayed to stop Grania going apeshit, like girls do.' He paused, aware of the failure of logic revealed by the next thing he was going to say. '*But* it was *Anansi* who got the big plank, and crawled out, and it was so scary I couldn't watch. She held Marta up for hours.'

'The whole thing can't have taken more than an hour and a quarter,' said Eric, calculating. 'Just as well, with the tide coming up.' He shuddered. 'Doesn't bear thinking of. Lucky Jake came back with the RIB.'

'If you were in *mud*,' said Mark rudely, 'you'd know it felt like hours. Anyway, I think she ought to get a medal. She couldn't stand up at all when they got her out. Her bad foot just sort of folded up. Jake says she must have had to lock onto the plank with her feet, like when you're climbing ropes in the gym. But she kept Marta up.'

'That's right,' said Jake the boatman. 'Clung on like a monkey, she must have been.'

'Jolly good show,' said the Hon. Sec., passing the group with a whisky on his way to the untidy cubbyhole he ruled. 'But I think, young man, the question should be asked as to what you were all doing down there without telling anyone.'

'Oh, that stuff,' said Mark evasively. 'Doesn't matter now, does it? I bet this is going to be in all the papers.'

'What is?' said Harry Glanville, strolling into the bar. 'What's been going on?'

When they began to tell him, he sat down heavily, so pale that Eric Rattray, unasked, put a glass of brandy in front of him. When they had finished, Harry pushed his untouched drink away and walked out to the car park. Marion was beside the car, chatting to Alan Tranmere who was still in his city suit. Both looked up in surprise as he wrenched the car door open.

'I'm going to Ipswich hospital,' he said. 'The girls are there, and it's my fault.'

Sheila and Alaia sat together between the two beds. The inert sleeping figures lay rolled in heated blankets, faces still streaked with mud. It was quiet in the side ward, insulated from the outer world. Through the high window a patch of pink sky showed that the rain clouds had cleared in time for the sunset. The women spoke occasionally in low voices, Sheila reassuring, Alaia tearful.

'They don't think she's in danger,' said Sheila, looking at Marta's pale face and black brows inside the swaddling blankets. 'Not now. They say she's up to the right temperature.'

'Why doesn't she wake up?'

'She's exhausted. The Sister said.'

'Anansi wasn't so hypo-hypothermic, was she? They said? I wasn't listening properly, I was too wound up with Marta – oh, my baby! Look, she's nearly snoring. She always snored, even when she was tiny.'

'Anansi's going to be fine too. In herself, anyway. There's something about the foot they didn't like. Blood supply, or something. I have had,' said Sheila gloomily, 'to ring Social Services, and leave a message. I hope they leave us alone.'

But Alaia was immersed again in Marta, who had turned over a little way in her sleep.

'She looks normal now! Look, pink in her cheeks!'

Sheila clucked some reassurance, then turned back to Anansi, who lay as still as a tombstone carving, her fine face upturned to the white ceiling, her breathing easy.

'Where *did* she get those looks?' Sheila asked rhetorically. 'Janice Archenlaw says her mother is a pug-faced little thing with a sulky mouth.'

Alaia glanced across, jolted by the mention of this forgotten, unseen mother. For the first time she focused properly on Anansi's quiet face.

'That child saved Marta,' she said wonderingly. 'Douai says she was amazing. Sheila, we are not sending her back into council care. Ever. She belongs to all of us now.'

'If she wants to,' said Sheila, gently. 'She may have had enough of Blythney, perhaps.' She reached out, and stroked Anansi's forehead with the back of one finger.

'I shouldn't have left her. Not with the boat on the beach. Any child would take a dare. I should have known that. Messing about in prisons interfering in her past, while all the time she nearly died. God forgive me. God forgive me.'

Harry drove fast, swerving round the series of roundabouts that led to the town. Marion, who had jumped in next to him to the bafflement of Alan Tranmere in the car park, tried to soothe her husband.

'It was *not* your fault,' she said. 'It was one of those things. She could just as easily have got the boat from the mooring. Anyway, if she hadn't sailed off with the others, Marta Markeen might have drowned in that mud, mightn't she?'

'I warned them,' said Harry. 'When the dog went in. I warned them. I think I told them it was deeper, downstream off Heron. I'm sure I did.'

'Marta wouldn't have taken it in,' said his wife. 'Anansi obviously did. She crawled out to her, you say?'

'On one of the landing-stage planks, according to Mark. Then Simon seems to have pulled Marta out – who'd have thought it? – and gone back for Nancy, but knocked her under when he fell. Hit his own head on the plank, but went on diving and grabbed her.'

'How long were they in there, those two?'

'Not long. Not long. The RIB came, with Jake and the two Carters. They were just in time to stop Douai going in after the other two. He was tying a rope round his waist. Christ!'

'It is not your fault,' said Marion. 'For as long as I can remember, Blythney children have been exploring the river. We did, Sheila's generation did, this new litter do the same. There's not many places where children still have that freedom.'

'They could all be dead,' said Harry bleakly.

'We've never had a death. Not a child. Only those teenagers from Catley who got drunk and stole the rowing boat.'

'I should have been there,' repeated Harry. 'Supervising.'

'Freedom,' said Marion sharply. 'Keep that in your head. Freedom. You fought for that.'

The car was at a standstill, Harry waiting his chance to swing right across the road into the hospital car park. He turned and looked at her. 'It's supposed to be women who make a fuss,' he said wonderingly. 'Look at us. Am I an old woman, do you suppose?'

Marion laughed. The car pulled forward, and Harry parked and walked rapidly towards the main doors of the hospital. An ambulance stood nearby, and glancing inside he saw that it was streaked copiously with mud. Two paramedics were preparing to hose it down. He shuddered then strode in, followed by Marion.

The nurse put her head round the door of the low-lit ward and said to Sheila, 'Mrs Harrison? Your husband and son are getting ready to leave now.'

Sheila followed her out.

Simon, a bandage round his head, was sitting with his arm across Douai's shoulders.

'Are you sure you're all right?' Sheila asked doubtfully. 'You took quite a crack on the head, they said.'

'Concussion watch,' said Douai. 'I have to check his pupils sometimes, and notice if he gets drowsy or confused.' He was reading from a hospital card. His spirits, Sheila was glad to see, seemed excellent. 'We've got a taxi home. I rang up to book it.'

'I'm sorry I haven't been with you all the time,' she said. 'Anansi's still asleep, but Alaia needs someone with her till Jonny gets back.'

'Where is he?'

'She asked him to go home for Marta's bear and floppy kangaroo. She got a bit upset when he didn't want to leave, so he gave in.'

'Does Anansi have anything he could get?' Douai asked abruptly.

Sheila and Simon looked at each other.

'I don't think so,' said Sheila. 'I never saw a toy anywhere in her room.'

'If it was me,' said Douai flatly, 'I would want Rabbit when I woke up.'

Sheila blinked. She had not seen Douai cuddle Rabbit for years, although the grimy blue creature lived permanently on a bookshelf in his room. She had never seen Anansi cuddle anything.

'Well,' she said, forcing brightness, 'you'd better get home. Simon, are you *sure* you're fit to?'

'We can't leave Vincent on his own,' said her husband. 'And Poppy Hampton is next door if the boys want to run round there for help. She sent a message saying there was supper laid out in our kitchen for us in case we got home.'

Sheila, guiltily remembering her treatment of kind pestiferous Poppy that morning, said, 'Oh, how sweet,' in a faint voice, and then moved across to hug Douai. 'Well done, darling,' she said. 'I haven't said that yet. But well done, and well sailed, and go careful. Love to Vince. I'll be home as soon as I can. You do see,' she hesitated, her arms still round her son, 'you do see that I have to stay with Anansi for the moment?'

'Of *course*,' said Douai, with infinite scorn.

Emerging from the lift, nervous in the hospital atmosphere, Harry saw Jonny Markeen stepping out of the one alongside with an armful of fluffy toys. Marion had elected to wait downstairs, saying 'She's your pigeon, really.'

'You heard, then,' said Jonny.

'I did. I feel responsible.'

'Bollocks. Grania and Marta were responsible, if anyone was. Or we were, for thinking that featherheaded Hampton child was fit to be out of anybody's sight for ten minutes in a boat.'

'I did warn them about mud,' said Harry. 'They saw the dog get into trouble. I did tell them.'

'Harry,' said Jonny, 'it is not your bloody fault. Anyway, it's your little protegée who saved Marta's life, full stop. One of your regiment. You should be bloody proud of her.'

'I am,' said Harry.

Together, they went into the side ward where the women jumped up to greet them. Marta was fast asleep; after a fond glance and an inquiry of the nurse, Jonny informed Alaia that he and she were going for a cup of coffee in the canteen and drew his reluctant wife away.

Sheila said to Harry, 'I am so glad you're here!' and flung herself on his chest.

'Poor little Sheel,' said Harry. 'It's all right now.'

'They'll whisk Anansi away, you know,' said Sheila through her tears. 'Serious accident while in care of foster parents – she'll be back in some local authority home before you can say "unfit carers".'

Harry pushed her to arm's length and gave her a little shake. 'Rubbish!' he said. 'She did *not* have an accident! She sailed her boat, perfectly competently, tied it up, witnessed an accident, and went to help. With considerable presence of mind.'

'Heroism,' said Sheila, nodding and passing her sleeve across her eyes.

'Beyond the call of duty,' said Harry. 'I tell you, there were already local newspapers ringing the club when I left, so Eric says. If we have to use media blackmail, we will. Anansi comes home to Blythney. Full stop.'

'If she wants,' said Sheila. 'If she wants.'

'Go and have a cup of coffee too,' said Harry. 'I'll sit here for a while.'

Swimming up towards consciousness from the deep, warm drowse of exhaustion, Anansi found her mouth blocked, her eyes dark, her limbs trapped by constricting mud and Marta gone, slipped away, horribly not there. If Marta went too far, the fuckilla man would get her. An inarticulate, animal cry of rage broke from her and Harry saw the arms and legs fighting against the enwrapping blankets. He reached his hand out, hesitated, then moved to the door.

'Nurse!' he called.

From the desk outside, the nurse appeared, and said, 'Ah, good. Waking up, dear?' She came to the bed and put her hand on Anansi's brow. 'Good, I think.'

The high, thin cry went on. Harry said:

'Can't we do something? She's in distress!'

At the sound of his voice, Anansi's eyes flew open. 'Harry!' she croaked.

The nurse said, 'Isn't that nice? She knows her grandad, all right,' and went back to her station, calling, 'If she wants a drink of something hot in a moment, call me.'

'Harry,' said Anansi again. Then: 'Sorry. Sorry I took your boat.'

'Doesn't matter,' said Harry. 'Not a bit.'

'It was out of order.' She closed her eyes.

'It was. But you made damn good use of it. You saved Marta's life.'

'Marta!' The big eyes snapped open again. 'Where's she gone?'

'Asleep. Look. In the next bed. She's fine. You saved her life, Nancy. You did.'

'I know,' said the child, closing her eyes again. 'So that pays off your sentry, then.' She gave a curious chuckle, then drifted back into a quiet sleep. Harry loosened the bonds of her blankets slightly, so that she did not panic again when she awoke.

It was many hours later that he understood what she meant about the sentry.

Chapter Twenty-five

Marta and her retinue of furry animals were home in two days. Two more were spent lolling in luxurious convalescence on the garden swing-seat, relating the drama to a stream of admiringly solicitous little friends. Alaia danced constant attendance with lemonade and Karen's best home-baked biscuits, and the weather grew hot and still. On the third day Marta walked with her father across the marsh to Coker's Quay, where a light breath of wind stirred the torrid air. Harry was there, fitting a new floorboard to the Whitecap to replace the one which had sunk in the mud during Jake's final rescue. He glanced up.

'Can I get in the boat?' asked Marta. 'I've almost, nearly, forgotten how all the ropes work. And I want to tell Anansi I know them, when I go and see her in the hospital.' She clambered down the steps, yanked the mooring line and stepped onto the bow of the dinghy. It floated back to its spot on the quiet water, and Marta sat frowning up at the mast, a hand shading her eyes. Jonny and Harry stood together, looking at her.

'The absence of trauma in that child,' said Jonny fondly,

'can only be a sign of imbecility. She hasn't had a single nightmare.'

'Has she not? Nancy has.'

'I suppose she was conscious, and thinking about the danger, for a lot longer. And Marta seems to have handed over entire responsibility more or less straightaway. She says she made angel arms, then Anansi came and held on to her, then she woke up in bed.' He paused. 'But then, Mart's always been looked after, all her life. Doesn't know any different. How is Anansi? Have you seen her?'

'I'm going again today. Sheila's been up every day. Says she kept waking up shouting, after every nap, but it's calmed down now. Douai went yesterday, so I stayed away.'

'What happened with Douai?' The three families had talked constantly in the days since the accident, and the old pattern of difficulty and dislike at Seafret was familiar territory. Simon had even been up with Sheila and spent an evening with the Markeens. He was still pale and bandaged, and Alaia observed to her amusement that Sheila was mothering him a great deal.

'Well,' said Harry, 'Sheila got there with Dow, and he said he'd rather see her on his own. So she showed him in and left them to it. When she went out, she heard Nancy saying, "Thanks for getting help so quick," and saying that he must have sailed really well. So then Sheila went for a coffee and hung about for half an hour, and when she got back the two of them were deep in technical conversation about racing boats and trapezes, and she felt like a bit of a spare wheel. Douai bought Nancy a present, too. Hid it under his chair, gave it her at the end, and ran off a bit embarrassed.'

'What?'

'Furry hippopotamus. Big green one from ToyBoy on the High Street. He got it as a joke, he said, because she was so good in mud.'

'Did she like it?'

'Can't be parted from it,' said Harry. 'So this morning I got it a baby, for portable use.' He pulled a paper packet from his pocket and showed Jonny a chunky green velveteen hippo, three inches long. 'Taking it in this afternoon.'

'I haven't quite clocked why she's still in there,' said Jonny. 'Not hypothermia any more, is it?'

Harry looked across the river and spoke flatly. 'It's the foot. The bad one. Sheila got told yesterday, because there's some problem about who gives consent for operations. There's a meeting fixed with the orthopaedic boss at the hospital. All she knows is that there's some hitch because the circulation was never terribly good, due to the foot being distorted, and it lost blood supply while it was cramped round the plank and she was going hypothermic. Anyway, they're not happy. Endless X-rays.'

'Look,' said Jonny. 'I am, as you know, a rich and vulgar merchant. If there is any question of her needing private treatment, here I am. You will tell them?'

'Yes. I will. We'll help too, if we can.'

'Because,' continued Jonny, 'every time I see Marta skipping around without a care in her empty little head, followed by Alaia with a warm jumper and a plate of biscuits, I think of that other child. I think of her lying in hospital without a parent in sight, limping round the town, spending her whole life at the mercy of some council official. It stops me sleeping properly. She saved Marta for us.'

Marta looked up from her preoccupations in the boat.

'I got it!' she said. 'I forgot about the spinnaker rope, that's what muddled me. Uncle Harry, when can we go and do the camp on Heron Island?'

'See? Not even the grace to be traumatized,' said Jonny. 'Would you bloody believe it?'

When they first brought Anansi a bedpan she was outraged. 'I can go to the toilet,' she said with stiff dignity. She sat up, and swung her feet out of bed. Momentary alarm crossed her face at the colour and limpness of the lame foot, but she set it to the ground with the other. The nurse stood by, impassively, until Anansi pulled her weight onto her feet, then caught her as she toppled towards the floor.

'Easy does it,' she said. 'Your poor foot isn't really ready for walking yet.'

Anansi glared at her. 'I'm not pissing in that – pan,' she said in disgust. 'I'll hold on to something.'

'You can have a crutch if you like.'

Anansi liked the crutch little better than the bedpan, but bowed to the inevitable. Her foot, obviously, needed a bit of time to get better. Only as the days passed did doubt set in.

The orthopaedic consultant was tall and tanned, with a rangy middle-aged athleticism. He raced Flying Fifteens down at Aldeburgh, so Jonny Markeen knew him. He had arranged a meeting with the two Harrisons to discuss Anansi's condition, and raised his eyebrows a little when Jonny appeared as well, together with Harry.

'What's all this, then?' he said. 'Who's in charge?'

'None of us,' said Sheila frankly. 'Social services in London, temporarily in loco parentis while her mother is in prison. But we as fosterers can refer the situation on to them. Jonny and Harry are here because they want to ask you about private treatment – they would fund it.'

'NHS will do quite nicely, I think,' said the surgeon. 'Although there might be an advantage if it comes to prosthesis.'

'Prosthesis?' said Sheila, startled. 'Surely you don't mean—'

'Let me take it from the beginning,' said the consultant, soothingly. 'It's very important that parents – er, carers – get everything straight in their minds so that they can support and inform the child's decision.'

'Decision?' Sheila was silenced by a quick frown from Harry, and subsided. Together, in appalled silence, the four of them listened to what the surgeon had to say.

The foot, he explained, had plainly been badly broken at the ankle many years before. He doubted whether it had ever been properly set or plastered at all. *Win Brindley,* thought Harry with a spurt of useless rage. *And that hopeless mother of hers. Just how difficult is it, to dial 999?*

'In cases like this,' said the doctor, 'in a young child, the bones will knit quite fast. But not always in the right position. Then the child starts getting mobile on the distorted foot, and that compounds the long-term problem. They learn to use the nerves and muscles in any way that gets them mobile. The irony is that the more determined and fit the child is otherwise, the more irrevocable the distortion gets. Though it may cause all sorts of other physio problems, backaches and so on.'

'We've always thought that Anansi gets around remarkably quickly, considering the limp,' said Sheila.

'She's wiry, she's light, and she's determined,' said the doctor. 'Which is terrific, in one way. But it means that things become irreversible. Right now – and probably for a good few years past – there is no operation which could correct the distortion of that foot.'

'But she gets around fine,' said Simon. He suddenly saw the image of the small, dark figure limping along the sea wall in the evening, and then remembered the outcome of one of those evening walks. He flushed, and glanced around, but nobody else had made the connection.

'She *did* get around fine,' continued the doctor. 'So everyone says, including herself. But not any more.'

As the silence in the little room deepened, he explained the rest. The circulation within the foot, dubious before, had become seriously compromised during the rescue. 'She must have clenched every muscle she had to stay locked into that position on the wobbly plank. She showed me how she was lying. But between that and the hypothermia, she's paid a price. Frankly, what she has now is a God-awful foot. Functionally it is all but useless.'

Jonny broke the silence. 'You're working up to suggesting amputation, aren't you?'

The surgeon nodded.

Harry broke in, 'You can't! She's not twelve yet!' In his mind, unrolling in nightmare procession as if they had been sprung from a box, were field hospitals and refugee camps and landmine zones: civilians, comrades, friends, men, women, children – limbless, helpless, enraged, embittered.

The surgeon saw his age and military bearing and understood immediately. 'Things,' he said gently, and directly to Harry, 'have changed very much indeed. Especially in rich countries like this. We're a long way past the clumping peg-leg. Keep listening.'

He pulled from behind the desk an assortment of prostheses: false feet of incomprehensible materials, pink shapes of lower legs, sorbo pads, surrogate ankles. He talked on. He enthused about something called the SACH foot – 'solid-ankle-cushion-heel'.

Finally he put the objects away in their box and said, 'You hated that, didn't you? Everybody does. There's a natural revulsion at the idea of cutting off a living, pulsing part of your body and replacing it with plastic and steel. It takes a special kind of courage even for adults to face it. But if you were to come to rehab for a while I could show you better things. I could show you videos. I could show you a fifteen-year-old boy who plays football for his school with a prosthetic foot. I could show you a chap who goes windsurfing on one, and a couple of very creditable ballroom dancers. I could introduce you to an ex-fireman who goes figure skating, three years after his whole foot was burnt to a claw. I could show you people walking around in ordinary shoes and trousers, and ask you to guess which ones had false legs, and you'd get it wrong. I could prove to you that this child will have better mobility and more peer acceptance with a prosthesis than she's ever had yet.'

There was silence. Then Simon said, 'And if we – she – they – decide not to?'

'Then she'll walk on crutches, with a foot more deformed than before, so that she won't even be able to cram ordinary shoes on it like she has been doing. And it will get infections more easily, and need frequent checking and treatment, and it will probably smell. And gangrene will be a constant danger. I tell you, this is an awful foot.'

He was used to silences, and sat back relaxed, waiting for them to digest this information. It helped, the surgeon thought suddenly, that there were four of them and that none was a blood relation. Usually it was parents to whom he made this speech; their guilt and neurosis would curdle the air. Now there was only superficial shock and sorrow, which turned rapidly to interest and hope.

'It's only a foot, after all. Not like losing a leg,' ventured Simon after a while.

'Well, we would prefer to take the leg off just below the knee,' said the surgeon smoothly. 'It sounds worse, but it works better.'

This time it was Sheila's turn to flinch. 'A girl's legs . . . as she grows up . . .'

'Indeed. A sensitive subject. I do not pretend that a false leg is any asset to a girl.' He leaned back, and looked at them while they thought. 'But movement – remember, to a healthy young animal, movement is life. I have girls who go salsa dancing on a SACH foot.'

'Well,' said Harry finally. 'Who discusses this with Anansi? You, or one of us?'

'Not social services,' put in Sheila quickly. 'There's nobody there that knows her.'

'She'll need her mother's consent, I daresay,' said the doctor. 'That's for them to sort out. But she's here, and this is the moment to do it. And if you,' he indicated Jonny, 'want to plough your ill-gotten gains from selling those daubs into a top-grade foot, I am not going to discourage you.'

'Look,' said Harry, 'could I suggest that you talk to her? She likes straight talking.'

'To be frank with you,' said the doctor, 'I already have. It shouldn't have happened before this meeting, and I apologize. But she is a very forthright child.'

The four of them stared at him as he went on, 'She asked me straight. Yesterday. Said, would her foot get better? She's noticed how blue and black it is, and she doesn't like looking at it. Chucks her towel over it if she's on top of the covers.'

'What did you say?'

'I said what we always say, that we could certainly get her walking again, better than before.'

'And?' It was Jonny Markeen doing the talking now, fascinated, his scarred face intent on the doctor's.

The surgeon smiled. 'She looked at me and said, "Not on this foot, mister. That's true, in't it?" And so I said, well, no, we might like to think about giving her a new one. And she said, "Cut this one off?" And I said, well, she wouldn't want two feet at the end of one leg. So she thought for a moment then said, "How long? I want to go sailing before they send me back."'

'Does she really understand?' asked Sheila. 'Has she thought about what it would mean to take your leg off every night and put it back in the morning?'

'Well, as I say, I am not supposed to discuss these things until parents know. But under the circumstances . . . Anyway, the next thing she said was, if she took it off for bed, would she have to hop to the toilet in the night? And I said yes.'

He looked around the group, with a faint air of challenge. 'I have never, ever before known a child that didn't flinch when it realized at that sort of daily level what was going to happen. The bravest of them, even the adults, go a bit blue around the lips at that point. But this one didn't. She just nodded and said, "OK, then." I tell you this, I really want to give that kid a very, very good foot.' He smiled, a little sheepish at his own descent from professional detachment.

'So she wants it done,' said Sheila. 'And you're telling us all this . . . ?'

'I am spelling it out to you so that you understand, as well as she does, what the issues are. When you're satisfied about what she wants, one of you will need to talk to whoever needs to give this consent.'

'How long . . .' began Simon. The doctor cut in, smoothly.

'The sooner the better. She's in hospital, she's quite well-adjusted to it, the limb is clean, she'll be off the antibiotics in a day or so. There's a necessary healing period between amputation and fitting which may be difficult for her, even with her courage. I'd like to get on with it, frankly. There isn't any reason she shouldn't be starting to walk before the school term starts in September.'

Harry opened his mouth to speak.

'Yes,' said the doctor. 'And sail, too. If she leaves hospital with the foot in its present state, and gets an infection, there'll be much longer delays.'

During this momentous meeting Marta had been left to amuse Anansi in the ward. When the party trooped into the children's ward to collect her, they were greeted by a peal of laughter from the far corner of the room. Marta jumped up from the floor where she and Anansi had been sitting over a brightly coloured puzzle. The hippopotamus had sole possession of the bed, apart from its plush green baby nestling under its chin.

'Hey,' said Marta, tugging at her father's arm. 'Guess what? Anansi's getting a cool new foot.'

When they had gone, Anansi climbed back into the narrow white hospital bed, and lay for a while with her two green hippopotami balanced on her chest, her arms loosely round them.

So they would cut her foot off, the old, twisted foot

that had made them call her Limpy in the playground, and brought her bad dreams, and haunted her with wondering for as long as she could remember.

They would cut it off, take it away. The thought made her slightly scared but strangely exhilarated.

She liked the big surgeon: he was kind, he had respect. Like Harry. He told her that whatever anyone said, it was her choice whether to give up on the old bent foot. He had been straight, too, no bullshit. Told her the fake one would not work easily straightaway. She would have to learn a new way of using her leg and her knee. She had wanted to know how she would find out how to do it right. He had put his hand on her arm then and said, 'You'll have all the help you need, I promise.' She had believed him.

She flexed her leg, experimentally, under the covers. Yeah, you could move it lots of different ways. So where was the problem? She had learnt to sail a boat quick, hadn't she? Could a leg be harder, with all day to practise?

'You might miss it,' Marta had said airily. 'Poor old footy!' Anansi considered that, too, but shook her head on the pillow, half smiling at the thought. Nah. Wouldn't miss it. Nor, she felt suddenly convinced, would she ever dream about the fuckilla man again.

'They take my kid,' said Tracey rhetorically, 'just for a holiday by the sea, *they say*. Then the next thing I know, they up and tell me, oh, by the way, they're cutting her leg off. It's diabolical. I'm her mum, I got rights.'

'It isn't quite like that' said Mark Hinton patiently. He was always patient with the Traceys, having infinitely more tolerance of their stubbornness, prejudices, vanities and failures of understanding than he could possibly muster for their middle-class sisters. 'It's an operation which the health authority inform us would greatly improve her mobility and quality of life. She's lucky to be able to get it so quickly.'

Marion was sitting beside him in the Holloway interview room, as representative of the Blythney group. She had been chosen after a protracted council of war between Harrisons, Glanvilles and Markeens at dinner. Sheila, it was felt, might be perceived by Tracey as a rival mother and resented accordingly. Simon was not even considered; in his new mood of amazed humility he accepted this meekly. Harry and Jonny were told by Sheila that if they were to meet Mark Hinton they would be red rags to a bull: an old military type and a self-made entrepreneur. Anathema. Only Marion, with her WRVS credentials, was thought suitable.

'Just don't wear tweeds, that's all!' said Jonny Markeen, who had struck up a considerable rapport with the feminine, formidable old lady during their contacts over Anansi. 'You don't have a camouflage jacket, or a pair of jeans, or a shell suit, I suppose?'

'Black,' said Marion. 'Black cardigan, pink blouse, I think.' The group laughed, but there was tension among them.

'She could say no,' said Sheila. 'And then there would be all sorts of problems. The local authority could overrule her, technically, but because the condition isn't lifethreatening I doubt they would want to. It would be easier if Tracey Cowper were convicted already, but imagine the press coverage if she was on bail. "They cut my little girl's leg off without me there."'

'There *is* always the chance of having the press on our side,' said Jonny thoughtfully. 'Medical Miracle Heroine, you know. There was a nice little showing of stories about the rescue.'

'We don't want to resort to that,' said Sheila sharply. 'It leads to nothing but trouble in the end.'

'I wish you'd tell Marta that.' Alaia grimaced. 'She couldn't get enough of posing for the *East Anglian Daily Times*.'

So Marion had met Mark Hinton, explained her position as fosterer's aunt, and now the two of them sat in the small bleak room confronting the tousled and defiant figure of Tracey.

Mark had brought cigarettes, and the younger woman smoked them one after another without apparent pleasure, stubbing the ends out viciously on the table. At first she had asked only after Kyra, in a stream of miserable rage at the system that kept them apart.

'She's my baby, she needs her mum. It's out of order, keeping us apart. I oughter be in a mother and baby unit. I got my rights. I want to see her, right? I don't want her in no home, full of perverts.'

Mark had answered her patiently, giving news of Kyra and two Polaroid pictures of the child playing happily in a suburban garden. Marion, despite her initial antipathy to this gaunt, brusque young man, honoured him both for his patience and the trouble he had taken to get the pictures.

'I visited her two days ago,' he told Tracey. 'She's happy. Children are happiest in the summer, out in the garden. She thinks of it as a little holiday. Don't worry.' After a while, he came to the reason for the interview. Marion noted that Tracey had not mentioned Anansi at all of her own accord. It was Mark who said, 'We have news for you, about your elder daughter.'

'In trouble, is she?' Tracey blew out a long stream of smoke and stubbed another cigarette on the Formica. She reached for a fresh one from Mark's packet. 'I'm not surprised. I always said she'd end in the nick or on the game, that one. I couldn't do a thing with her. Bad blood, she's got.'

'She's not in trouble,' said Mark 'She's in hospital.' Briefly, he told the story of the rescue and outlined the problem of the foot. Again, Marion felt a prick of unwilling admiration for him. When he had been told the story himself, he had not seemed moved or interested, merely observing that these expensive middle-class hobbies obviously had their drawbacks, and that he preferred to send disadvantaged children on properly run training cruises with recognized organizations. None of this priggish disapproval, however, was being relayed to Tracey. He merely told her the facts, baldly and professionally.

This was when Tracey began emoting about her rights. In moments the subject was returned to Kyra.

'I s'pose you'll be back next week saying you want to cut my Kyra's arms off. What am I supposed to do, stuck in here?'

Marion itched to say, 'Keep off the drugs, for one thing.' She had sharp eyes, and did not think that all the puncture marks on Tracey's arms were old ones. She held her peace.

After a few more rambling paranoid diversions, which further fuelled Marion's suspicions, Tracey concluded: 'I'm not signing nothing. Not while I'm in here. They can give me bail, and give my Kyra back, then I'll think about it.'

Mark glanced at Marion. He had, she knew, been entirely won round to the idea of the prosthetic foot; the orthopaedic surgeon had rung him, and talked as one professional to another. She thought there was appeal in his look, and nodded.

Speaking to Tracey for the first time since the initial pleasantries of introduction, she said, 'Could you and I have a private chat? Mr Hinton has to speak to the governor, I think.'

'Is that about my going to a mother and baby unit?'

'Among other things,' said Mark evasively. The chances of a child as old as Kyra being reunited with a mother in prison were, both of them knew, virtually nil. But he rose and stepped out of the room to lean on the cold wall, eyes closed, recouping his strength for whatever came next.

Inside the room, Marion said without preamble, 'I don't want to waste your time, or mine. But tell me. Was it Win Brindley who kicked her, or one of the others?'

A stream of profanity made her flinch briefly, but she held her ground. It resolved itself into: 'What the fuck do you know about Win Brindley, Lady Muck?'

'Only what Charlie told me,' said Marion imperturbably.

'Charlie? He's in Germany.'

'No, he isn't. And he says the kicking was nothing to do with him. It can be proved. He was in Travemünde at the date it happened. There are military records.' Marion in fact knew nothing of dates, but the ploy worked. Tracey put her cigarette down and let her tousled hair flop over her face, curtaining it almost completely as she stared at the pitted table top.

'I tried to stop Win,' she said. 'He was crazy with drink. He was an arsehole, like all of them.'

'So why,' asked Marion, 'didn't you take her to the hospital?' She looked directly at Tracey, her gaze unwavering. The game of bluff was making her heart beat faster, and filling her with a kind of shame: this was, after all, a poor thing, a casualty at the bottom of the society which had set her, and Harry, and Blythney, securely and comfortably on top. The thought of Anansi walking steadily into the future, up the hill away from Tracey's world, spurred her on. She kept her stare level.

'Win din't want any trouble,' the young woman said finally. 'No police trouble. We was still trying to make a go of it, him and me. He said kids got better quick and it was best to leave her.'

'Where?'

'In the bedroom. Mostly. She did get better, anyway.'

'She limped,' said Marion. 'Badly. If she'd had it set, she would never have had to limp for the next eight years. She wouldn't need to have the foot off now. *You* did that.'

'It's not my fault,' said Tracey defiantly.

'Yes, it is,' said Marion.

'It's that Win Brindley. He was an arsehole.'

'You were an adult. Anansi only had one parent to defend her. That was you. You didn't do it.'

'You can't prove nothing, not now.'

Marion merely looked at her. Tracey looked back, with pure hate. For a long moment they held one another's eyes. Then, the dull look returning to her eyes, the younger woman said, 'So, I'll sign for it. Whatever. But I should have give that kid up years ago. I tried, only she got out of the home and came back. That kid never brought me no luck. She's bad blood.'

Marion rose, and looked out into the corridor. Mark was still there, as she had expected. She signalled to him to come in, and the matter was concluded. Afterwards,

306

she told Harry, she felt depressed and dirtied for days. But Anansi's left foot was taken off two days later, on the last afternoon of the Blythney junior regatta; and when she came round from the anaesthetic, Douai and Harry were waiting in the ward.

'You won this,' said Douai, handing her a flat leather trophy case. 'I came third in the Laser Twos and sixth in the handicap. Vince lets me sail his boat, because he's playing tennis with Janie all day long.'

Anansi, still groggy, pulled herself up in the bed, regarding with equal amazement the high protective cage beneath the blanket and the leather box.

'Whassat?' she said. 'What you mean, I won it?'

'Open it.'

Inside the case was a flat, silver-plate medal bearing the arms of the Blythney Yacht Club and the words:

Seamanship Award 1999
Presented to
Anansi Cowper
For Lifesaving

'You have to be a member to qualify,' said Douai. 'So they've made you an honorary life member. The last one was the *Duke of Kent*!'

Anansi looked at it, fuddled, for a few moments. The marks cut on the medal, curly and important-looking, meant almost nothing to her.

'Read it to me? Harry?' she asked.

And he did, in a steady voice. But even as her smile spread and her cheeks flushed with pleasure, he realized with a sinking heart that it was not only walking on a false foot that she now had to learn. The wave of admiration and emotion that had borne her on since the rescue would not carry her all the way. The child still had battles, and must be armed. She couldn't even bloody *read*.

Chapter Twenty-six

'It's been a funny summer,' said Bethie Cotten to Susannah Rattray. Susannah, nursing her baby in the first pale-gold days of September, had come to Bethie's to keep her company while she packed away the holiday house until half-term. Now, the dozing baby on her shoulder, she sat in the kitchen rocker in catlike contentment.

'Funny for me,' she said. 'That is the *last* time I spend the summer like a barrage balloon. Spring or autumn babies only.' She had gone into labour late on the night of the mud rescue.

'I meant in the town,' said Bethie. 'First the stuff about the Harrisons, then Penny taking off with the girls, and Alan having this thing with the *nanny*—'

'I have to say,' said Susannah, 'that even after what Penny said, it was a bit of a shock when she took off to London and the girls went up for a spell with her, but the nanny was still nannying Alan!'

'Well, good luck to him,' said Bethie. 'Nice Suffolk girl, Janet. She'll be cheaper to run than Penny, I should think.'

'All the same! How's she going to get along with his friends?'

'As well as we let her, I suppose.' Bethie gave the worktop a final rub, and said, 'There. Ready to go. I do dread going back to London, every time.'

'Eric says we might move down here full-time,' said Susannah. 'For precious mousie's sake.' She kissed the baby's head. 'He could commute.'

'Like Simon Harrison?'

They giggled. Simon had got a job. It was the wonder of the town, their faded celebrity author going to work in Framlingham every day, on the *bus* – but only, Sheila said defensively, until he got a little car of his own. He didn't want to deprive her of the Volvo. The job was for a small high-class poetry publisher running a profitable sideline in gift books. He was liaising with writers and European photo libraries. It gave him time for his own writing. He was working on a new kind of book, a departure.

The Blythney wives were agog to know what Sheila thought of this development, and of Simon's meek return, but she chatted less these days. She also organized less, and seemed detachedly content about most things. She spent a lot of time with Alaia Markeen. But that was natural, the others supposed, since the two little girls were still inseparable.

'Marta's teaching the black child to read, it seems,' said Susannah, this connection having made itself in her mind.

'So she says. Actually, I think Marion Glanville's in charge. Marta's role is to pester Anansi to read her own favourite books.'

'She surely won't be able to go to school? With such poor reading, and that foot?'

'Sheila says she will. When the walking's settled down. Jonny offered to pay for private tuition at home but apparently it's better to keep everything normal-looking, for those social services.'

'Who was the black man there last night? At the Harrisons'.'

'What?' Bethie was agog. 'I didn't see—'

'I think he stayed the night. I saw him saying good-bye and being driven off by Marion. Wonderful looks, film-starry.'

'What on earth can be going on?' Bethie was seriously annoyed now. This story was getting beyond her.

The dusk was coming earlier now; sunset colours came too soon. On Coker's Quay, with the tide swirling past in fast equinoctial flow, Harry Glanville was stooping to the damp lines of a new mooring. He too was reflecting on the oddest of Blythney summers. Charles Darwin Cowper's emotional visit the night before had sobered him.

It had gone well, as well as he had ever dreamed in his most sentimental moments. Anansi had stood up on her new foot and held out her hand to her father with what truly looked like recognition. The two had built memories together, talked of walking by the docks and Nanna Beverley and a black toy duck called Rasta which he said she liked best, and which after a while she claimed faintly to remember. With all his heart, Harry had wanted to see this as a happy ending; yet it was not.

The man meant well, had large extravagant plans, boundless charm and a real love of his lost daughter, but he could not be relied on. He had no home nor any stability fit for the raising of a child. He would also, Harry judged, be only too ready to be distracted by any new racket for getting rich quick. It was not out of the question that he would end up back in prison.

Harry looked across the river, empty now, regaining its dark ancient dignity after the summer flurry of bright sails. Even less, he thought, could be hoped of the poor, fuddled, furious mother awaiting her trial in Holloway. When she signed the operation consent, Tracey had also formally asked for Anansi to go into care permanently. She had repeated the words which haunted Harry and Marion: 'She never brought me no luck anyway.'

Marion, doggedly, had asked if she could visit her again and bring some pictures of Anansi with her new foot. Tracey, through the medium of Mark the social worker, had refused to see her.

So it was up to them, now. All the same, Harry thought ruefully, the Blythney group was no fair replacement for true parents. They would try all right; Harrisons, Markeens, Glanvilles would not give up Anansi lightly now. For the six remaining years of her minority they would, if allowed, see her through school, tend body and mind, and do their best to find work for her errant father. If she was taken away, they would keep a space and a bed always open for her in Blythney. All their fates were bound together. At least, thought Harry, the law provided that Anansi's own wishes would come to mean more and more as the years of growing went swiftly by.

But he hoped with all his heart that they would be able to keep her in this safe place, for a time at least. One day in hospital she had talked to Sheila about the possibility of inviting Kyra for a holiday, 'to paddle'. Marta in particular was entranced at the idea of an even littler match girl, too young to object to being given the role.

Harry bent to adjust his mooring on its rusty ring. They had to accept, he thought, that all the well-meant patronage and friendship in the world would never convert this wild thing into something else. Whatever they did for her, whatever they gave her, this awkward, downright, gallant alien would never become a comfortable Blythney child. She would have no true family or home until the day came when she founded one of her own. The storms of adolescence would not go easily for her. Pretending was in vain, happy endings elusive. Harry told himself these things, fiercely, as he tied the last hard knot in the wet mooring line.

Still, there were things to be done. Tomorrow she would be twelve years old. In secret, in his barn, he and the youngest lad from the boatyard had rebuilt Sheila's old Whitecap dinghy and, defying ill luck, renamed it. When Anansi came down in the morning, walking with her stick across the rough marsh track, she would find it alongside his boat and know that it was her own, to steer by her own star.

He looked down at the new name on the stern. He hoped she liked it. She was, under Marion's tutelage, showing a pleasing taste for 'fancy words'. So the boat, in her image, was simply called,

Tenacity.

Harry smiled at his own sentimentality. The brat was, he thought, as likely as not to paint it over and call it after a rock star. So what? A parent might be affronted by such behaviour, but these days he felt the mental advantages of his own old age, his nearness to the river mouth and the wide eternal ocean. He at least could take any snub she could throw at him, any whirl or eddy of her turbulent years of growth. He should live six years, surely? More, with luck.

That his last years should mingle with her first ones filled him with joy and wonder. The privilege of watching her beginnings was all the greater because her life would have a longer course than he could hope to see.

It would flow on, as determined in its course, as unpredictable, as faithful, as compounded of bleakness and beauty as the river itself. In the end, like every life, it would find its way to the sea. Harry looked at the two boats: the comfortable battered darkness of the old one and the bright brittle varnish of the new. He raised his hand to them in gentle ironic salute. Then, whistling up his dog from the rabbit-haunted heath, he set off for home.